REVENUE MAN

REVENUE MAN

(The emergence of Tubal McArthur)

STÉ MCCOINNICH

The manufacturer's authorised representative in the EU for product safety is Authorised Rep
Compliance Ltd, 71 Lower Baggot Street, Dublin D02 P593 Ireland
(www.arccompliance.com)

Troubador Publishing Ltd
Unit E2 Airfield Business Park,
Harrison Road, Market Harborough,
Leicestershire LE16 7UL
Tel: 0116 279 2299
Email: books@troubador.co.uk
Web: www.troubador.co.uk

ISBN 978 1 83628 198 6

British Library Cataloguing in Publication Data.
A catalogue record for this book is available from the British Library.

Printed and bound by CPI Group (UK) Ltd, Croydon, CR0 4YY
Typeset in 15pt Garamond Pro by Troubador Publishing Ltd, Leicester, UK

MIX
Paper | Supporting
responsible forestry
FSC
www.fsc.org
FSC® C013604

Dedicated to the men and woman of the Boards Investigation Office who often worked in the most difficult of circumstances. Work hard and play harder, we are united in a lifelong brotherhood. But the most credit of all goes to my wife Sue, supportive and always proud of me, we have shared so many experiences along the journey of a life together.

Prologue

I am destined to live as an enigma.

Or so a subliminal voice prowling the dank recess of his perplexed mind informs him. To this soul, daily life is often tolerated by navigating around uncomfortable events. These events, to him, visited frequently, requiring a strong lager antidote whenever the mood took him. At least this is what he came to believe as he battled through his formative years. He will not entertain liability for self-perceived character flaws or transgressions driven by alcohol though. It's hard enough hosting his internal demons' daily battle, pitching stifling shyness against the desire to be noticed. This young man, if truth be told, suffers as the unwitting bi-product of a familial timeshare – the human equivalent of an apartment in Tenerife; school terms with the parents, loving but dysfunctional insular perfectionists, and all holidays at his maternal grandparents', witness to a quasi-transient patriarchy, built on making money and socialising in degenerate company. So, our hero experienced little continuity from either side throughout his childhood years to mould his emotional soul. Despite this, inner strength and determination have guided him to where he is today.

The family always regarded him as 'the clever one', but

spontaneity and overt signs of intelligence never really appealed to him. What does being 'clever' mean anyway? It's all relative, I suppose. He is tenacious though and will work through problems until he has a solution, sometimes even the right one. At school, the teachers labelled him 'conscientious; a stock descriptor for one who hands in homework but contributes little else to the class. Although, occasional flippancy, masking his lack of comprehension, surfaced, almost Tourette-like, by the unleashing of a witty quip that had momentarily churned around in his brain before his mouth seized control and independently spat it out. A dangerous dereliction in the 1970s at a South London secondary school that trawled its teaching staff from a caustic blend of redundant army officers or practising psychopaths, often both. Discipline must be maintained. Corporal punishment the go-to response. Their disconcerting arsenal of pain ranged through T-squares, slippers, plastic cricket bats and board rubbers although the religious education teacher, not disposed to such worldly possessions, would spontaneously smash a dissenter's head down onto the nearest desk. Fundamentally though, our protagonist's early life was afflicted by a deep-rooted desire to batter into submission the spectre of introversion conflicting him. To counter his demons, an alter ego that fronted out life's challenges and sought a higher station grew within him. True, this would take some moulding to escape the reticence of his developing years. As he bloomed post-puberty, self-medication seemed the answer; a trait not discouraged by family. Or perhaps those who should nurture, failed to notice.

He was always a big lad, and what fourteen-year-old, you may ask, doesn't want to spend his school downtime ensconced in one of the family's smoke filled tombs of a betting shop or T-cutting and bashing out 'cut and shut' cars for auction! A life where school holiday evenings were spent in pubs and clubs with his grandad's ingratiating punters buying this pseudo adult frothy pints of light and bitter and cheap gassy lager. The regular entertainment as diverse as joining the night's end singalong at the piano or catching his Glaswegian aunt clobbering some disrespecting soul over the head with her stiletto heel at bingo. Certainly, such a life put paid to developing any long-term external relationships. Other than school time, he was never in one place long enough to work out how to keep friends. Delinquents might envy such an upbringing, but loneliness was the dominant emotion held by our hero. In his quiet moments he often wondered if his tribulations were the result of poor nurturing or just a genetic cock-up.

So here he is, Tubal McArthur, mixed Scots English, born and bred south of the Thames with a questionable biblical name passed through the family from his three times great-grandfather in Victorian Bethnal Green. Now everybody calls him 'Mac', but schooldays vested Tubal with the impudently obvious nickname 'Tubby Tubal', although being selected to play rugby as a prop forward for the school certainly kept the bullies away. Tubal only remembered being on the receiving end of an unsolicited punch off the playing field once. Minding his own business walking home one night, he felt a dull thump in the back of his head, knocking him forward. Ears ringing, he turned in shock ready to receive anything else that might come his way. Before him stood a lanky, scruffy, brown-suited lad, a bit older with fine, wispy hair delicately sprouting along his top lip as if puberty was a late train held outside the station. A startled look on the lad's face transformed into a nervous smile as his arms widened in submission. His sweaty palms opened and, now posing no threat, he spoke.

'Sorry, mate, I thought that you were someone else,' he blurted as he ran off down the road.

Tubal said nothing and carried on home. The blow didn't

register as much as those occasionally wielded in anger upon him by his mother's frying pan. But Tubal is tough. The school rugby master, Mr Mallory, often enforced how strong Tubal was by inviting visitors to training sessions to scrum down against him. Tubal always felt uncomfortable with that. Away from the rugby pitch, Mallory, a colossus of a man, enjoyed wielding his king-size slipper upon any class urchins who challenged him. Tubal was never on the receiving end, but Mallory had an unsavoury penchant whereby he'd agree not to report pupils to the headmaster if miscreants accepted extra whacks of his velvety punisher. Thinking back, Mallory was probably only ten or so years older than Tubal. In later years at another school, Mallory's behaviour, undoubtedly more developed and predatory, earned him a lengthy time at Her Majesty's Pleasure before opting to top himself.

It is true. During Tubal's early years, he generally seemed able to avoid confrontation and would certainly prefer to make a joke about something than fight. He did try to get on with everybody despite an entrenched preference not to. But Tubal liked to be different and would seek ways to present his introverted persona to an audience blissfully ignorant of his occasional inner turmoil. Propelled by his parents, Tubal decided to stay on at school. He could now customise his sixth-form uniform, choosing a shiny silver-buttoned, navy-blue blazer; a wide-lapelled and double-breasted affair Tubal adorned with the school badge sewn roughly onto the breast pocket. Matched with black drainpipe trousers and blue brothel creeper shoes, Tubal felt the embodiment of his love of 1950s rock and roll and the resurrection fuelled by the BBC's *It's Rock 'n' Roll* programme on the wireless. He became a prolific contributor to the student magazine, *The Mechanical Badger*, continued playing rugby for the school and spent his spare time decorating an empty storeroom to form a new sixth-form common room. Life was looking up, and Tubal even had the opportunity to meet girls once at his all-male educational Stalag's sixth-form disco; drinking from a Watneys Party Seven with an end-of-night snog to Led Zeppelin's 'Stairway to Heaven'. Tubal decided to grow his hair like Robert Plant, but his curls erupted into a bush more reminiscent of the hippie afro-wearing 'Hair Bear' from the Hanna-Barbera cartoon. The only thing missing now was the wherewithal to study and his chosen subjects of A level English literature, history and economics were poor bedfellows for a seventeen-year-old paint-slopping, satire-writing, chunky Elvis. And so autumn 1977 became Tubal's educational swansong. Although betting shop duties filled his summer holiday days, the nightly lure of clubs and entertainment were more befitting of this new young adult. Tubal no longer needed school; he needed a job, and a variety of offers came from kudos-seeking punters, which he naively accepted. 'Just write this letter and you'll be in.' So, he did, and he wasn't! Tubal reluctantly accepted that he had to create his own destiny. Already perched on the periphery of a nefarious world, there was only one place for this reluctant bookmaker's apprentice to go. A place to grave-turn ancestors and aghast living kin: Tubal applied to join Her Majesty's Inland Revenue.

To his great surprise, Tubal was invited to an interview. What to do now? When the day came, he made it clear that he could not after all envisage himself working in an office. Tubal said that he wanted to work in a role that got him 'out and about in the fresh air'. He had no idea what working for someone outside the family meant, let alone what the Government would expect of him. In his heart, Tubal didn't really want to go to work, but summer was over, and he'd already surrendered any further academic fortitude. The interviewer, a little round man with a pyramidal moustache, walked from his desk and opened the top drawer from his bank of grey metal cabinets. Tubal imagined that this held the perfect role for him filed under 'N' for 'Non-office jobs for adolescent office work applicants'. Or perhaps he was looking for his bowler hat and umbrella. After thumbing through some papers, the man asked Tubal a few innocuous questions and then called his secretary into the room.

'I think he'll do,' he said.

The secretary wrote something down on a clipboard, clutched it closely to her breast and promptly left the room. That was it. He was in and, unbeknown to Tubal then, on a path to a destination alien to himself and certainly the majority of the Revenue's own staff.

Tubal was initially posted to a South London office within a mile of his Lambeth birthplace. The District Valuer's office dealt with property valuations for the local council to levy building rates. Daily he would visit houses, factories and shops, getting information on building conditions, taking measurements and recording the extent of dereliction. He was let loose in some of the most challenging environments in London around crumbling council estates, the old Thames wharves and Surrey Docks. Regeneration then still awaited the birth of the London Docklands Development Corporation. The term 'yuppie' had yet to embark on its transatlantic flight from the USA and the 'sarf' London indigenous people of Tubal's birth cultivated and expanded his worldly acumen. He felt happy being posted away from a stuffy office, and his new job allowed him to maintain a degree of independence. More importantly, the office was built over a pub, and days catching up on paperwork meant a pub lunch with colleagues. There were no worries about the boss. A creature of habit, he had his own bolthole for his daily half of bitter and a sandwich away from the minions. Within too long, by religiously developing his time management skills,

Tubal found it possible to fit in five pints of lager, pie and chips and a few games of darts in the lunch break. Downside was the hiccups that often meant afternoons concealed in the filing room stooped over trying to drink a glass of water upside down or entrenched in the toilet holding his breath. Still, this was a true education, and Tubal's loose apprenticeship in the betting shops and car auctions of his teens became augmented by his development as a mid-twenties all-round 'geezer' on the mean streets of Southwark. Still, soon it was time to move on, and although Tubal felt confident that he'd been sufficiently trained to draw a floorplan of the Taj Mahal or calculate the weight of steel in the Eiffel Tower if required, he now needed a new challenge. His inner personality remained reticent, but Tubal had perfected an external presentation of confidence that gave him chameleon-like properties in adapting to his surroundings. An opportunity then arose that Tubal felt strangely drawn to. It promised travel, kudos and promotion. Without hesitation, Tubal applied for, and was accepted into, the enigmatically entitled department known as Technical Division T2A/4.

So, there we are. This is Tubal. An enigma, perhaps. Will others see him this way? Who knows, but we can't let that spoil his fun now. Tubal's on a switchback ride in a clandestine world of catching criminals, disrupting racketeering and enjoying the tremendous esprit de corps of playing fast and loose with a skilled and highly effective group of misfits. He is Tubal McArthur, Criminal Investigator, Boards Investigation Office, known colloquially as 'The BIO' part of 'Technical Division'; a highly effective force operating in dirty, dangerous places. The imagination may now be running wild. Well, let's see.

Chapter One

Life ambled on to 1986 and day one of Tubal's rebirth as a fledgling investigator. The Robert Plant locks have been shorn and he's scrubbed up and Paco Rabanne-scented in smart Farrah trousers and grey jacket. Although not his idea of sartorial elegance, wide-rimmed glasses now adorn Tubal's maturing features and shade the steely cold blueness of his eyes. The brothel creepers are away on three steps to heaven, replaced by sensible black brogues. This is the new external Tubal and his inner ego must surrender to the new chapter in his life.

As Tubal settled into the classroom, he was one of ten trainees all embarking on their new career. Nearly all men and a good span of ages, but Tubal finds he's the youngest: twenty-five years old and newly promoted to Executive Officer. He had not realised the uniqueness of his promotion until faced with older colleagues who, like him, had moved through the ranks rather than been fast-tracked from university. As Tubal looked around him, he surmised that the recruitment section had selected individuals on their diversity, as no common denominators ostensibly shone through. Perhaps that's the point. Only one of them was destined to work alongside Tubal. Paul Ramell, ex-Royal Navy from Chatham in Kent, tall but slightly stooped with wispy blond hair tousled into a curl at the front. Paul smoked incessantly and spoke measured and slow between draws. A creature of conformity moulded into a blue tonic suit who later became famed for his hogging a favourite seat at the bar and daily prescription of two pints of Young's Bitter. Tubal took to him instantly and thought that they would likely become good friends. Turned out that the trainer, Eric, was a matelot Paul served with in the Med until they lost contact years ago. Tubal banked upon their reunion working to his advantage, hoping that Eric would smooth the way for him to ingratiate himself with his new colleagues. Tubal desperately wanted to get through the training successfully and make a name for himself. A return to the world of fifteen-metre tape measures and technical drawing was not on his agenda.

The other trainees were destined for each of the small regional teams seeking new blood. Paul and Tubal would join one of five teams delivering investigative capability for London and the South. Allocations to teams was somewhat of a misnomer as all units operated nationally on the UK mainland. Northern Ireland was special and represented by a small clandestine unit known as 'London office' over a shop near Waterloo Bridge. Their operating zone was referred to as 'over the water'. The rooms that Tubal and his new compadres were sat in once held Italian prisoners of war used to clear bomb damage from nearby Kingston-upon-Thames. In 1948, the whitewashed, single-storey, prefabricated huts were allocated as 'temporary' Government offices, and rumour had it that modernisation was due sometime this millennium. Steelworks for the anti-aircraft battery that protected nearby industry sat overgrown with weeds and some talked of a secret bunker secreted in the ground below. The site was discretely tucked away, dissected by the A3 and enclosed by branches of the main railway line to London from Guildford and Portsmouth. There was even a private access path to the railway station, although bowler-hatted commuters were long gone.

After a morning of introductions, photographs and form filling, Eric kicked off the afternoon by contextualising what the new cohort was doing there.

'You are not interested in Joe Public's tax affairs. Your role is purely criminal investigation, working directly under the command of the Board of Inland Revenue,' he said.

It sounded very grand, although Tubal couldn't imagine himself in response to the question, 'Who the fuck are you?' answering, 'As far as you're concerned, I'm the Chairman of the Board', although one of Eric's anecdotes told of such a retort from an unnamed officer. He explained that BIO was historically a unit to identify and prosecute internal theft and corruption but had taken on the mantle of investigating all criminal offences against the Department. Their core work now was to prosecute the misuse of tax exemption documents in the construction industry by organised criminal gangs including those 'over the water'. Tubal had no idea what these documents were.

'You are one of a small but select group of people identified as having the aptitude to do this work. Don't balls it up.' Eric sounded serious.

The unit was nearly sixty years old. It had remained covert in the public's eye and had only recently been expanded. Tubal's predecessors were few and traditionally had remained until retirement or death. This was a career move for people with no desire to go anywhere else, selected from the peripheral of the organisation. People with wherewithal for the task without pandering to tax collection targets or feigning moral reprehension at deviants operating in the 'cash-in-hand' society. Tubal felt that he was made for the role.

The basic practical training was looming, but Eric first enlightened the class with the history behind why the

Department needed BIO. He transported the trainees back to the recession of 1920 to 1922. High taxation rates were harming industry and preventing economic recovery, they were informed. The Government reduced the basic rate of income tax to 10% with a zero rate for the impoverished working man. Generous tax allowances, able to be claimed retrospectively, were awarded to married men with children to stimulate population growth. Investment income from share dividends and bank interest remained taxed at source, however, thereby allowing the newly tax-free proletariat to claim any taxed investment income back from the Inland Revenue.

It was no good; Tubal's mind had begun to wander. To him, this resembled a return to schooldays. He had always enjoyed history but wouldn't choose income tax 1920 to 1922 as his specialised subject on *Mastermind*. As reminisces of schooldays churned around his head, Tubal noticed a wry smile on the face of Debbie, one of the regional recruits. Tubal felt a little bit intimidated by Debbie, bordering on scared, and she was looking straight at him. Debbie Condon, older woman, brash, ultra-confident 'up North' lass; all long lashes, satin-pink lipstick, blue eyeshadow and skin-suffocating fake tan laid by mechanical digger. A mahogany amazon crowned by an expanse of jet-black hair framing the artwork of her face. A welcome distraction to this cohort of men. Our budding but woefully inept Don Juan had felt a lustful attraction towards Debbie on first sight. An attraction that evaporated when her lips parted to speak. Debbie felt compelled to speak loud and dirty. There was no kill switch. In the morning coffee break she had held court, regaling everybody with her tales of sexual conquests and enlightening all as to why she kept a cucumber in the fridge on standby for lonely evenings: Tubal decided he wouldn't fancy going round for a salad. So yes, to Tubal, scary. This was no debutantes' finishing school, but he suspected that her future endeavours might require a tad more decorum.

'So, what does all that mean then, McArthur?' Eric had twigged Tubal's digression.

'More people got tax rebates?' Tubal replied cagily.

'What it means is that a new growth industry developed – fraud. An opportunity not lost upon some self-serving members of the Department,' Eric retorted in dramatic prose before explaining further. 'If people were too poor to pay tax, they were hardly likely to have investments. Their identities became ripe to be stolen by internal fraudsters who held their fiscal information. This is the root of why you are here today.'

Eric referred all present to the case of D H John, an 'established clerk to the Surveyor of Taxes', sentenced to six months' hard labour in 1924 for fabricating a tax repayment of over £450.

'Mr John was the first known perpetrator of an "internal" fraud,' said Eric. 'Other internal cases progressed during the 1920s, but it was a case in 1928 that led to the establishment of the Boards Investigation Office.'

At last, Tubal thought, *Eric has got to the point.*

Ernest Waddell, Assistant Inspector of Taxes at Nottingham, thought that he had created the perfect crime. His job allowed him to travel around the territory, giving him access to addresses where fraudulently generated tax repayment cheques could be posted to and collected by him. Waddell commissioned printers and plate makers in Northamptonshire and Oxfordshire to create dies and other instruments that enabled him to create counterfeit share certificates, company dividend and bank interest warrant counterfoils. By fraudulently stealing the identities of people who paid little or no tax, Waddell then falsified documents to state that tax deductions had been made from these bogus investments. These he sent to the

Nottingham Tax Office where staff processed them and posted a tax repayment cheque to the claimant's address. Nothing would link him with the fraud and his rank meant that he could authorise repayment without challenge.

'Or so he thought,' Eric continued 'As in a lot of the cases that you'll see, an alert is often triggered by the simplest of errors. Those on the take are often exposed when they go on holiday or even spend an afternoon at the dentist. A colleague takes a phone call from an innocent dupe or a financial institution checking a payment, and that's it, game over. Beware of the workaholic, particularly those who are very guarded about their work.'

A bit of a generalisation, Tubal thought as Eric educated all on Waddell's eventual nemesis.

Francis Moyland suffered badly in World War One but had returned to his position as a tax officer at Nottingham Office. Moyland's managers had written him off in career terms, but he was a tenacious individual despite his social confidence being blighted by recurrent bouts of shell shock. Francis was given a small office at the back of the filing room and delegated the laborious task of auditing all of the dividend warrants and other documentation submitted to support tax repayment claims. He was fastidious in examining every document, his zeal built upon the premise that he could resuscitate his career. Moyland's final report highlighted a pattern of common denominators that cast doubt on the authenticity of many repayment claims issued in Nottingham. An investigation was launched, and the trail led back to Waddell, who was arrested and later received five years' imprisonment for stealing £6,000.

'That's about £125,000 in today's money and probably not even the full loss,' Eric emphasised.

Eric placed an acetate of a 1928 report from *The Guardian* on the overhead projector. The report informed them that the printers and plate makers Waddell commissioned were charged with forgery. Luckily for them, they were acquitted after their defence argued that if Waddell could dupe his educated tax inspector colleagues, what chance would these artisan fellows have; they had fallen prey to 'one of the cleverest scoundrels in the country'.

'So, there you are. The shit hit the fan. A huge embarrassment all round. An inquiry was held, and the Board created the Investigation Section in 1929 to pursue enquiries of a personal and confidential nature. The BIO was born.' Eric's history lesson was over.

Tubal hoped that his further training would concentrate on the practical elements required for the job. He was not disappointed. Over the following two weeks, Tubal learnt about evidence gathering, constructing case files, basics of criminal law and surveillance techniques. There were sessions on using an SLR camera, operating handheld, covert and vehicle radio sets and the frequencies he was to use. Although the main radio frequency is unique to BIO, Eric reported that occasionally the Post Office came through on the airways. The General Post Office (GPO) have something called a 'Book Room'. This was discovered when passing the central post office sorting centre at Mount Pleasant in the City of London on one of Eric's training exercises. Nobody had any idea what this was, but when a strange voice came over the radio, it became too good of an opportunity for the more juvenile-thinking members to pass up.

'Book Room,' the voice would say.

Some joker would pick up the radio handset, push the transmit button and reply, 'Book Room.'

No matter what the mystery caller said, the budding entertainers replied with the words 'Book Room'. The GPO had no idea who or where their antagonists were and both sides got fed up pretty quickly. Still, it broke up the monotony of sitting in London traffic. Not that the cars issued for use were going anywhere fast; a fleet of wedge-shaped Rover 213 and 216, mostly in red with a black aerial protruding from the boot. Not very covert to those in the know. The Rovers were great in the city but had the acceleration of a sloth with gout when chasing a 'suspect' round the North Circular. Tubal felt enlivened to learn that all BIO vehicles, including his own car's registration number, were marked with a 'police eyes only' identifier to prevent unwelcome or corrupt eyes revealing their identity. It became clear to all that the limitations of the Road Traffic Act would have to stretch at times to secure the end goal. Tubal briefly perceived the personal benefits of this free reign on the road before reminding himself that he had absorbed himself into a position of responsibility. He would be a fool to jeopardise it. Besides, Tubal had already sown his automotive wild oats in his teens. In his manor, driving licences and speed restrictions were deemed gratuitous impediments to honing skills behind the wheel. He had somehow managed to avoid police attention until after he passed his driving test late at a comparatively mature age of twenty-one.

'Yes, I'm sorry, Officer. It was how fast? Oh dear. The carburettor was sticking, and I put my foot down to clear it. You followed me for how long? No, I didn't see you.'

A guilty plea to Camberwell Magistrates and a £30 fine followed, teaching Tubal a valuable lesson: always check your rear-view mirror.

The two weeks of structured tutoring flew by. Tubal felt relieved but apprehensive that he was still only partially equipped to meet the role. Eric had made it clear to the group that the best way to learn was by doing the job. From now on, success was in each investigator's grasp if they applied themselves.

'How do you think you've done, Mac?' Eric took Tubal quietly aside.

It was the last Thursday evening before the group split up and returned to their base teams on Friday lunchtime. Days normally ended in the Orleans Arms, the unofficial out-of-hours base that provided sustenance and solace to work-weary investigators most lunchtimes too. Tonight's session at the Orleans was a celebration of new friendships and skills mixed with trepidation. There were no formal assessment, and Tubal's future lay in the gift of Eric and the training team.

'Well, I think I did OK. There was a lot to learn,' Tubal expressed tentatively.

'No, mate, you'll be alright, no problem. It'll be good to get some young blood.' Eric's brief riposte lifted the weight from Tubal's shoulders.

'Same again, Mac,' Paul muttered from behind, a Senior Service cigarette clasped within clenched teeth.

'Yeah, go on then,' Tubal responded, 'I am always thirsty, mate.'

It's going to be a good night, Tubal thought as he spied Debbie at the bar. She seemed to have mellowed during the two weeks and was back to Manchester tomorrow.

'You alright, Deb. What can I get you?' A new confidence lurked within Tubal as he moved towards her.

Everyone else had stayed in local guest houses, but Tubal lodged at his grandparents. Ironically, the HQ of his family's business interests was less than two miles from the office. The wheeling and dealing of Tubal's youth omnipresent yet the familial connections aligned with South London villainy now felt inconsequential. Part of Tubal's armoury but not relevant to the here and now: reserved for weekends, bank holidays and weddings, of which there were many. After all, no one in the family had been convicted of any crime since Tubal's great-grandfather's street bookmaking days in the 1950s. Even that was a lottery in the gift of the local police sergeant; gift being the operative word. So, for now, Tubal was happy and would stay put.

'No, love, you're alright; I've got one here,' Debbie replied, eyes transfixed on a muscled guy at the dart board.

Tubal felt that he was in a no-win situation. He had to get back for Horlicks with his nan, so an iced cucumber sandwich with Debbie was definitely off the menu, despite Tubal's Red Stripe lager-fuelled bravado.

'OK, Deb,' he whispered as he returned to Paul and Eric.

The beer monster element of Tubal's brain contested it, but he was in the early stages of a hangover, and tomorrow was beckoning. It was time to call a taxi and get some sleep.

***

In what seemed like no time at all, Tubal was up, showered and off on the long walk back to the office for the last day of training. Despite a few sore heads, the class were upbeat and ready to roll.

'Morning, gentlemen and Miss Condon. I'm pleased to say that you have all passed the training and will start operationally on Monday. I have for each one of you your deputation signed by the Inland Revenue commissioners.' Eric called everybody's name out in turn. Nobody clapped.

'Tubal McArthur.'

Tubal walked to the front of the room and collected a small leather wallet containing his photograph and a silver badge with the Inland Revenue crest on. His authority was neatly printed on watermarked white card.

This is to certify that T McArthur, whose photograph and signature appear opposite, has been appointed by the Board of Inland Revenue, *Somerset House, Strand, LONDON WC2 to be an* investigating officer *and he is authorised to carry out investigations on behalf of the Board of Inland Revenue.*

Tubal silently read this and felt that he finally belonged to something. He was an investigating officer or IO for short. The rest of the morning was spent on admin and the alluring world of expenses available to claim, one unique concession being that anyone still working past 8pm was entitled to £10 towards a meal and an extra hour's overtime to eat it! It didn't register with Tubal at first that he would have to work a twelve-hour day before qualifying for the allowance. Still, £10 is enough for a good curry.

'A meal receipt will be required and no, you cannot claim for alcohol.' Eric made his point.

Tubal had to buy his own drinks. *Well, I suppose that's what overtime is for*, thought he, single with only self-gratification to concern himself.

End of morning it was back to the Orleans for a liquid lunch and to wish the regional compadres au revoir. Tubal and Paul then spent the early afternoon with the experienced IOs amassed at the bar for their Friday debrief. Five operational teams covering London and the South, each with six IOs and a senior officer. Judging by the camaraderie and constancy of whip money being laundered for full pints of Young's finest, Tubal guessed that a fair percentage were in the Orleans. Soon, he and his buddy would meet their new partners, experienced IOs to develop their new-found skills.

'Hello, mate, I'm Marty McIlhenny, the liaison officer in the Registry. It's my job to know about you, Tubal McArthur.'

Before him is a large bear of a man, dwarfing Tubal's five-feet-eight frame, pale-skinned with wild, unkempt blond hair and eyebrows contrasted against a full ginger-tinged beard. Marty winked as his hand shot out, grasped Tubal's tightly and harmoniously shook the right side of his body.

'Fancy a drink?' Marty asked through hair-muffled lips.

Before he could answer, a cold pint of lager was ordered for Tubal. It seemed as if refusal wasn't an option.

'That's great, thanks,' Tubal replied.

Marty explained that the Registry was where intelligence was collated, and his role was to liaise with the police and other investigative agencies.

'Mostly involves meeting in pubs and sharing bits of information. If you need to know anything, come to me,' Marty said. 'Oh, and when we leave here, pop down to our afternoon Tea Club.'

And with that, he was off to the other end of the bar.

'I see you've met Wookie.' Paul was back beside Tubal.

'Wookie?' he replied, puzzled.

'That's what they call Marty the liaison guy, like in the *Star Wars* films,' Paul answered.

It made sense to Tubal now, although he felt sure that Marty was not covered in hair under his suit. Unless he shaved it.

Once they'd had their fill for the day at the Orleans, everyone retired to base. Paul and Tubal returned to the classroom. They didn't know where else to go but found that Eric had already left for his home office up the M1.

'OK, Paul, where's this Tea Club then?' Tubal slurred.

It was getting late in the afternoon, and nobody appeared to be doing any work in the rooms that they passed. As they ambled around the corridors and building spurs, Tubal and Paul found themselves audibly directed towards their likely destination. One of the rooms emitted clouds of cigarette smoke and loud whooping noises. This had to be the place. Tubal gingerly pushed the door open to witness what could be described as orchestrated mayhem. Around the room the walls were decorated with press releases, Page 3 model cut-outs from

The Sun and what appeared to be IOs' deputation photographs superimposed onto compromising pictures. At the far end there was a group playing cricket darts with the arrows flying over seated men chain-smoking and swigging tea. Some Tubal recognised from the Orleans but others were new to him. Between them and the door, Tubal could see Marty stooped over a much shorter, younger man as they moved crab-like around in circles akin to sumo wrestlers. The younger man's legs flailed around like spindly nunchucks as he tried to keep his balance. Upon catching sight of Tubal and Paul, the pair parted and invited them in. The younger man spoke excitedly, his voice jumping an octave through his breathlessness.

'Hello there, I'm Padraig Smith. Paddy. Welcome to the Tea Club.'

Tubal had been cocooned from the main throng until then. Whether that was for his benefit or theirs was anybody's guess, but he was past the point of no return. Monday would be a new beginning. An introduction to their teams and the partner who would nanny them for the unforeseeable future. Tubal felt like the Exchequer's virgin bride in an arranged marriage with the unknown.

Chapter Two

Tubal's first six months at BIO were over and he had passed his probation period. On his first operational day, he had been allocated to Group Two, one of four teams tasked with routine criminal investigations, leaving Group Five as a specialist resource. Tubal's life had now blended into a culture of early rising and working late into the evening. It was absorbing work, and he took to it well. Harry, the Senior IO, had found the perfect partner for him. Somebody whose demeanour and complete lack of trepidation when faced with potential for aggravation starkly compared with Tubal's. True, Tubal could front out any situation, but this was different. He and his partner both had the quiet exterior, but this fellow was one piercing blue-eyed, blond coiled spring that took no prisoners. A highly efficient IO fabled for his chasing down and thumping a road rager whilst on route to his own wedding. Nathan Bronsky, or 'Nutty Nat', was a few years older and a great deal fitter than Tubal. A quarter Polish and a quarter Ukrainian from his absent father's side, and the remaining half Tasmanian devil they guessed. Although that was not strictly true, as Tubal had already been introduced to Nat's mother: a demure, softly spoken South Londoner whom Nat doted on. Maybe his irritability was founded on Slavic testosterone and resentment at his father leaving before he was born. No one was brave enough to call him 'Nutty' to his face and, despite his tenacity and sartorial elegance, Nat was about as cultured as Noddy. He always looked serious, but if he found something humorous, his eyes lit up and his tongue leant out of the left corner of his mouth. Once any self-believed witty comment imparted his lips, his eyes became fixed on you for a reaction. A simple smile normally worked, but no reaction, often borne out of miscomprehension by the unaware, invoked a cold stare and a curt, 'What's up with you, arsehole?'

They worked a range of cases together but predominately tax exemption certificate or 'lump' fraud in the construction industry. This, Tubal had discovered, was a scheme that allowed building workers or 'subbies' to receive tax-free pay from construction companies on production of a voucher, the '715', authenticated by a '714' certificate containing their photograph and signature. Very similar to a bank card and chequebook but with their picture scowling back. These certificates had a three-year life before expiry. Subbies also receive a book of twenty-five vouchers and hand over a 715 in exchange for their gross pay. The contractor then sent the 715 vouchers to the Revenue and the subbie settles with the taxman at the end of the year. Simple. Trouble was that each voucher could receipt a figure of up to one hundred grand. It was therefore possible, if an unscrupulous contractor purloined a blank book of 715s, that they could write off up to £2.5 million to a subbie who may have disappeared long ago. Thereby a huge illegal market had been created that cost the Exchequer £50 million a year. It was Group Two's responsibility to track down and prosecute those subbies and contractors that abused this scheme. Although Nat and Tubal worked as partners, they each maintained their own portfolio of cases to investigate.

***

It was a Thursday afternoon. Tubal had spent his time monitoring contractors who had submitted 715s which have been reported as lost or stolen by their holders. There are genuine cases of course, but some dishonest subbies do falsely report their 715s lost, stolen or even befalling a disaster such as fire or being shredded by a hungry pet. These 715s miraculously later turn up at a contractor's office bearing an array of handwriting yet an authentic-looking signature for the 'loser'. This then begged the question: how did the contractor get them? Experience had taught Tubal that the voucher book, with a photocopy of the 714 certificate, had most likely been sold to a dealer for a few hundred pounds, if not less. That was if you discounted a genuine theft by a psychic signature forger. Dealers can make 10% of the voucher's face value. The contractor would write off the whole amount to pay a cash-in-hand workforce or reduce their own profit for tax purposes. It was seriously big money. Potentially a book could be worth a quarter of a million pounds on the black market. The most ruthless of the dealers were 'ghosts' unknown to the UK tax and benefits systems. Their success was reliant upon paramilitary masters 'over the water' compelling them to pay commission in order to operate. This was organised crime working covertly within the building of Britain's infrastructure. Generally, the subbie 715 sellers have little interest in what happens to their documents. The more astute voucher sellers will keep their head down, systematically harvesting single 715s. They've worked out that reporting the loss or theft of 715 books will prompt an unannounced visit from the BIO boys to ask awkward questions.

This Thursday felt different though, as if a defining moment was within Tubal's grasp. He had placed a number of subbies on a central 'stop list'. Once their 715s were submitted by contractors, the central processing office extracted these and posted them onto Tubal. Typically, these 'stops' included a mixture of reported thefts, sold vouchers surfacing after a seller's prosecution and suspicious 715s needing further scrutiny. They usually arrived mid-week, giving Tubal and Nat an incentive to bundle the case files into the car and spend the evening knocking on doors. Afterwards, they would end up at a predesignated curry house to meet other IOs for a drink, debrief and to fill their boots on the ten quid allowance. Nat always said that this social interaction was endorsed by senior management. It promoted camaraderie, apparently. Tubal wouldn't argue with that notion, let alone challenge Nat's contention.

'Hey, Nat, have you come across a company called BUR or Boteler Urban Regeneration Limited?' Tubal asked. 'They've used one of my booksellers.'

'Never heard of them. Hang on a minute, mate, I'll speak to Marty in the Registry; he can check his database.' Nat was away through the door before Tubal could speak further.

Tubal followed behind him. He didn't like being left out and certainly didn't want Nutty taking all of the glory if it transpired that he was actually onto something. As Tubal entered the Registry, Marty had already accessed the central intelligence system.

'BUR are a new company that have bought up swathes of London dockland for regeneration,' Marty reported. 'They are the ones building the Pilgrims Pyramid entertainment complex at Rotherhithe. The site where the old Surrey Docks is being filled in.'

Marty had access to systems that were beyond the reach of most IOs, although it was planned that each IO would get their own computer over the coming months. Up until then, each IO had to research their targets remotely, relying on paper files and the filling in of forms to get information from local tax offices. The computers will give them everything at the touch of a button. *Very 1984*, Tubal thought when told; well, 1987 to be exact.

'The contract is worth millions according to the *Construction News*,' Marty continued. 'One of my Special Branch contacts has a marker on it, don't know why. What's your interest?'

Tubal pulled a wad of 715 vouchers from the envelope he was holding. 'A subbie coughed to selling two books of vouchers for fifty quid each a few months back. Robbie Quinn in Stevenage. Got two years in prison,' Tubal briefed Marty. 'BUR has submitted five of Quinn's 715s. A round sum ten grand on each so far and there's still a whole book outstanding.'

Marty took the vouchers from Tubal.

'Looks like these have been topped and tailed,' Marty referred to the signature and Quinn's address, which had been completed by him as part of the deal. 'Who did he sell to?'

'Wouldn't say. Classic unknown, never-been-seen-before man in a pub story. Quinn got the shock of his life when Mac told him that this invisible man's clients had already written off over a hundred grand in his name.' Nat jumped into the conversation.

'There's a similar batch of five from another subbie, Thomas Cole, again ten grand a piece,' Tubal interrupted, 'reported nicked from his van. Lives up in Essex, Basildon.'

Tubal had been keeping an eye on Cole for a while and had collated a preliminary history for him. Six months earlier, Cole reported that his van was broken into while left overnight in a pub car park. The only things stolen were his 715 vouchers and no report of theft had been made to the police. Cole had made no mention of his 714 certificate when he wrote to the Revenue requesting a replacement book, but his vouchers were surfacing with a signature matching the one on his file.

Until then, there hadn't been a great deal of money on them. Now BUR had submitted both Quinn and Cole's vouchers, receipting substantial round sum amounts dated at weekly intervals. This might be expected of a subbie with their own workforce, but Quinn was in Pentonville and Cole was a one-man band groundworker.

'Looks like we'll be in Basildon tonight then,' Nat replied. 'I'll drive. Get your stuff and we'd better hit the road.'

So, on this Thursday, it looked like Tubal had bagged himself a major investigation into Boteler Urban Regeneration Limited. Later he would put the company and their subbies on a stop list to get all of their submitted vouchers sent to him. But then they were on their way to interview Thomas Cole: downside being that Nutty Nat was driving and Tubal had left his spare underpants at home. Not that Nat was a bad driver, it's just a whiff of open road triggered a slamming of his right foot on the throttle whilst simultaneously weaving in and out of traffic in a game of automotive dare. He loved his car: a jet black, 2.8-litre fuel-injected MKIII Capri. Its aggressive styling matched him perfectly, but its low-slung seats played havoc with a big lad like Tubal. Nat enjoyed smoking in the sanctity of his car and the ashtrays bore testament to this. Tubal might have the occasional cigar, thinking it might sober him up at weddings, but, despite bathing in other people's smoke most of his life, cigarettes never appealed. Fresh air suited Tubal far better, although he realised his mistake as soon as he opened the Capri's air vents as they flew along the North Circular.

'What the fuck did you do that for?' Nat spoke through the peppering of cigarette ash and leaf mould infusing them from the ashtrays and deep recesses of the dashboard.

'I wanted some fresh air,' Tubal replied as he dusted himself down.

'Well now you see what fresh air does.' Nat scowled towards his partner and slammed his foot on the gas in a fit of pique.

The rest of the journey was driven in silence, Nat sulking and Tubal slapping dust from his clothes and removing debris from his nose.

They finally arrived at Basildon Police Station around 5pm and asked to speak to the collator, if they hadn't already gone home. This was normal protocol to ascertain if there was a history of violent behaviour or anything else relevant to Cole that they should know. Luckily the collator was still around and happy to help, always a bonus in itself. A search of his card index revealed no intelligence on Thomas Cole. For Tubal, he was just thankful that the diversion had given Nat time to cool off before they went off to confront their man.

Thomas Cole lived on the sprawling Laindon Five Links housing estates at Somercotes. Linked courtyards separated the houses and parking was a toss-up between a cul-de-sac with no escape route or around a large central green provided for recreation. Either way, strangers were visible a mile off. This was an area of dark alleys and dingy corners, and the police knew it colloquially as 'Alcatraz' after the prison colony. Nat, true to form, went straight into the cul-de-sac as the least visible but riskier option. Tubal approached Cole's front door tentatively. The doorbell was detached and hung forlorn from its wire connecting it to the door frame. Wooden board replaced the bottom glass door panel that had likely been kicked in and 'Baz', a graffiti welcome to visitors, adorned the porch brickwork. Nat impatiently leant across Tubal, took a coin from his pocket and rapped it hard on the door frame; five times in quick succession. Another of his tactless habits guaranteed to wind people up. Almost immediately, a make-up-encrusted, red-lipped, bleach-blonde woman snatched open the door. A waft of body odour-tinged sugary cheap perfume blew past, diminishing the elegance of her business suit.

'Is Tom in?' Tubal enquired.

'Oh, I thought you were a mini cab. No, he's not in from work yet,' she replied. 'Who wants to know?'

'No bother, I'll try him later.'

'Please yourself.' The woman turned off the hall light and shut the door behind her. She walked past Tubal without looking back. The house was now in complete darkness.

'I'm not hanging about round here,' Nat said. 'Let's find a pub.'

Finding a pub was easier said than done. The developers installed cable TV in every home, but public houses were deemed superfluous in the world of 1960s new towns. After driving off the estate, they pulled up outside their only option, the Plough and Tractor, ironically titled in such expansive fields of bricks and concrete. A rather odd structure looking like a mobile home had dropped from space onto the roof of a bungalow; regimented bricks and glass downstairs contrasting with dirty beige cladding adorning the overhanging oddity on top. Tubal guessed this would appeal to Nat. He wasn't a fan of the Orleans, or even drinking particularly, but he enjoyed the seedier side and spent long Friday lunch breaks unilaterally surveying the strippers at his local. As they entered the Plough and Tractor, the air held a stale blend of spent alcohol, burnt cooking fat and cigarette smoke. Tubal felt the stickiness of the dank, drink-sodden carpet beneath his feet as they approached the bar.

'Two pints of lager please, mate,' Nat jumped in to order, furnishing Tubal with the notion that perhaps he did have at least one redeeming feature after all, 'and some change for the pool table.'

This was just what Tubal dreaded. Nat wanted to play

pool. This establishment was not likely to attract suited and booted passing trade for a post-work aperitif, let alone those hogging centre stage by commandeering the pool table. More significantly, bending down to cue the ball caused Tubal's glasses to roll down his nose, adding blurred vision to his natural ineptitude at the game. This did not feel like a natural environment for Tubal, not in someone else's territory, but it allowed them to kill time until they tried Cole's address again. It was still quite early, and witnesses to Tubal's three-nil thrashing by Nat were few until a scruffy, dirt-sodden man in tan safety boots placed his coins on the pool table. Tubal is saved.

'I'm done here, buddy.' Tubal handed over to Nat's new challenger. 'It's all yours.'

Nat vigorously chalked his cue ready for the challenge. Tubal relaxed, relishing the chance of a break from Nat's excited bellowing each time that he had beat him.

'I'll get another round in,' Tubal called over to Nat as he approached the bar.

As he put the pints down on a spare table, Tubal looked across at Nat's new friend. He looked familiar. Tubal plucked a small passport photograph from his breast pocket and discretely held the image in the palm of his hand to study closely. Although somewhat dishevelled with several days of stubble caked with sweat and dust, Tubal was certain it was his mark for that evening: Thomas Cole. Nat was too engrossed in his game, so Tubal kept his discovery quiet as he slowly sipped his amber nectar. There was no point leaving the pub until he did, and intelligence might be gained from observing Cole for a bit. A judgement call had to be made. If Cole was clearly in for a session, Tubal decided that he would have to confront him here while he was alone and sober. There was no point risking any evidence gained, only for it to be kicked out of court.

'Better put your money down if you want another thrashing,' Nat shouted over. He had beaten Cole and would now be insufferable.

'No, I've had enough,' Tubal called back. 'Your drink is here and won't drink itself.'

Nat joined Tubal back at the table. Cole had taken up a stool at the bar.

'We'd better go round and give another knock after this,' Nat said.

Tubal showed him the photo held in the palm of his hand.

'I think that's him,' Tubal replied. 'If he's not left by the time we've finished our drinks…'

He had spoken too soon. Out of the corner of Tubal's eye he had spied Cole quickly moving towards the exit. Hopefully he was heading for home. They decided to wait to give Cole time to sort himself out and would then shoot round to knock on his door.

Fifteen minutes later, the Capri was fired up and steaming back to the ruefully dingy cul-de-sac at Alcatraz. Where the Capri had nested earlier, a battered former GPO van was stood. Nat peered through the grimy windows and spied a crudely printed invoice headed 'Tom Cole Groundwork' in the nearside footwell. As they approached Cole's address, the visibility of the hall lights provided the second clue that he was back home. Tubal rushed forward and gave two hard knocks on the door. Nothing. Nat pulled his coin out, but this time Tubal's bulk prevented him from claiming the narrow doorway. Tubal knocked again and an outline approached from behind the top panel of frosted glass. The door slowly opened.

'Mr Cole, Thomas Cole?' Tubal enquired. His head nodded to confirm as they introduced who they were.

'Didn't I just see you both in the Plough and Tractor?' There is a degree of foreboding in Cole's voice.

Tubal resisted the urge to lie that they had been watching him for weeks and knew what he had been up to. Maturity has improved his psyche to the extent that his thoughts only occasionally impulsively spurted from his lips these days.

'Yeah, that's right, but I didn't know it was you. We had just popped in to use the toilet.' Oh well, Tubal lied about the lying. 'Can we come in to talk about the 715 vouchers you had stolen?'

Thomas Cole moved aside, and they were shown into his living room. The TV blared out an advert for soap powder, yet the air was pungent with the odour of sweat-soaked socks and stale tobacco. Tubal could see Nat gagging. He fought to speak without inhaling the odour through his nose. The plan was that Tubal would lead the interview while Nat took contemporaneous notes. They hoped by the end to have a witness statement of use against the contractors submitting Cole's vouchers at the very least. In reality, though, nobody knew how this was going to pan out or how far Cole could be pushed. Everything depended on gut feeling and gauging reaction when the stolen vouchers were shown; the little tics, sucking in of air, sweating, even crying. As Tubal gained experience, he gained confidence in judging the situation. Thomas Cole sat back on a faux leather armchair engrained with splashes of white gunk. He'd had no time to change out of his work clothes. Nat and Tubal perched on the edge of a candlewick throw-covered sofa, minimising surface contact and taking the most sanitary option.

'Can you explain how and when your vouchers were stolen?' Tubal spoke over the TV noise. 'And can you turn that telly off.'

Thomas obliged with the TV, but there was no respite from his feet. The quicker this was done, the better for their airways. A customary tale unfolded, one where the dates and locations differed but the storyline remained the same. Thomas recounted that he left his van at the Plough and Tractor overnight. In the morning, he discovered his van had been entered and the vouchers had been removed from the glove compartment. Nothing else was stolen and he never rang the police or his insurance company as he might have left the door unlocked and didn't think the vouchers had any worth. *Bollocks*, Tubal thought.

'So, there wasn't any damage to your van then?' he said rhetorically. 'How did you know someone had been inside?'

Thomas didn't answer.

'Can you show me your 714 certificate?' Tubal continued.

'Yes, of course. I always keep it safe in my wallet.' Thomas reached into his trouser pocket and pulled a brown leather case sporting a patina of dust into the open. 'Here it is, safe and sound.' Thomas handed the certificate to Tubal, who placed it on the floor.

'And nothing else was stolen?' he repeated.

'No, sir,' Thomas said after a short pause.

'How would the thief know your address?' Tubal kept the questions coming, but Thomas looked perplexed and didn't seem to comprehend what he meant.

No response came back. It was time to put some pressure on. This did not stack up. Thomas would need to see what Tubal had been keeping from him.

'What do you know about a contractor called Boteler Urban Regeneration or BUR, Tom? Down in South London.'

'Nothing. Never heard or worked for them.' Thomas had found his voice.

'They seem to know you, Tom,' Tubal hit back, showing Cole the first voucher. 'Ten thousand pounds. How do you explain that?'

Thomas sharply sucked in air, his eyes transfixed on the 715 voucher. Tubal swiftly presented the next one in the sequence.

'Another ten grand a week later and then each week for a further three weeks. Fifty thousand pounds in five weeks.' Thomas was handed each one in turn.

'They're nothing to do with me.' Thomas secreted globules of sweat from his brow as he spoke. 'They must be the stolen ones.'

'So, who did you last give a voucher to from the stolen book?' Tubal asked.

'Nobody, it was a new book that I was keeping spare in the van.'

'Were any of the vouchers written on?' Tubal looked at Thomas, who was now shaking his head. 'So how did your address and signature get on there?'

'Don't know. It looks like my signature, but someone must have copied it.' Thomas's hands shook as he answered.

Thomas Cole was in a corner; even if somebody had copied his signature, they would need the certificate as a guide, and this was quite firmly held beneath Tubal's left foot. His address could be found out from the telephone directory, but even a master forger needs something to copy.

'I don't believe you, Tom. The contractor has a copy of your certificate and is adamant that you worked and were paid fifty grand to supply labour. What really happened to your 715 book?' Tubal subconsciously lowered his voice as if BUR had heard the false statement leave his lips.

'It wasn't me; I haven't earned that money. Look around you – I'm skint.' Thomas paused and put his head in his hands. 'The missus is doing two jobs just so we can live.'

'It's not just the Boteler vouchers; I have others here, same writing on the address and your signature. Looks like the book was signed up in one go. Did you sell the book, Tom?' Tubal pushed further, knowing that more than half the missing book had yet to surface.

No response, but that's OK. Silence could be a valuable tool compelling people to fill the gap. Thomas was gazing at the floor and Tubal sensed that he needed a few minutes to contemplate the significance of what was being said. He probably had no idea where the vouchers would end up or how much money was to be put on them. You could guarantee that the contractor, to save their own skin, would be resolute that the subcontractor they employed was the genuine certificate holder.

Nat had caught up with the notes and put pen and paper to the floor.

'This is not looking too good, mate. You've been taken for a ride, and somebody is earning a shit load of money off your back,' Nat spoke directly to Thomas. 'I think you signed up the book and sold it with a photocopy of the certificate.'

Thomas rose from his seat and walked to a small serving hatch through to the kitchen. Picking up a cigarette, he lit it and returned. Slumping back on his chair, he took a deep breath and spoke.

'I'm a bit too fond of the horses and it's got me into a shed load of debt. The wife doesn't know. She'd kill me. A bloke on site said that he could help me out and put me onto a contact of his. I was offered a grand for the whole book. I just didn't think. This was the answer to my prayers, but the money is blown now.'

Nat removed his screed from the floor to record Tubal's next words.

'Thomas, I must inform you that you do not have to say anything, but anything you do say will be written down and may be used in evidence,' Tubal cautioned. 'I will ask you a series of questions, and they and your answers will be written down. When we are finished, I'll invite you to sign this Q and A as a true and accurate record.'

A hurdle had been breached and the relief in Thomas's face as the burden lifted from him was clear to Nat and Tubal. He gave no name for his illegal temporary benefactor, but he did describe him as a large, stocky Irishman, over six feet tall, with a big stomach, dirty glasses, bushy grey beard and bulbous nose. The Irishman drove a four-wheel drive Landcruiser from where he removed a rucksack and counted out £1,000 in cash, all new notes, for the fully signed book and a copy of Cole's 714 certificate. Not much to go on in the scheme of things but Tubal's suspicions were confirmed, and he'd notched up another bookseller, another 'cough' to his hit list. This was how his peers would judge him, and another success had been chalked up for the office.

It was late by then. As they shot back to Surrey, Nat and Tubal chatted incessantly, dissecting and speculating on the evening's proceedings. The next day, Tubal would tidy up the papers to prepare for a charging decision. Next time he'll see Thomas Cole will be in court. But first, it's a celebratory chicken dhansak at the Akash and a catch-up with any other IOs drifting back from their night's entertainment.

Chapter Three

The weeks blew past in a hurricane of self-sufficiency, sustenance and shag pile. Three or more months had passed, and Tubal's life had changed exponentially with an annulment from his grandparents' patriarchy and a move to his own flat overlooking the Thames at Surbiton, that icon of suburban life. Weekends are cherished. Golden hours for slumber and seeking an assemblage of social pursuits outside of the biological family. He had a new family now, coagulated by comradeship, camaraderie and curry. What he didn't have was the time or opportunity for romance. Not that he hadn't tried, but Tubal had zero ability to read lascivious cues and lacked the confidence to pursue primal attraction, leaving him prone to surrender to sexual trysts with insatiable cousins or sloppy drunken kisses from disconsolate girls at parties. He lacked the wherewithal to resist and, frankly, it would be impolite. But, for now, Tubal's work absorbed him. At the most inopportune moment, thoughts and hypothesis on current cases emerged from nowhere and challenged his mind. Inspiration may bloom in the early hours, curtailing blissful sleep. The sanctuary of his morning shower was often invaded by line of enquiry ideas popping up in his head, diverting Tubal's concentration and triggering amnesia as to which of his bits he had already washed. Still, he was loving life, and the investigation into the Pilgrims Pyramid development and BUR gathered pace. Nat had been up with Tubal to visit Robbie Quinn in prison, and Quinn confirmed that the BUR vouchers were amongst those sold. His zero knowledge of BUR and the fifty grand was corroborated in a witness statement; indisputable of course as he was detained at Her Majesty's pleasure at that time. More importantly, Quinn relented and gave a description similar to that given by Thomas Cole for the 'man in the pub'. What's more, Tubal had a name; the Irishman was called 'Patrick'. Well, nobody said it was easy! Fortunately, Marty maintained the national intelligence database and 'Patrick' was appended to the other unique identifiers and descriptions for the ultimate prize: the dealers. In BIO case hierarchy, taking out a dealer was the pinnacle and an asset to one's career path.

There was also a new lead on BUR. They had submitted their annual subcontractor return, which included the Quinn and Cole payments. It also highlighted subcontractors issued with a 714C, or company certificate. These certificates had the company name, registration number and company secretary's signature printed on them but no photograph. They are issued to limited liability companies with a high turnover or large geographical spread. Better than that, the main contractor could validly pay untaxed amounts against a company invoice. There were no 715 vouchers, just a copy of the 714C. Boteler Urban Regeneration Limited had paid a total of £1.5 million to one such 714C company, Gilmore Angell Limited. Significantly, this company were no longer believed to be at their North West London business address, and letters to the company secretary, Devereaux Angell, were returned 'gone away'. To Tubal, it further felt like he had uncovered a major fraud case, but to prove criminality required direct evidence against the string pullers at BUR. Firstly, though, he had to identify the Gilmore Angell Limited invoice supplier and speak to Devereaux Angell, the original 714C holder. Things were moving quickly, but then an undeniably predictable event saw Tubal's destiny unexpectedly swerve again.

The Rover 200s had been letting the IOs down and the skill of their sole motorcyclist was increasingly the difference between an evidentially worthwhile surveillance op and an early stand-down with a greasy compensatory gut-buster breakfast. Finally, the Treasury puppet masters had realised that the bad guys could be ignominious in flouting speed limits and traffic laws and did not politely wait for the cloned Rover fleet to catch them up. Christmas had come early with the supply of new fuel-injected, fat-tyre, automotive power houses of diverse makes and colours, each with covert aerials and communication systems. Nat was beside himself and took the new Vauxhall Cavalier SRi on a solo call to follow up a lead.

'I'm going to put this through its paces,' Nat whispered to Tubal as he left the office, eyes bright and tongue protruding left.

'I'm sure you will,' he responded with his now practised Nat response smile.

And that was it. Next thing Tubal knew was when the Group Two boss, Harry, called the team together to tell them that Nat had broken his leg and was in hospital. Obviously, the pace was a bit too much for him as Nat booted the SRi up a slip road onto the A4, bounced off the rear tyres of a tipper truck and flew through the window of a carpet shop. BIO was now depleted by one car, one IO and facing a compensation claim for untold shards of glass within the shag pile. What's more, Tubal was now partnerless and Harry could not operate with an odd number. Fate had dealt him an opportunity. Yes, Nat had moulded him into the IO he was becoming, but his unbalanced, intolerant view on life had become a hard master to pander to. Now was Tubal time.

There was only one place for him to go now, and Tubal transferred to Group Five the next day. He viewed this as an exciting uplift as IOs on this team worked fluidly without the need for formal partnerships and focused on targeted surveillance operations into dealers. Tubal felt that he could fit straight in and progress the work he had already started. What's more, due to the importance of the Pilgrims Pyramid development, Tubal's investigation into BUR and partial identification of 'Patrick' had come to the attention of Grenville Allonby, the group leader responsible for authorising high-profile BIO operations. Allonby had never been a BIO officer himself and perceived them as an insignificant and maverick inconvenience to his daily schedule of pursuing mega-rich tax-evading individuals. A rather sycophantic individual with a reputation for diving under tables and biting the inner thighs of powerless female subalterns, Allonby was trusted by his Somerset House superiors to operate worldwide in seeking reparation for UK PLC. Tubal had no idea why he was interested in his case, but that was something for his new Senior Investigation Officer to concern himself with. So, that afternoon, Tubal mentally prepared for relocation to Group Five with a long lunch at the Orleans to toast Nat's fortunate escape and his breaking free. The remainder of the day passed swimmingly, if not a smidgeon alcohol-fuelled. Tubal slept well that night.

***

'Morning, guys, I'd like to welcome Mac to Group Five. I think that most of you know him, but we'll get the formalities out of the way,' George Craig, the SIO, addressed the room as they gathered for the morning coffee break. 'Can you all please introduce yourselves?'

George was a no-nonsense Scot from Edinburgh with a twinkle in his eye that belied his ability to hoodwink you into a false sense of security, wondering whether you were the butt of his dour humour or likely to encounter serious shit. Tubal had spent the first part of the morning in his office hearing what George expected of him and briefing him on his caseload. Now Tubal's new team waited impatiently to embrace him into the fold and to get on with the rest of their day.

'Mac knows me already; I'm Paddy Smith,' the human nunchuck from the Tea Club spoke first, his polished Surrey twang giving no quarter to their shared Gaelic heritage.

Next was Paul Ramell, Tubal's mate from day one and another one of the reasons he felt glad to get a place in Group Five.

'Hiya, Mac, great to have you on board.'

'Thanks, Paul,' George replied. 'Terry, you're next.'

'Hello, Mac, I'm Terry Burton.'

Tubal hadn't met Terry before; he wasn't one of the Orleans or Tea Club crowd and kept his own company. He was known to Tubal by reputation though, as this preceded him as the IO with the most nicknames, mostly derogatory and normally based upon his latest blinkered faux par. A squat, toad-like individual, bespectacled with a speckled grey mop of hair tousled into a crown to conceal encroaching baldness, Terry was oblivious to the amusement his naivety and trivial attempts at one-upmanship often generated in the downtime chatter. Tubal nodded in recognition as Terry smiled inanely at him. He decided that he would reach his own conclusions about Terry in the field of play.

'Alright, mate, you know me, Stevie Nixon if we're going formal.'

Stevie was the motorcyclist and an invaluable asset to all of the teams working out of their Surrey bolthole. Very much the loner, Stevie spent all of his spare time restoring a 1952 Vincent Black Shadow an uncle left him in his will. He lived for life on two wheels and perfected his surveillance roadcraft on secondment to MI5 following tours with the Royal Military Police.

'Hi, Stevie, I'm looking forward to working with you full-time,' Tubal chipped in.

'Nice to meet you, buddy, Zahid Khan, everyone calls me Sid.'

'Looks like it's only me left then, Felicity Francis, Flick.' A soft hand extended towards Tubal's and gently held it as he felt a glow radiate through his fingers and head towards his cheeks.

Tubal sensed that he'd held eye contact for a nanosecond too long and hoped he wasn't blushing.

'Right, that's it then, back to work,' George ordered. 'Mac, there's a spare desk opposite Flick. Let me know if you need anything.'

So, that was it. Tubal had moved to Group Five and felt a new independence sweep over him. Each IO had their own portfolio of cases, and although George had strategic control, each of the team would lead the rest when pursuing their own cases.

'Fancy going out with me tonight?' Flick had manoeuvred behind him and spoke gently over Tubal's right shoulder. Her voice tinged with rural Kent brogue.

Tubal swivelled his chair round to face Flick.

'Workwise you mean?' he joked as he nervously fumbled with his workstation keys.

Flick looked straight through Tubal, either dismissive of what might be an innocent question or just ignoring his flippancy. Tubal guessed that Flick was a little bit older than him. Her long, honey-streaked hair was tied back, and Tubal noted that she was casually dressed in pink trainers, faded denim jeans and a thin, beige, baggy V-neck jumper shrouding generous but curvaceous contours visible in shadow as the sun glinted through the room's dusty windows. From a distance, Flick could be mistaken for a vapid pawn in the crowd, a demure vista, until she spoke, and a hint of wickedness sparkled with sweet intensity from her delicate hazel eyes framed behind stylish oval glasses. Tubal felt an instant warmth in her company.

'OK, I'm free this evening and I want to check out an address anyway,' he quickly added.

Flick smiled sweetly. Over the next few hours, an itinerary was planned as each consulted the other on their night's objectives. Tubal's was simple: to visit the last known addresses of Gilmore Angell Limited and find Devereaux Angell, de facto secretary, wife of the managing director and holder of the 714C certificate. This fitted in with Flick's plans as she wanted to scope out a surveillance job planned in the same area of North West London during the coming days. She sought to reconnoitre the target address under cover of dusk but before the night drew in.

'If we head over to Cricklewood first, I'll have a shufti at the business address – it's up by the railway yards off the Broadway,' Tubal briefed her as they made their way to the car. 'I'll drive if you like.'

First day on Group Five and Tubal knew he had hit the ground running. The journey over to Cricklewood consisted of long silences and small talk as these two strangers sat cocooned together in the new pool Peugeot 309 GTi. Flick and Tubal knew next to nothing of each other but were not yet comfortable with asking personal questions. Instead, Tubal peppered the journey with anecdotes along the way.

'See that old hospital building, I was born there,' he'd suddenly exclaim at random moments. 'That house there used to be a brothel. Outside the tube station over there, my great-grandfather used to be a street bookie from his flower stall.'

Flick said very little in response, but Tubal sensed that her work preoccupied her mind. As they approached Cricklewood, her inner thoughts vocalised. 'This job of mine, Mac. It's the first op I've planned on my own, so I want to get it right.'

'You'll be fine, I'm sure.' Tubal bid to reassure Flick, knowing that he would also be under the spotlight. 'Here we are, Hampton House, I'll park up and we'll have a look around.'

Gilmore Angell Limited's office was no more than a single-storey prefabricated cabin enclosed by corrugated iron fencing. Two large padlocked meshed metal gates served as the entrance and gave a view of the area within. The yard was empty with no sign that a company supplying over a million pounds of labour operated. Flick joined Tubal from the car, and they walked along to a section where the cabin windows faced out onto the road. Through the dust-coated glass, Tubal managed to make out the company name sign written on a panel lying on the floor. All around it were remnants of charred and shredded papers strewn randomly. It was obvious nobody was around. As Tubal turned to Flick, he became conscious of a third presence exiting from a van that had just pulled up.

'Can I help you, mate?' the uniformed security guard asked as he walked towards them. A dog barked from the rear of his vehicle.

'Yeah, I'm looking for the people who run this yard,' Tubal replied.

'They've done a moonlight flit. Must be months ago now. What do you want with them?'

'I'm owed some money. Nothing for you to worry about.' As he spoke, Tubal and Flick moved towards their car and jumped in.

Once fastened back in the Peugeot's bucket seats, Tubal

fired the engine and drove away before Mr Security had any further questions. Next stop was the address he had for Mrs Angell: a large Victorian house split into flats on Kilburn High Road.

As they approached the front door, Tubal scanned the names marked on the entry phone system. A blank space alongside the bell push for Flat 6, alleged home of Devereaux Angell, stared back at him. Tubal had no idea if she still lived there with her husband, but both needed locating fast. A buzzer sounded as he pushed the dull metal button and waited for the intercom to crackle. Nothing. He pushed again and waited for a good ten seconds. No reply.

'Oh well, time for plan B.' Tubal nodded at Flick as he pushed the doorbells for the ground-floor flats and waited for the first one to answer.

'Hello,' came a cracked elderly voice from the box, 'who's there?'

'Sorry to trouble you but I have a letter to hand deliver to Flat 6,' Tubal replied. 'Can you open the front door please?'

Flick was already leaning against the door as it clicked and swung open. The mystery voice remained safe and secure within their home as the two IOs mounted the stairs to Flat 6. Outside, Flick stood back, leaving Tubal to knock on the door whilst simultaneously pressing his ear against the wood to listen for signs of life. Still nothing. Tubal pushed the letter box open and peered inside. Somebody was living here, but who? Suddenly, a child crawled across the hall floor from one room to another.

'There's a baby in there,' Tubal whispered to Flick.

'Hello, can you come to the door please.' He raised his voice as he called through the letter box. 'My name's Tubal McArthur and I'm looking for Mrs Angell.'

A figure stooped to pick the baby up and edged towards

the front door. Tubal withdrew his fingers from the metal letter box as it snapped back into place. After a few seconds, the door fell back and strained against the security chain. Through the gap, Tubal made out a young black woman dressed in a white bath robe peering out at him.

'There is nobody of that name here,' she said in a soft Caribbean lilt. 'I don't know a Mrs Angell.'

Tubal produced his deputation and identified himself and Flick as BIO officers.

'This is the address we have for her. How long have you lived here?' Flick asked.

'I don't, this is my boyfriend's place, Eric Warner. He's lived here about six months; I'm just visiting.'

'Have you seen any post for this address that doesn't belong to Eric?' Tubal enquired.

'Everything goes into the letter box downstairs and gets left if it's not for Eric.' The young woman removed the chain and directly faced them.

'Can you open the letter box for me?' Tubal requested.

'Well, I suppose it's alright; Eric works on the buses and won't be home until late. Hang on, I'll grab the keys.' The young woman disappeared back inside before returning with the baby clasped to her chest and shut the door behind her.

Downstairs in the hallway, a bank of locked boxes with post slots stood against the wall. Taking a small bunch of keys from her dressing gown, the woman handed the baby to Flick and opened number six. Inside was a wad of post secured by an elastic band. The top envelope was marked for the attention of Mrs D Angell, Gilmore Angell Limited. Tubal quickly flicked through the rest, knowing that, realistically, he would need to open and examine the post back at the office to look for evidence.

'If it's okay with you, I'll take these and redirect the letters back to the Post Office.' This wasn't exactly true, but Tubal said it anyway.

'Do what you like; Eric puts it all back in the post anyway when he has time,' the young woman muttered as she gathered the baby and remounted the stairs. 'Goodnight.'

Flick and Tubal returned to the car and made their way over to Kilburn. Tubal's work for the day was done. Flick was targeting the girlfriend of a dealer who had absconded to Ireland after being found guilty of fraud. In his absence, the courts gave out a lengthy prison sentence, meaning that he would go directly to jail if they located him. A week ago, Flick had a breakthrough with an anonymous telephone call informing her that the dealer and his girlfriend were still seeing each other. On the back of that, Group Five planned a surveillance operation on the girlfriend in the hope that the two would meet up. As they parked near the target address, Flick took a small notepad from her pocket and noted possible plotting positions for the cars and an observation point, or OP, for the IOs maintaining eyeball on the address. It didn't take long to scout round and find the exit points from the target's tidy mid-terrace house. Basically, there were two: front door onto street; back door into a public convenience of an alleyway serving druggies, dogs and dossers. Although Flick had it covered, likelihood was the secret mistress would come out the front.

'OK, Mac, I'm all done. What do you fancy to eat?'

'How about a few pints and a curry?'

'Yeah, I'm up for that.'

Group Five wasn't that different after all, and Tubal had survived his first day.

Chapter Four

'Stand by, stand by, all Hawk units,' Eyeball transmitted from the covert OP as all units stirred into life.

Flick had briefed everyone early in the morning and issued each pair of IOs with an Operational Order containing photographs and known information for the day's targets, Shauna Brady and, if all went to plan, her fugitive boyfriend Gerry Murphy. The group left Surrey at 6am. It was Flick's theory that if Shauna went out during the day, it probably wouldn't be too early. The intelligence team had already confirmed that she doesn't have a job or any known reason to leave her Kilburn home. Each of the vehicles was assigned a 'Hawk' prefix denoting that they are a London and South operating BIO unit. As was normal on these jobs, the team was working blind and expected a long day ahead with no idea of the outcome. Although it was believed that Shauna was unemployed, her name was linked to major players in 'lump' fraud. On at least two occasions, she has been found in bed with known dealers when the police crashed through their front door in the early hours. That being said, they had no corroborative information on how Shauna spent her day. However, if the information was kosher and it led to Murphy, that was all that they were interested in.

Terry had the eyeball, otherwise known as direct sight on the target, through the reflective glass windows of the nondescript Sherpa Van's back doors. He could see all but nobody could see in. The team had been parked up in their allocated positions for a while, but it was still only breakfast time and some were caught napping when Terry repeated the message.

'Stand by, stand by, all Hawk units. Female wearing red coat opening front curtains, all Hawks acknowledge.'

'Hawk Two acknowledged,' Flick spoke first as the Officer in Charge of the operation. George could be heard whistling some unrecognisable tune in the background.

'Hawk Three acknowledged,' Tubal responded quickly by pressing the radio transmit button secreted by his right thigh. Paul had already started the 309 GTi's engine, waking Marty and prompting his sharp exit out of the back door ready to drive the Sherpa off the plot.

'Hawk Four acknowledged,' Paddy completed the inventory for the cars present. Sid was driving.

'Hawk Five, ready, willing and able.' Stevie's muffled voice transmitted as he helmeted and mounted his steed parked behind Hawk Four where he'd sat waiting for the action to start.

The anticipation had been building since dawn and Tubal and Paul had been parked up in a side street for what seemed a good few hours; Paul enjoying his smokes and Tubal listening to Derek Jameson on Radio 2. Marty always fell asleep on jobs; not that he was used much these days. Getting up early was alien to him, but they needed him to make up numbers. Occasionally he would wake up and impart pearls of wisdom.

'Do you know, Mac, if you grew a beard, it would give your face more character.'

Tubal would ignore him and he'd return to slumber. The adrenaline always kept Tubal awake on these operations. He was

41

too interested in what was going on around him. Plus, as all of the cars were new, he didn't fancy waking up and finding the tyres slashed or graffiti etched into the paintwork. On these jobs you're looking to be the grey man that nobody notices. Generally, people aren't interested and, if they are, that's where the ability to twist truth into fiction without blinking is an asset.

Terry was in the worst position as he was stuck in the van on his own. He had no chance of relaxing as the Sherpa was as close as they could risk, and Terry was the only one with 'eyes on'. He had also been awarded a new nickname that week, although he didn't know it, with the fitting sobriquet 'Terry Two Sheds' after a discussion about the weather and George telling the team that his shed had flooded.

'Well, I've got two sheds,' said the toad, so that was that.

'Stand by, red coat confirmed as Subject One. It's an off, off, off, walking towards white Mini, black roof, Papa Index… stopping at vehicle.'

All vehicles maintained radio silence whilst Hawk One continued the commentary.

'Door open… subject into vehicle, confirm white Mini, black roof. Subject wearing red coat, blue jeans, black hair tied back. Stand by.' A long pause ensued as all Hawk units waited for further information. 'Manoeuvring, manoeuvring, it's an off, off, off. Hawk Three take over commentary as you are now the lead vehicle behind the target.'

Paul waited until the Mini was travelling before he and Tubal gently eased out to follow at a safe distance. As the vehicle closest to Shauna, they were designated as the eyeball.

'Hawk Two permission.'

'Go ahead, Hawk Two.'

'We're your backup, over.'

'Roger Hawk Two.' Tubal felt comforted that Flick and George were within a safe distance from them and could take over the eyeball if they showed out at this early stage. It didn't matter where the others were as long as they followed the radio traffic.

'Currently one for cover, subject held at junction with Alpha Five… it's a left, left, left Kilburn High Road.' The 309 GTi was held up by a vehicle in front of it. If they didn't move soon, they'd lose Shauna in the traffic. 'Hawk Five make ground,' Tubal instructed.

'Hawk Five acknowledged.' In the rear-view mirror Tubal saw Stevie flying down the wrong side of the road to assist. The encouraging roar of the BMW quietened as he swung past them and forced his way onto the Kilburn High Road.

'Hawk Five now has eyeball, speed two zero heading north in slow-moving traffic.'

'Hawk Three now on Alpha Five, four for cover.' Tubal and Paul were catching up and realised that the bike would be compromised if traffic remained at twenty miles per hour.

'Hawk Four permission. We now have the eyeball junction of Glengall Road,' Paddy's excited tones burst onto the airway before Stevie could answer.

Paddy and Sid had shadowed them via the side streets and found themselves directly behind Shauna. The team were enslaved to the London traffic and going nowhere fast.

'Roger Hawk Four, eyeball to you.' Stevie had pulled into a loading area in the seconds before the convoy passed him.

Paddy kept the team updated as they edged towards the major interchange between the A5, North Circular and the M1. Shauna had barely looked in her mirror, but the risk of now losing her was at the forefront of everybody's mind.

'Hawk Four, convoy check.' Paddy prepared for a change in eyeball at the junction if necessary.

'Hawk Three is backup,' Tubal transmitted quickly. They were now directly behind Hawk Four.

'Hawk Two, two for cover behind Hawk Three.'

'Hawk Five making ground to junction.'

'Hawk One, we're way back but tagging along,' Terry Two-Shed's voice croaked from the sluggish Sherpa.

'Roger that all Hawk units... nearside indicator on... approaching junction... it's a left, left, left signposted North Circular,' Paddy's voice had jumped an octave, 'held at roundabout, offside indicator... moving onto roundabout, not one... not two... third exit A406. Eyeball to Hawk Three.'

That was the cue Paul and Tubal needed and they now focused hard on their prey. Shauna had committed to the North Circular eastbound and floored the Mini away from them. Hawk Four pulled back as Paul slammed the GTi into fourth gear and eased past them, backed up by Hawk Two in his slipstream. Shauna's Mini was no match for the Peugeot as they made ground towards her, the three-lane highway allowing Paul to blend into the unsuspecting traffic at a distance but still maintaining eyes on the Mini. With all Hawk units in pursuit, any deviation by Shauna was covered; they just had to sit tight until she made her next move.

Time moved expeditiously as the group continued east with no certainty of destination. Shauna appeared oblivious to them, or anything else for that matter, and any risk of showing out was quickly mitigated by swapping the lead vehicle. This irregular convoy moved quickly, dissecting the Essex suburbs before the target turned off the North Circular and sped along the A12 before diving down into the Blackwall Tunnel. As they followed, the radio traffic cackled and died, futile for the minutes spent in this cavernous space deep under the River Thames. Still onwards they flew until the signal returned with the splurge of daylight that led them into the bleak wastelands of North Greenwich. Flick and George had the eyeball as they left the tunnel with Tubal and Paul tailing just behind.

'Exiting Blackwall Tunnel, no deviation, speed three five miles per hour,' Flick updated the team. 'Stand by, nearside indicator…'

The Mini exited left and moved through a maze of homogenous council flats before parking outside a terrace of steel-shuttered cottages awaiting either demolition or renovation. At the end of the terrace, Tubal noticed a public house or PH, as he and Paul held back to observe. Hawk Two tailed off and made ready for Shauna's next move.

'It's a stop, stop, stop,' Tubal updated. 'Stand by, subject exciting vehicle. Walking towards PH The Pilot. Can any footmen take?'

'Hawk Two Foot out.' Flick emerged from the road behind Shauna.

'Hawk Four Foot backup.' Paddy appeared beside the 309 GTi and crossed over the road towards The Pilot.

As Paddy walked past, Tubal could just about make out the transmit button clutched in this man-child's hand with part of the connecting wire dangling out of his covert radio shoulder holster. Tubal knew Paddy quite well by then as a fellow Orleans drinking buddy but, at times, he acted like an excitable public-school leprechaun.

'Tuck it in, Paddy,' Tubal burst onto the airwaves. There was no time for protocol.

'Roger that Hawk Three.' Paddy fumbled with his jacket to conceal the dangly bit.

'Two Foot has eyeball. Subject has entered PH. I'm going in.'

'Four Foot will follow.'

With Paddy and Flick now in The Pilot, Tubal assumed operational control. The cars and Stevie parked up ready for the next move and excitement was rising. If Shauna was meeting Gerry, they'll need to get the police there fast.

'Hawk Three to Two Foot maintain radio silence. Can you hear me? Give one click for yes, two clicks for no.' Tubal always chuckled to himself at the second option for this question.

One click was heard.

'Can you see Subject One?'

One click heard.

'Is she alone?'

Two clicks heard.

'Is she with Subject Two?'

Two clicks heard.

'Roger that. Is she with a man?'

One click heard.

'Do you recognise him?'

Two clicks heard.

Tubal settled back and waited for any update. Flick was in a position to observe from within and Paddy was probably having a swift pint . There was not much Tubal could do other than check the radio reception every now and then. This seemed a bit of a trek for Shauna's lunch, but whatever the story, there was no sign of Gerry.

Suddenly it all kicked off again.

'Rapid clicks heard, stand by, stand by,' Tubal acknowledged Flick's signal that Shauna was back on the move. She could only have been in the pub for ten or fifteen minutes. Not much of a liaison and perhaps only a two-pinter for Paddy!

'Hawk Three has eyeball on vehicle,' Tubal continued.

Paul manoeuvred so that they could follow the Mini in whatever direction it headed. Tubal could see Shauna's car but she would be unable to see him. Flick and Paddy were out of the game until the coast was clear and their drivers were in a position to pick them up. This left Paul and Tubal in the one car with the bike as backup to maintain control until the others caught up.

'Subject One is out and walking back towards vehicle. Holding a large white envelope in left hand, still walking... still walking... at vehicle... now entering,' Tubal updated, giving Paul a chance to throw his spent cigarette out the window. He clicked his knuckles ready for the off.

Shauna was on the move again. She had placed the envelope in the car and the route out committed her back onto the Blackwall Tunnel approach with no option but to run southbound. Paul pulled back and let her go, knowing that they could make ground once she cleared the junction.

'Hawk One permission.' Terry's voice interrupted the game plan.

'Go ahead, Hawk One.'

'We have just got through the Blackwall Tunnel. Have we missed anything?'

'Hawk One, hold back and listen to commentary. Subject is southbound on the tunnel approach,' Tubal quickly spurted out.

It was one thing the time that they had taken to catch up, but Tubal couldn't risk interruptions to the commentary with only two assets currently on Shauna's tail. The *London A to Z* lay open on Tubal's lap, telling him that the road shortly merged with the A2 to Dover. It was crucial that they didn't lose her here.

'All Hawks make ground, major junction approaching.' Tubal had no idea what the current state of play was but he could see Hawk Five gliding along their offside and knew that Hawk One was plodding along somewhere behind them.

The Mini was some way ahead of the 309 GTi, cruising along in the left-hand lane. Paul accelerated to get closer. Shauna appeared oblivious to the world around her as they hovered comfortably a few cars back on her offside. All of a sudden, without indicating, she veered left off the tunnel approach, crossed the safety chevrons and glided up the slip road, taking her away from the A2. In Tubal's wing mirror he spotted that Hawk Five had mitigated Shauna's move, manoeuvred the bike into lane one and put his left arm out to slow down following traffic. Taking the hint, Paul swiftly swung across the carriageway onto the slip road to put them back on track. Stevie flew past on their nearside as Tubal quickly updated himself on the map to prepare for Shauna's next move; either she will head back to the Blackwall Tunnel or take the scenic route through South London. He conducted a quick convoy check, leaving Paul to shadow the Mini as Shauna queued to exit at the upcoming roundabout. All of their compadres had returned to the fold ready for her next move.

As Shauna moved onto the roundabout, the GTi was held back by traffic. Hawk Two took the initiative and steamed up the inside lane, backing them up as they slowly edged along the road. Stevie was already perched by the roadside to give a direction.

'Hawk Five has eyeball, not one, not two, third exit, A2 Central London. Hawk Two can you take?'

'Roger that. Hawk Two now has eyeball, A2 no deviation.' Flick's brogue floated through the airways.

If Shauna was going back home, she had chosen the tortuous route, via slow, grinding seas of traffic struggling to cover ten miles an hour, if that. *It's mid-afternoon*, Tubal thought, *surely, she isn't heading back to Kilburn in the rush hour?* All they could do was sit tight and prepare for any sudden stop or deviation without warning. Tubal wished something would happen soon; he needed the adrenaline kick to keep the pangs of hunger and need for a piss at bay.

Hawk Two held position on the A2 for quite some way through South London. There was no need to change the lead vehicle at this snail's pace. They expected to be entrenched on this road to somewhere for some time yet. Even if Shauna did chance to look in her mirror it would more likely be out of boredom than trying to ID the driver behind. If she was to turn off the A2, the 309 GTi was strategically placed to furnish new eyes if required. Tubal could sit back and people-watch for now as they edged along. Then suddenly:

'Offside indicator, moving to lane two at traffic signal signposted Rotherhithe… it's a right, right, right. Hawk Two following. Back up move forward.'

Paul accelerated fast up in Hawk Two's slipstream and swung right as the traffic lights blinked to amber. Tubal looked back behind them to see the motorbike and Hawk Four pull out from the stationary traffic, fly down towards oncoming vehicles and shoot across the junction in a game of automotive Russian roulette against the red light. All but the Sherpa made it to safety. Their whereabouts would have to wait until the next convoy check.

Shauna was heading straight in the direction towards Surrey Docks, one of Tubal's old stomping grounds. Flick had surrendered the eyeball back to Tubal in Hawk Three and the team were making steady progress as they shadowed the derelict basins of Father Thames. *It certainly looks a lot different from when I was last here*, thought Tubal. The old dock machinery he remembered was dwarfed by the tower cranes and concrete reinforcing pillars forming the skeleton of the phoenix rising from the mud and silt of the waterfront.

'She's stopping, mate,' Paul exclaimed.

Tubal jolted back from reminiscing and pressed the transmit button.

'Stand by, stand by. Subject pulling over to nearside. It's a stop, stop. We are going past. Hawk Four can you take eyeball,' Tubal hurriedly transmitted.

'Roger that. Hawk Four has eyeball,' Paddy replied.

Paul took the next road left and pulled over. Tubal unbuckled and pushed the passenger door ajar ready for a quick exit. As they came to a stop, he leapt out and jogged up to the main road in time to see Shauna lock the Mini and walk towards a row of Victorian villas. Tubal could see that Shauna had the white envelope from The Pilot in her hand as she walked along. Paddy was left to maintain commentary as he had the best view from his car. On the opposite side of the road Tubal spied Flick closeted behind the graffiti-strewn panels of a bus shelter. Her hair was now held under a baseball cap, and she had donned a mottled denim jacket to change her appearance. Both waited for Paddy's further instruction.

'Subject has entered premises via outside steps. No number visible and no eyeball on subject. Any footman assist?'

'Three Foot can take. I have visual,' Tubal let Paddy know.

He had already spotted the building Shauna went into. It looked like a house from a distance, but as he moved closer, he was able to report that the property was actually office space covering three levels, including the basement, or what Tubal's nan would call the 'airey'. Stone steps climbed up to an elevated entrance hall on the ground floor. Tubal casually stopped outside the offices, pulled his notebook out from his jacket and stared at a blank page as if he had found what he was looking for. The front door was still open, and he could see a varnished wooden board with the current occupiers' names slotted into it. There was only one way to see where Shauna might be.

'Three Foot to Hawk Four. I'm going into the building.'

Tubal wasn't really comfortable with this but he was exposed from the rest of the team and backing out would not be seen as an option. Inhaling deeply, he moved confidently up the steps, expelling waste air and dread from his lungs as he walked into the foyer. There was nobody there, just muffled voices resonating from behind closed panel doors. Tubal prepared to make a mental note of the occupants but there was no need. As he raised his head, Tubal's eyes focused on four words already engrained in his memory: Boteler Urban Regeneration Limited. This wasn't their head office address, so it might be a site office, he guessed. The information board informed him that BUR occupied all of the upstairs rooms, but Tubal's thoughts turned to the question, *where is Shauna and what is she doing here?* More to the point, could Gerry Murphy be here? At that moment, an upstairs door closed and Tubal heard footsteps growing louder on the creaking wooden floorboards. A figure on the landing crowned the stairs before him. It was Shauna, and she was heading straight for Tubal. Ever the gentleman, he stood aside, allowing her to glide past as he discretely transmitted rapid clicks. Shauna smiled as she mouthed, 'thank you' and left the building. Tubal thought it funny that all day he'd been following a description of a red coat and blue jeans in a white car. Shauna's face had been a mystery to him other than a monochrome photograph. Now he had the real thing before him, an older-looking face of wearied porcelain divergent against her bright emerald eyes and coal-black hair.

'Hello, you lost?' a voice was heard from behind Tubal. He turned to see a matronly woman, probably in her fifties, peering over her glasses at him from the ground-floor office doorway.

'No, it's OK. I've got the right number but the wrong road. I'm meeting an old school friend, haven't seen him in years,' Tubal quickly answered as he exited onto the entrance stairs to make ground on Shauna.

Over the airways the team chatter burst into the covert receiver squatting in Tubal's ear. Shauna was already in her Mini and preparing to drive away. He waited on the stone stairs knowing that he would need to sprint back to the 309 GTi when the coast was clear. From his elevated position, Tubal could see over the advertising hoardings lining the pavement opposite. The foundations and polyhedron outline of the Pilgrims Pyramid development spread before his eyes. He momentarily felt overawed by the responsibility placed upon him for kicking off this investigation. Seeing the BUR office and the scale of their development made everything real to him. It was one thing jousting with booksellers trying to make a fast buck, but this was big business by powerful people. Tubal never expected that he would get so close this early in his investigation.

'It's an off, off, off, no deviation.' Paddy's voice broke Tubal's thoughts.

Shauna continued in the direction of Central London. Once out of her mirror view, Tubal made his move. Paul had manoeuvred the Peugeot round and was perched on the corner where Tubal had left him. He ran towards the car and bundled in, Paul gambling that Tubal's arse had actually hit the seat as he roared out into a gap in the traffic.

'Hawk Three permission,' Tubal called breathlessly.

'Go ahead, Hawk Three.' It was Flick who responded this time.

'Quick update. Subject visited offices of Bravo Uniform Romeo. Not carrying anything when she left.'

'Roger that Hawk Three.'

The 309 GTi caught up pretty quick albeit a little way behind the plodding Sherpa, but the team seemed to have everything within their control. Shauna remained south of the Thames until she reached Lambeth, where she veered north over Waterloo Bridge and drove down into the Strand underpass. As she emerged in Holborn, her driving behaviour changed completely as she moved from the two-lane throughfare, turning into a maze of narrow side streets. She was either lost or something had spooked her.

The team were now in dangerous territory as, for the first time that day, they might be compromised, especially as three IOs had already been within breathing distance of Shauna. The last thing they wanted was to lose her, although from Tubal's perspective the day had already been productive. Nevertheless, their objective was to locate Gerry Murphy, and that remained the priority. Flick returned to the airwaves, taking the decision to cover the main exit routes from the side streets with the cars, leaving the van on the main thoroughfare. Stevie would discretely follow Shauna on the bike whilst the others remained blind to her whereabouts until she resurfaced. Time passed slowly as they waited, and the day's adrenaline started to dwindle away. Tubal was feeling famished now, and as he sunk into the GTi's bucket seat, tiredness threatened to absorb him. At least his paralysed bladder had been emptied.

'It's a stop, stop,' Stevie's voice jolted Tubal upright. 'Lincoln's Inn Fields, she's getting out and walking onto the recreation green.'

Tubal grabbed his spare jacket and sprung out of the car. It was quicker to walk towards Shauna's location, leaving Paul to navigate the car through the traffic. As he reached the location, Tubal spied Flick and Paddy emerging from opposite corners of this historical playground of lawyers and surgeons. They all had Shauna in view across the grassy oasis as she headed towards Holborn Underground Station. Stevie updated the vehicles: if she was abandoning the Mini, they would need every asset on the ground.

Tubal was still the furthest away. With her back to him, he took advantage and sprinted closer to Shauna. All those curries and sitting around had begun to take their toll on him, but Tubal felt relieved that a modicum of residual fitness from his rugby days remained. As he approached, Shauna left the square of Lincoln's Inn Fields and walked into a cul-de-sac. At its end,

Tubal could see an alleyway that he knew led into Holborn itself. He thought it unlikely that any of the vehicles could get round to there if Shauna took public transport. Everything now rested on the three of them on foot and they could not risk getting too close. *Perhaps we'll have to come back another day*, Tubal thought.

Without warning, Shauna stopped, turned round and walked back towards their position. Tubal pulled his collar up and drifted into the doorway of an office block. Flick was positioned opposite him and her hand discretely signalled to Tubal that Shauna had veered right. As he moved out from the doorway, Tubal just caught sight of Shauna pulling back the front door of a pub sited on the corner of the lane.

'Three Foot to all Hawks. Subject has entered PH, The Ship,' Tubal updated the vehicles.

Flick and Paddy moved towards Tubal. It looked as if there were two exits from the pub both facing where they were located. They needed to get someone in there fast.

'Hawk One is now located in Holborn.' Terry Two Sheds awoke from his easy driving day around London.

'Roger that, Hawk One. Can you please enter PH and locate subject?' It wasn't really a request, but Tubal was the newbie in Group Five and thought politeness might help.

Terry acknowledged. Within a minute, he and Marty appeared down the alley and walked into The Ship. Tubal being less than six feet tall, he could not see through the mottled glass into the bar area as the door closed behind them. What he could see was Marty's mass and mane of hair bobbing along the clear glass panels topping the window frames. He moved through the compact drinking area and disappeared momentarily before his head came into view and Tubal saw his body rise slowly upwards.

'It looks like Marty is going upstairs,' the ever-helpful

Paddy disclosed. Paddy relayed that there was an upstairs dining area, after telling them that he sometimes drinks in The Ship. All they could do now was wait; confident that they had Shauna contained, Flick decided not to jeopardise the office's Little and Large in the pub by sending them messages.

It had started to get cold for those lurking outside the pub. Rough sleepers jostled their sodden sleeping bags and cardboard bedding into the doorways around them, ignored by the footfall of weary office workers seeking home comforts or solace through excessive alcohol or amorous liaisons with colleagues. The three IOs slotted somewhere between the two: sober loiterers whose purpose was of no interest to those passing by. Suddenly, Terry exited The Ship and gestured for them to move back into Lincoln's Inn Fields.

'Shauna's getting ready to leave but Gerry's in there. They've had a meal together. All very lovey-dovey. Made me blush,' Terry joked. 'Marty's at the bar now.'

Flick updated the vehicles and directed them towards the location. Everybody needed to get this right otherwise the whole day was wasted, and Gerry might never be in UK jurisdiction again. A judgement call was needed: it was too risky to confront Gerry in the pub, but if they took him down in the street with Shauna, they might never know what she was doing at Pilgrims Pyramid. The ideal position would be if Shauna went home alone daydreaming of her romantic tryst, oblivious to Gerry's night of incarceration pending transfer to a prison cell for at least the next two years.

Rapid clicks heard. Each of them dispersed out of sight ready for whatever was to happen next. All eyes focused on Shauna as she left The Ship and ambled back to her car. She was alone and of no further use to them that night. Stevie acted as the insurance policy, shadowing her back to Lincoln's Inn Fields. He'll send confirmation that Shauna had left the area before

Gerry was tackled. Flick was happy to let her run. Adrenaline pumped back into Tubal's veins; all of his senses heightened in anticipation of circumstances that were previously alien to him. Detaining fugitives was not their normal work, and the rest of the team looked edgy. George the boss had jogged to a telephone box to call for police backup. When he returned, he had brought a copy of Gerry's arrest warrant from the car. Just as George arrived back to join them outside The Ship, Marty appeared, and Stevie messaged that all was clear. They had the green light to go.

Before a plan could be hatched, Gerry burst out onto the street. George signalled for them to hold back momentarily until Gerry was clear of The Ship. Dealing with Gerry was one thing, but igniting a punch-up with would-be alcohol-fuelled saviours was not good practice. The burly Irishman turned the collar up on his heavy coat against the chill night air as he ambled into the darkness of a service road opposite the pub. Flick radioed Stevie to cover the opposite end that led back into the bustling thoroughfare of Holborn. There was no sign of the police and the options were dwindling by the second. As soon as Stevie appeared at the opposite end, George signalled for Tubal and Sid to follow down behind Gerry. Paul was dispatched to await backup and the rest would follow down at a slower pace. Gerry wasn't moving very fast, and even at Tubal's walking pace, they quickly gained on him. Stevie moved towards them, parked the bike in the centre of the road and dismounted. *At least he's got a crash helmet on for protection*, Tubal thought. Gerry stopped momentarily, as if he'd twigged something was wrong, turned round and walked back towards Tubal.

'Excuse me,' Tubal spoke now to stop and engage with Gerry. 'Can I have a word?'

Gerry ignored him, sidestepped Sid and silently walked

on. Now they had the advantage of three behind him and up to five in front if Marty moved quicker than he drove.

'*Gerry Murphy*,' Tubal shouted. '*Revenue officers, stand still.*'

At that, Gerry started to run but stumbled to the ground as Paddy caught his right arm and locked it. As he climbed back to his feet, Sid grabbed Gerry's flailing loose arm before any damage was done. Tubal caught up and studied a man whose dishonesty defined him. A man living in the shadows, a ghost plying his trade hidden from official records. Within seconds, the transfixed look of desperation melted from Gerry's eyes into slowly dripping tears. The realisation that he was caught overwhelmed him. Gerry sharply exhaled as tension drained from his muscles and, with a nod of the head, a smile emerged on his face.

'OK, lads, you've got me,' was all Gerry could say before a woman walking her German Shepherd appeared from the dark.

The woman must have heard Tubal shouting and witnessed the ensuing commotion. She ignored the huddle around him and spoke to Gerry directly.

'Are you alright? Have you committed a tax fraud?'

Gerry laughed as Flick ushered the woman away and told her not to interfere. She had broken some of the tension, but it was too early to relax. They had their man but no means to transport him away.

The small talk with Gerry was nearly exhausted when Tubal spied Paul walking towards them. Behind him was the unmistakeable outline of a Metropolitan Police Rover, all fluorescent stripes reflecting off the now glaring building security lights. One of the police officers left the car and ambled up to them. His colleague stood by the driver's door and watched.

'How are you doing? I'm George Craig the SIO here. This

is the fella I rang about – Gerry Murphy – and he's wanted on a return to prison.'

'I don't know anything about that. We were minding our own business, and your mate here waived us down with his cigarette.' The officer gestured towards Paul. 'I suppose you'd better let me know the story.'

George produced the arrest warrant, and after a bit more banter, Gerry was spirited away to meet his fate. And that was that. A long and productive day was at its end. Eventually they would make their way back to Surrey but at that point, a celebratory drink and a bite to eat was called for.

'I know just the place,' said Paddy.

'I'd better get the bike out of the middle of the road then,' Stevie replied.

Chapter Five

The stack of post liberated from Devereaux Angell's address appeared pretty unremarkable as the compressing rubber band pinged from around it. Recently, time to concentrate on his own cases had been a rare commodity for Tubal. After despatching Gerry Murphy, the team were tasked to one of Grenville Allonby's investigations into a wealthy Middle Eastern businessman living and working tax free within UK jurisdiction. This was a one-off and not something ordinarily within their remit. Allonby kept his cards to his chest, giving them very little information, but that was of no concern as, frankly, they didn't give a shit. The brief was to confirm if this individual resided with his alleged estranged family. If he was there, Allonby concluded, he had lied to the authorities: objective achieved. Such was the secrecy, the team had to pack overnight bags and were sent to a hotel near Somerset House following Allonby's monotone-voiced briefing. Tubal found it strange that the hierarchy perceived that these minions might be loose-lipped if at home but safe in a hotel bar full of strangers. Still, they managed a good meal, a few beers and a hangover-soothing cooked breakfast before saddling over to the target address the next morning. The case sensitivity required use of a remote camera concealed within their Ford Escort van. People sitting in cars near the address would likely trigger calls to the police, or worse: private security contractors employed by some of the residents. Sid drove the van to the observation point and walked back to the other Hawk units concealed several streets away from the businessman's Hampstead property. Paddy monitored the live feed on the video monitor and, before too long, was reporting typical morning chores for your average suburban family: kids driven to school in the Bentley; domestic staff sweeping the driveway; chauffeur polishing the Aston Martin. A pretty boring morning until…

'Stand by, stand by. Two males entering drive of subject property carrying small suitcases,' Paddy informed them, followed by a pause. 'Entering side door now. Out of sight.'

They all quietly waited until the commentary resumed. After a while, a garbled hiss emitted from the car speakers and Paddy's message, if that's what it was, became inaudible. Before they could try and make contact back, all of the radios went kaput, and communication was lost.

'Do you think that we've been rumbled?' Tubal questioned George, who had partnered up with him that day.

'Well, it's never happened before. Could be something to do with those guys with the suitcases,' George replied as they drove away to find a signal for the radio phone issued to them for the day. Time to update Allonby.

It was likely, in Allonby's assessment, that the suitcases contained radio jammers. This seemed plausible but didn't address how anybody knew that they were there. Every precaution had been taken by the team, and Allonby, regardless of his reticence, did not vocalise any concern to George. They couldn't help feeling that they were pawns in a game where only one player made the rules. So that was the end of that. The job was pulled, and they all scooted back to the office.

'Most of this is of no help at all,' Tubal called across in

Flick's direction as he shredded the overdue Companies House return reminders and advertising flyers addressed to Gilmore Angell Limited.

If he was going to find out what had happened to their 714C certificate, Tubal needed a clue to Devereaux or her husband's whereabouts. There was not much to go on so far. As he reached the bottom of the pile, Tubal slit open the last of the official-looking envelopes. This one was personally addressed to Devereaux Angell. As he removed the contents, Tubal's eyes focused on the Midland Bank logo and the realisation that he might have finally found something. Midland was not the known banker for Gilmore Angell Limited. The letter was dated more than six months earlier, seeking confirmation of the new account holder. Tubal already knew that the £1.5 million had been paid by BUR, so the bank must have received the details from elsewhere. Bingo! Tubal now relied on his contact at the bank's fraud department to guide him to the new account holder and give a clue to Mrs Angell's whereabouts. A quick telephone call and a little practised charm sowed the seed. After all, Tubal decided, it was payback time for a couple of mortgage frauds he'd helped her put to bed recently. There was no rush, but if she comes up trumps, he will harvest the fruit on his return from a relaxing lunch down at the Orleans.

The team had been working flat out recently. By Tubal's reckoning, it was reasonable to seek revitalisation and a creative catch-up with the congregation at their place of worship. He had got to know everybody quite well by now as they all virtually lived in each other's pockets. Even Terry had become bearable if you accepted that the only work that he volunteered for was the driving. So, they had started calling him 'Parker', albeit that Flick was the closest analogy for Lady Penelope and Tubal isn't too sure how enamoured she was with Terry. He's not with the crowd at the Orleans due to some domestic chore or other to deal with, an excuse of course. In Tubal's time at BIO, he had come to accept that, despite the closeness and camaraderie, people's private lives remained distant and of little consequence. His was simple, a solitary but uncomplicated life mostly alienated from his past. Talk of domesticity, wives and partners held little consequence to Tubal. He spent his off-duty time at his Surbiton bolthole consumed by music, lager and singing along to Billy Joel. That is how Tubal relaxed; his working days are driven by other indulgences.

'You're looking very philosophical.' Flick's voice broke Tubal's reflection. 'What you thinking?'

Tubal gulped down his lager before replying. 'I'm just trying to piece this case together. There seems to be more and more loose ends, but if I can move forward soon, I'll be happy. Plus, we still don't know what Shauna Brady was doing at BUR or who she met in the pub.'

'Might just be a chance encounter, but I'm happy to help you find the answer.' Flick smiled gently, as she tended to, and walked away.

Tubal followed her to the end of the bar. Marty was holding court and spoke excitedly in his customary short, sharp phrases muffled by the unkempt face fur smothering his lips. Each stanza interjected with, 'No. No. Listen.' The more he drank, the more he regaled with tales of previous BIO exploits. Tubal observed silently as Marty's peers unashamedly turned away as if they'd heard it all before. He didn't seem to notice them, but Tubal sucked up Marty's anecdotes enthusiastically, despite the incongruous feasibility of some of what he said. It was like he was reinforcing the mythology of the office, and Tubal was happy to listen for a while.

'You talk a load of bollocks. Don't be fooled by it, Mac,' Paddy called from across the bar.

'Mind your language, young man,' Marie the barmaid playfully chastised him.

It's not as if the clientele would mind. The staff at the Orleans tolerated a lot from the IOs but always with good humour. They know what they are about but never question these miscreants who evaporate after lunch yet reappear at night in their same working gear carrying the malodourous aroma of freshly consumed curry.

Having put the world to rights, they all headed back to the office, late but in time for tea. There was one thing Tubal had to do before he graced the Tea Club and the afternoon's sporting activities. Diverting through the maze of corridors, he returned to his desk in the Group Five room. Sitting by the phone in Terry's scrawny handwriting was a message for him to ring Midland Bank. As he hastily dialled the number, Tubal inwardly hoped that he'd get the answers he needed. Within seconds, the call went straight through to his contact, who confirmed that she had the information. She would fax it straight over on the secure line. Both of them were in a bit of a hurry and time for small talk would wait until the next time one of them wanted something off-record. Tubal waited by the fax machine, his anticipation rising like the wind building from his lunch and his vivid imagination raced ahead. Tubal's case was one of the largest the office had dealt with, and he felt blessed that it had fallen on him to investigate, a rookie in the Department. In his subconscious, however, there lurked a fear that he was being set up to fail or only allowed to carry on until one of the experienced IOs took all the glory. *Perhaps that's just my pessimism emerging*, Tubal thought and consigned this dread to its box temporarily. Within a few minutes, paper rose from the cluttering machine and a Midland Bank coversheet emerged, followed by facsimiles of communications about Gilmore Angell Limited. Tubal snatched these from the fax machine, sat down and studied them closely. There wasn't much content, but the information revealed gave him exactly what he wanted. Tubal now had two substantial leads to follow up in tracing the 714C certificate and uncovering how this defunct, non-trading business was supplying over a million pounds of labour to BUR.

Devereaux Angell had confirmed to the bank that Gilmore Angell Limited had been sold following her divorce and the Angell family no longer held a financial interest. This cleared up the issue of Mr Angell, and he was no longer of interest to Tubal. Mrs Angell signed the bank account transfer papers from an address in Kent. The new company secretary was named as Joseph Patrick Sweeney, although the contact details for him were as sketchy as Tubal expected for a company now operating beyond legitimacy. For Sweeney, the company secretary designation only held relevance to orchestrate the 714C fraud, and Tubal knew already that he was unknown to Companies House. He did recognise Sweeney's business address though. South Bank House was a suite of offices often used for temporary office accommodation or as a mail drop. Tubal's forefathers knew the building as part of the old Lambeth Doulton factory and its current guise featured regularly on BIO's intelligence database. It was going to take a bit more digging to find Sweeney's true whereabouts, but the pièce de résistance stared back at Tubal from the paper: Gilmore Angell Limited's new bank account details. Tubal anticipated that there might be a bit of a battle with Grenville Allonby to use his HM Inspector of Taxes statutory powers to get full legal access to the account. But Tubal knew that for the sake of protecting the Exchequer, he must blitz the case and identify all of the BUR payments. In the short term, that would be the only way the full extent of the deception could be found. If he waits for BUR to submit their next annual subcontractor return, Sweeney, and those behind him, would have dissolved into the ether.

Tubal couldn't be bothered with the Tea Club anymore as he had these new leads to research. He was also looking forward to an early night.

'Not coming down, Mac?' Tubal hadn't seen Flick walk in behind him. 'What you up to?'

'I've just got this.' He turned and handed her the bank info.

'South Bank House. They're normally quite helpful,' Flick replied. 'I'll go up there with you if you like. I can always flutter my eyelashes.'

'I'm not sure that will work, but yeah, OK.'

'No, but seriously, I had a case up there recently and they might remember me. They don't like being used for dodgy dealing.' She moved alongside Tubal and placed the fax back on his desk.

'Actually, Flick, it's been bugging me about Shauna Brady. The bloke she met in the pub. What did he look like?'

'Truth is, I didn't take a lot of notice. He wasn't Gerry and I was concentrating on Shauna. I'd probably recognise him again though if I saw him.'

Flick sounded almost apologetic, but having been out on a few of these surveillances, Tubal knew how easy it was to develop tunnel vision.

'I was hoping that you'd put a description on Marty's system,' Tubal continued. 'I was going to ask him, but that's pointless this afternoon.'

'There's nothing on there. We weren't in the pub long anyway before Shauna was off.' Flick sat back at her desk. 'You know, Shauna knows all the crooked people in this game. I don't believe in coincidences, but you never know.'

'You could be right.'

Tubal didn't believe in coincidences either, and Shauna needed to be placed at the back of his mind for now.

'I wouldn't mind spending a few days following this bank stuff up, if you're free,' Tubal asked.

'Sure, you can pick me up from home in the morning if you like.'

Flick looked up at Tubal as she spoke. He felt sure that he'd detected just a hint of pulsating eyelid.

Tubal spent the next half hour planning for their road trip and hoped that the outcome would match the effort. As he carried himself home, the only certainty was his impending date night with a culinary delight from the freezer.

Chapter Six

Tubal arrived at Flick's a little earlier than planned. It had been a while since the sartorial elegance of a suit and polished brogues were last slung on, but he was out meeting the public this time rather than skulking in the shadows. As he dressed that morning, there was no escape from the beer-baby bump that now sat idly over his waistline; not surprising really, given his current diet and lack of exercise. Other times, Tubal could conceal the spread under baggy, casual clothes and no one other than him cared, but the threads that day were unforgiving and he felt a tad uncomfortable. Inherently, Tubal sought to look the part if there was an occasion for dressing up and he relished his own appearance, glimpsing himself in each mirror that he passed. Even as a child, his grandparents dressed Tubal in white shirt, black tie and Crombie overcoat just to walk through East Lane market and have a photographer's monkey sit on his shoulder. Funerals and weddings always required expensive suits and dodgy ties that Tubal would later regret wearing. Since joining BIO, his vanity had evolved and the bottle-thick glasses had been traded for blue-tinted contact lenses. Tubal's optometrist had highlighted to him that such accessories accentuated the colour of his eyes; this appealed to him. His hair had now grown back; wildly rolling onto Tubal's shoulders in ringlets of frizz that deserved a trim but divorced his appearance from that of an archetypal civil servant. Tubal did buy a bowler hat once at a jumble sale, his motives more *A Clockwork Orange* than *Yes Minister*, but he never wore it. His head was too small and never suited a hat. As he recently had a bit of spare cash with only himself to spend it on, Tubal purchased a gold signet ring with the Playboy bunny logo on. Rings now decked his digits like a Gipsy king to augment the Edward VII sovereign Tubal inherited from his Scottish great-grandmother. Growing up, his grandad often accepted gold from his Romani punters and instilled in Tubal that if you had gold, you would always have money to fall back on. So here he was, fat but feeling a hundred dollars.

While Tubal waited outside Flick's place, he played around with the radio. If they were to spend the day in the car, they should at least have some decent music to listen to. Well, that was his opinion.

'*Fuck off.*'

Tubal heard a door slam and watched Flick storming towards him from the source. As she climbed into the passenger seat, he momentarily feigned obliviousness to her apparent disquiet. Then curiosity took hold.

'Come at a bad time, have I?'

'Shut up, Mac, and just drive,' Flick spoke sharply. 'I don't want to talk. He's an arsehole.'

Tubal hadn't considered that Flick had a resident arsehole. She'd never mentioned him and Tubal was happier believing that she was devoid of external male company. But it was work he needed to concentrate on and, like him, Flick had dressed for the occasion, replacing the ubiquitous faded jeans and loose-fitting jumpers for a cleavage-baring white blouse, fitted jacket and skirt combo that placed her bare, shapely legs far too close to Tubal for comfort.

'I want to head over to Kent first.' Tubal handed Devereaux Angell's new address to Flick.

Flick said nothing as she extracted the road map from its lair and flicked through the pages as if planning a route. Tubal roughly knew where he was going but felt happy that Flick had something else to focus on. Hopefully, she would calm down and the smiles that he had come to expect returned to brighten her face. Tubal just concentrated on the road ahead and listened to the morning sounds on the radio.

Mrs Angell had moved to St Paul's Cray, a once-ancient settlement transformed in the 1950s with its neighbour St Mary Cray when a vast council estate housing ten thousand people was built alongside the country farmhouses. Members of Tubal's extended family were transported there from London's war-scarred streets, tin baths and insanitary plumbing. He knew the area for its unique characteristics forged through a hybrid community of bankers, businessmen, builders and blaggers. Tubal didn't know what had led Mrs Angell here, but these 'Crays' were famous for two things: their fifty-acre nudist camp and, perhaps more pertinently, prominence as home to the largest settled community of Romani and Irish travellers in the UK. It was his guess that Mrs Angell had links to the Irish community here. He hoped so. If she had become a naturist, his allegiance to Queen and Country did not yet extend to stripping off in public; Tubal would have nowhere to keep his pen and notebook for a start.

'You ever been to a nudist camp?' Inexplicably, Tubal's thoughts had again vocalised.

'What?' Flick had no idea what he was on about.

'Oh! Don't worry about it, I was just thinking out loud.' Tubal sensed by the look on her face that Flick was a little perturbed at the verbal aberration of his inner thoughts.

He felt obliged to explain but chose not to. The journey

was passing quickly, and Flick had closed her eyes in silent slumber, leaving Tubal to navigate his way around the M25. They weren't too far away, and he needed Flick to guide him in for the final stretch. Tubal cranked the noise of the radio up a little, hoping she'd take the hint.

'Nearly there. Can you tell me where to go when we come off the motorway?' He spoke over the noise of the radio and waited for a reaction.

Flick stretched her arms out, yawned and sat proud in the seat before realising that her skirt had risen when her dozing body had twisted towards the door pillar. Quickly pulling at the seam, she grabbed the map book onto her knees.

'What's this music, Grandad?'

'I don't know – it's the radio,' Tubal answered with the newly acquired knowledge that Flick didn't appreciate Radio 2. 'Can you direct me to Mrs Angell's address from here?'

Flick opened the index and thumbed towards the page matching the grid reference. As she studied the maze of streets and configurations, Tubal sensed that she was having difficulty. And then the classic sign: she turned the map upside down and spun the page round to find their bearings. Tubal pulled into a lay-by and waited.

'Do you want me to look? I know the area a bit,' he offered after a pause.

'No, I can work out where we are. It's just that some of the estates are a mass of cul-de-sacs and squares with no vehicle access.' Flick had removed her glasses and was squinting at the page. 'There we are, got it.'

Tubal pulled away and let Flick take control. At least she had stopped talking to him in monosyllables. After all, he was the innocent party in whatever had kept her in a foul mood that morning. Perhaps his crime was talking to her at all.

The next twenty minutes flew past as Flick directed them

around crescents and rows of houses built back to back in grids. Devereaux Angell's address sat at the centre of one of the more recent additions: wood-clad terraced houses interspersed with two-storey blocks of flats and cul-de-sacs to access neat rows of identical garages. A myriad of alleyways linked these properties, but only one roadway around the perimeter gave vehicular access. It all looked neat and tidy. They parked up and, from the boot, Tubal grabbed the black, cloth-covered folder that held the case file and his notepad. He looked around at the palpable homogeny of a scene that, perhaps cynically, Tubal predicted as a developing blighted landscape but, until then, the trim gardens and whitewashed facades contrasted starkly with the older properties nearby. As they turned and navigated their walk into the development's heart, Tubal's senses were assaulted by a heavy, musty aroma burrowing into his nostrils and watering each hydrogel-clad eye. He guessed that it originated from an adjacent building that was partly concealed by high panel fencing, its presence betrayed by a billowing white vapour dispersing up into the sky. Tubal saw Flick's finger and thumb pinch her nostrils together as they sidled into a courtyard shielded by red-brick garden walls on one side and a terrace of identical dwellings on the other. The air there remained unsullied and provided a welcome release. As they crossed a deserted children's play area, Tubal could just about make out the block writing affixed to a low-level block of flats, Keturah House. This was the place they were after. As Flick followed him up the grey concrete stairs to Mrs Angell at number four, Tubal felt perturbed about the curious smell that tarnished the tranquillity of their surroundings. Stepping gingerly amidst the potted flowers lining the path, he approached the front door and pressed the bell. The pad of clicking footsteps was immediately audible behind the door, which sharply swung open. Before them stood a woman of inscrutable age, in Tubal's eyes anywhere from thirty to fifty, dressed in a knee-length beige pleated skirt, matching high-heeled shoes and silky cobalt-blue blouse straining under the burden of her heavy cleavage. Her make-up was barely noticeable except for the light shadow complementing her emerald eyes. Jet-black hair tumbled over slightly hunched shoulders. On facing her unexpected guests, she swept her fringe to the side as Tubal spoke.

'Mrs Angell, Devereaux Angell?'

'Yes, can I help you?' The lady's voice had a soft Irish lilt.

'My name is Tubal McArthur, and this is my colleague, Felicity Francis. We are from the Inland Revenue Investigation Section.' He held out his identification. 'Can we have a word with you please?'

'Yes, my love. What's it about?' Mrs Angell stood back from the doorway without waiting for an answer. 'You had better come in.'

Flick followed behind as they were led into the living room. Without invitation, Tubal and Flick planted themselves either side of a snoring Pomeranian snuggled in the centre of a slightly worn white leather sofa.

'Are you on your way out somewhere?' Tubal enquired, sensing that her attire suggested she might.

'Oh no, darling. I'm just rattling round the flat in case a handsome suitor calls.'

Tubal blushed. He couldn't help thinking that Devereaux had a certain older woman sex appeal about her.

'First things first. Would you like tea?'

Our host seemed to welcome their company yet strangely hadn't pushed the reason for their visit.

'Mrs Angell…'

'Call me Dee please, God knows why my mammy named me Devereaux.'

'Tea will be great, but we've come to ask you about the company, Gilmore Angell.' The dog raised its head, yawned and, on hearing Tubal's voice, snuffled back into a fur ball.

'Oh yes, now let me get that tea.'

With that, Dee left the room, leaving Flick and Tubal with the nonchalant dog and a china menagerie of Beswick animals gazing at them from within fusty glass-fronted cabinets dotted around the room. After a few minutes, Dee returned with three mugs of anaemic tea and a plated crescent of assorted biscuits on a melamine tray. She placed this on the coffee table betwixt them and a mock Georgian TV cabinet.

'I love my horses, as you can see from my cabinets. Help yourself to a biscuit. Now what do you want to know?'

Dee nudged past and positioned herself on a rainbow-striped snuggler chair that contrasted sharply against the rest of the decor.

'Quite simple really, I want to know what has happened to the 714C certificate for Gilmore Angell Limited.' Tubal came straight to the point. No reason not to.

'Ah well now, not that simple. It was all my ex-husband's baby, but as I helped with the books, he wanted me to be Company Secretary.' Dee continued, 'Things started going bad over a year ago as there just wasn't enough work to make the business viable. The bastard sold off the plant and buggered back to Dublin, leaving me to sort out the rented yard in Cricklewood. I lost my flat over it. Luckily, I managed to get a council place over here near family.'

'Do you like it here?' Flick interjected before Tubal's question was answered.

'Well, it's not what I'm used to. Then there's the pease pudding smell from the factory.'

'Oh, that's what it is,' Flick retorted.

'And the 714C?' Tubal countered before any further digression.

Dee stood up and walked over to an antique-looking writing bureau. One of those with a pull-down 'fall' front that, when unlocked, reveals an inlayed writing surface and pigeonholes for correspondence. Tubal knew about such things. He was given an Edwardian writing bureau for his seventh birthday. Tubal wanted an Action Man.

'If you bear with me a sec, I'll see how I can help you.' Dee shuffled through a visible pile of papers, tidily ensconced within the bureau's inner recess.

They silently waited, partly to allow Dee to concentrate but mostly in deference to their canine friend who now nuzzled comatose against Flick's right thigh.

'Here we are: Mr Sweeney.' Dee lifted a ragged brown envelope and drew the contents out onto the writing surface. 'Pat Sweeney was a freelance site agent used by my husband. He wanted to buy the company but was too late as everything had been sold off by then.'

'Have you met Mr Sweeney?' Tubal asked.

'No, I had nothing to do with anything at site level. All I know is that Gilmore Angell had no plant, contracts or business premises, but my ex-husband believed this man when he said he could resurrect the business. All we had left was the company registration at Companies House.'

'And the 714C certificate,' Tubal added.

'Yes, but that's of no value if we are not trading,' Dee replied confidently as if she genuinely believed it was true. 'So, I sent the certificate to Pat Sweeney and signed over the company bank account to him. It's nothing to do with the Angell family now.'

'Do you have Mr Sweeney's address?'

'Only a business address in London. Let me see. Yes, South Bank House in Lambeth,' Dee read from a slip of paper held in front of her. 'This is the only address I have. My husband might know, but I don't fancy your chances much tracking him down.'

Dee was right. Even if they had his address, Southern Ireland was totally outside their jurisdiction; a fact known only too well by adversaries returning there. At least in the North their powers held even if house calls required armed convoys chaperoned by the Royal Ulster Constabulary. Something Tubal had yet to experience.

'So, Joseph Patrick Sweeney. Is that who we are talking about?' He sought to resolve the discrepancy over the name.

'Well, that's what the bank said, but the only name I heard was Patrick Sweeney,' Dee replied.

'Do you know anything else about him?' Flick joined in.

'Not much. I know that my husband said the man was always on the go and hardly slept, an insomniac.'

'And what about company invoices and other paperwork?' Tubal asked.

'I sent Pat the template for the invoices and any copies of the 714C that I had signed,' Dee replied. 'I had no use for them.'

While Dee thumbed through her records, Flick and Tubal sipped their tea, giving Tubal time to think through the basics, just in case he had missed anything. It was important that he get Dee's testimony down in writing without alerting her to the link with Pilgrims Pyramid. More important was the date that the 714C and bank records changed hands.

'Oh, I forgot about this.' Dee shook an envelope, ejecting a key out onto the floor, which she stooped to retrieve. 'Pat had use of an old Landcruiser of ours – this is the spare key.'

'Was that sold by the company?' Tubal asked as Dee inexplicably handed the key to him.

'I don't think so. To be honest, my ex probably just let him have it in lieu of wages or, more likely, because he couldn't be arsed to get it back.'

'So do you think that the Landcruiser is still registered to Gilmore Angell Limited in Cricklewood?' Tubal asked. 'Do you have any further details or the registration number?'

'I have no idea, my love, all I have is this key.'

Tubal felt slightly deflated. In his mind, he had anticipated the finding of the key, or at least the vehicle details, as the days eureka moment. Instead, he found himself with Cinderella's glass slipper secreted in his hand. Flick's eyes transfixed upon Tubal as if she knew his next move. He rolled the key between his fingers.

'Do you mind if I hang on to this?'

Flick's eyes widened, forcing her eyebrows upwards as Tubal spoke. Clearly, she hadn't read his mind at all.

'I can pass it on to Mr Sweeney if I see him.'

'Well OK, if you want it. I don't know what use it is to you, but I've certainly no need of it.'

Dee manoeuvred back down onto her chair.

Tubal didn't know what he was going to do with the key, but he felt that it might come in handy. The important thing was that Sweeney had the original Gilmore Angell Limited 714C certificate in his possession. They spent the next hour getting Mrs Angell's recollection preserved in a witness statement, and then it was time to leave. As they rose sharply from the settee, the startled dog propelled itself onto the floor. They thanked Dee, said their goodbyes and exited back into the pungent chickpea air.

'So, what *are* you going to do with that key, Mac?' Flick collared Tubal on the walk back to the car.

'I dunno. It just seemed better to have it than not,' he replied. 'Let's have a spot of lunch and head up to South Bank House so you can work your magic.'

Chapter Seven

A welcoming smile radiated from the concierge's face when he spied Flick leading the way up the steps into the exquisite ceramic tile and terracotta-encrusted rainbow-bricked building adorning Lambeth High Street.

'Hello, Miss Francis. How are you today?' the tall, immaculately dressed custodian enquired politely as he held the sturdy Victorian door open.

'Fine thank you, Gladstone. I'm surprised you remember me,' Flick responded. 'As you can probably guess, we are looking for some information.'

'Yes, of course. Please take a seat.'

'Hello, mate. I'm Tubal McArthur.' Tubal placed his hand into Gladstone's and consciously clasped it tightly in the way that men believe they should, their perceived masculinity shining through.

Gladstone shook his hand blindly, his eyes fixed firmly on Flick, who had sat in the velvet padded chair in front of his station in the reception area. As Gladstone manoeuvred back behind his desk, Tubal moved towards him and explained the reason for their visit. Gladstone rose up again and entered a small office behind him. After a few minutes, he returned with an A4 manila folder and opened the cover. There was hardly anything in it.

'Look, I shouldn't really be showing you this,' Gladstone spoke quietly, 'but if you ask the questions, I'll answer them as best I can.'

Tubal had the impression that Gladstone wanted to help as much as he could. There were obviously rules that he had to follow, but he guessed from Gladstone's blazer badge that he was an ex-military man. He certainly carried himself as such, so he probably felt that it was his duty to help them. Tubal therefore made certain that everything that he wanted to know was covered. If he missed anything, he felt confident that his wingman Flick would pick it up. Fact was, despite their informal approach, if Tubal thought that there was anything of evidential value being withheld, he could seek a court order to obtain it. This way just made life simpler. In any case, despite the warm reception and the consequent ease at getting the Gilmore Angell Limited information, no new evidential nuggets were extracted from the sparse records. Effectively, South Bank House was what's known as a 'dead letter' office; post addressed there accumulated in a locked pigeonhole in the wall in the foyer to await the hirer's collection. Gladstone did not recall Sweeney, but box holders had a key and, in return for a monthly fee paid by standing order, they could visit any time day or night. The only documentary evidence held at South Bank House was a basic rental agreement. Tubal had Gladstone copy this in case he needed it later to match the handwriting.

'So, what happens when the post arrives?' Tubal asked.

'I sort it out and place anything for the rented boxes through the slot at the top,' Gladstone replied. 'To be honest, I only ever recall putting the odd bank letter for that company in their box.'

This is what Tubal had suspected – Sweeney had no need of an office, just somewhere legit for banking purposes. It was likely that all other transactions were face to face with those he's working with. They thanked Gladstone for his help and made tracks back towards the office. Although Tubal was getting a feel for this work, he bowed to Flick's experience to work out what to do next. If, as suspected, this was a 714C scam, BUR would be looking for regular cash supplies to pay their ghost labour force. Group Five had taught Tubal that these cases typically involve the contractor issuing a cheque payment against the rogue 714C company invoice. Up to 90% of the invoice value was then couriered back in cash and used to pay the site workers without the kerfuffle of tax deductions. If any questions were asked, they are Gilmore Angell's men. The reality, though, was that these 'skins' were open to exploitation by the anonymous gang masters that pick them up from rendezvous points such as Cricklewood Broadway at 5.30am each morning. It was a world where human labour was a commodity, where men are expendable, and circumstance often dictates that they slave for minimal reward: akin to prostitution without the sex. Flick churned over what they knew as they travelled back to base and concluded that, yes, they must chase the money, but the only way to find Sweeney was to witness what happened to the cash. That means sitting on the bank until the cash courier makes an appearance. The quicker Tubal put his case to Grenville Allonby the better.

'What you doing now, Mac?' Flick asked as Tubal prepared to drop her home.

'Nothing much, drop the car off and probably get something to eat.'

'Fancy a drink? I don't want to go home yet.' She sighed. 'I need some time to think.'

'OK.' Tubal didn't need much persuading, and it was still quite early, as if that mattered.

He knew of a nice Thames-side pub equidistant from both their flats. Flick went back to Tubal's and, after dumping his bags and case papers into chez McArthur, they slowly made their way along the shoreline footpath before reaching The Old Ferryman. It was a balmy evening and the tables overlooking the river invited them to perch wearily and unwind with the sound of murky water lapping against the mooring wall. Flick had already promised the first round as Tubal moved to saddle one of the vacant weathered benches. As his leg swung between the bench and the conjoined table, an arm linked with his and pulled him backwards.

'Do you mind if we go inside?' Flick released her grip on Tubal and disappeared from sight through the antiquated ale house's brass-furnished old oak door.

Tubal followed behind and headed past Flick at the bar to claim one of the snug booths. It was quiet in there tonight with most of the clientele out admiring ducks or eating basket meals on the terrace. Flick rejoined Tubal shortly, carrying a welcome pint of lager and a Guinness for herself. They hadn't really spoken to each other much in the car, so conversation quickly turned to the day's events, before the predictable talk of office politics – who was doing what to whom. It didn't really matter what was true or whether their perceptions had legs, this was the way of things: speculation and conjuncture sidelining the monotony of daily routine. Time passed quickly, energized by more liquid tongue loosener, yet they both remained guarded about revealing anything about themselves. Despite this, Tubal sensed that a pervasive tenderness, albeit conflicted by circumstance, existed between them. He would have liked to believe that they were kindred spirits, each desiring the warm throes of intimacy. Alcohol and romantic naivety generally bring out such delusions in Tubal and generally, he lacks the courage to unilaterally test his impulses. Someone once told him that, as a Capricorn, any prospective lover needed to strike pre-emptively. Tubal did recognise this need in him, but the cold truth was, they were workmates; there was a line that should not be crossed.

'What are you going to do for food, Mac?' Flick held out a menu.

'No, I'd better go. I'll get something from the freezer when I get home.'

Tubal didn't relish the idea of going home alone, but he needed a good night's sleep. The following day he would draft a report for Grenville Allonby and make an appointment to see him. They both rose from the booth and made for the exit.

'I'll walk you home if you like,' Tubal offered.

'Thanks, Mac, but it's not necessary. I'll see you tomorrow.' Flick leant forward and gently kissed him on the cheek.

Chapter Eight

Tubal made it to the office early to make a start on his report. Palatable nutrition had, in deference to his rebuttal of Flick's invitation, evaded him once home. Only an ancient Vesta curry could be found in the bowels of his freezer, possibly a housewarming gift from his mother and barely edible. Tubal had never understood why more raisins than meat appeared in the diarrhoea-coloured slop. Terry broke his concentration and started a surreal conversation about not understanding *The Rocky Horror Picture Show*, one of Tubal's favourite musical films. Tubal queried the sexual orientation of a cast member, questioning whether or not they were gay. Terry acted aghast at the suggestion with the quip, 'but they live in Guildford', before exiting to drive one of the bosses up to Solihull. As he chuckled to himself at Terry's pomposity, Tubal began collating together everything that he currently held for the Pilgrims Pyramid contract and the developer Boteler Urban Regeneration Limited.

Allonby will question every aspect. Tubal supposed that this was justified as Allonby was putting his neck on the line getting the Production Order signed to obtain what Tubal required from the Midland Bank. As was the way of things, he had to follow protocol and George, as the Senior IO, had arranged and would accompany Tubal to meet with Allonby later that day. No matter how competent Tubal thought that he was, junior staff are not tolerated to present their work in the corridors of power without an appropriately graded senior officer as chaperone. Ironic really, as there are no such qualms when Allonby invites himself to the office piss-ups and exerts his smarmy seniority over the younger women in the typing pool. That's when a chaperone really is the sine qua non.

So exactly how far had the case come? With all of the chasing around after the Gilmore Angell 714C, Tubal must recount the larger picture. As he typed, he chased backwards and forwards through the case file to ensure he had enough to convince Allonby that accessing the Gilmore Angell bank account was a proportionate response and justified further investigation into BUR. So far, Tubal had documented the two booksellers, Thomas Cole and Robbie Quinn, emphasising that BUR used their 715 vouchers to the tune of £100,000. Next, he highlighted the witnessing of Shauna Brady visiting the BUR site office opposite the Pilgrims Pyramid development, although Tubal reckoned that Allonby would not appreciate the potential implications of this. If so, sod him, but Tubal felt that it was relevant, given Shauna's connections. This only left his reason for accessing the bank account. Already Tubal has identified £1.5 million paid to Gilmore Angell Limited by BUR, but that had only taken him up to the end of the previous tax year. Any payments made more recently wouldn't show up until the middle of the following year. It was clear to Tubal that the company were operating outside the control of the legitimate 714C holder. Joseph Patrick Sweeney, was now Group Five's number one target, had no official profile in the UK and operated in the shadows. All things considered, Tubal believed that he must act quickly; the tax lost exceeded £400,000 and would inevitably multiply. Chicken feed in Allonby's corporate tax enquiries fought in palatial offices and sealed at the client's expense over a Johnnie Walker Blue in the bar of some far-flung lavish hotel. Yet to the racketeering boys over the water, this was serious money, and Sweeney's venture screamed for their attention. This was not just about the money. If Tubal was right, funds generated from any commission paid by Sweeney or his masters could be used to threaten the fragile security of the six counties.

'Morning, Mac, you alright?' Stevie broke his concentration. 'You heard the news about your old mate, Nutty?'

Since Nat's accident, Tubal hadn't had time to keep in touch with him other than to sign the obligatory get-well card. Some of the old team did go up to see him, so Nat probably wondered why Tubal couldn't be bothered.

'No, mate, what's that?' he replied.

'He's coming back next week, but they're sending him on a driving course in Devizes first.' Stevie spoke quickly as he hurried out of the room.

Jammy bastard, Tubal thought to himself. He would have loved to go on the driving course, but the guv'nors obviously wanted to minimise the risk of Nutty writing off any more assets. The rest of the office learn on the job and pray they don't hit anything, particularly shop windows. Tubal began to recount his early post-driving licence days. He had a drinking buddy, a police officer, who had completed the advanced driver training. On their way to and from country pubs, he would push Tubal to drive at maximum speed on whatever side of the road gave maximum vision. With hindsight, Tubal now thought that his buddy was a bit of a control freak; nevertheless, if they timed it right, they could leave rural last orders in Kent and still get back for 11pm closing in South London.

'What does that road sign mean, Mac?' he would say, pointing to the circular white sign with a slanted black line across it.

'National speed limit applies,' Tubal would smugly answer.

'No. It's a GLF sign. Double de-clutch, change down and Go Like Fuck,' he would say, and Tubal blindly followed.

Tubal found it a great way to boost adrenaline and sharpen his reactions, but at BIO he was doing it legally. OK, not quite legally, but the police markers on the vehicles warded off any unwelcome attention most of the time.

'Nutty's back next week then.' Paul poked his head round the door, neatly knocking red glowing ash from the tip of his cigarette to the floor.

Tubal seemed to be the only person who didn't know. Not that he cared much.

'Yeah, so I hear,' he replied. 'I hope he's not looking for his old partner back.'

'No, you're alright. Word is Debbie Condon's coming down to work in London. It'll be a match made in heaven.' Paul chuckled.

Paul was right. Both were devoid of any moral compass, but Tubal couldn't imagine Debbie putting up with Nat's idiosyncrasies. Fireworks would surely follow: not least if Debbie's somewhat tactile leanings towards men she fancied became known to Nat's wife.

'Two o'clock train to London, young man. Report on my desk by one,' George interrupted.

'No problem. I'm just tidying up my briefing paper now, George,' Tubal answered, knowing that the distractions meant he had a way to go yet.

'Chop, chop then. You can update me on the way.'

The pressure kept rising that morning, not least because everybody wanted to talk to him about Nutty. Tubal was struggling for time. Hitting the procedural points needed to keep Allonby happy was the main issue, rather than the case facts and chronology.

'Alright, my lover?' Flick's faux country bur broke his concentration. 'You look like you need a bit of help.'

Flick's appearance couldn't have come soon enough. The others were either out or busy and, in any case, she probably knew the same as him about the case. Tubal was happy that he could keep George and Allonby on side with Flick's input. The next hurdle would be his surviving the Somerset House meeting in one piece.

The morning was soon over. Report wrapped up and ready to roll. Tubal met with George in his office before they walked up the private footpath and onto the station platform for the 2pm train. The journey into London didn't take long, and the bracing walk across Waterloo Bridge freshened up the senses ready to face the reluctant puppeteer of their irregular brotherhood. Tubal had by now visited Somerset House many times but remained enthralled by the iconic magnificence of this neoclassical palace. What's more, the courtyard was a blessing as IOs are among the few people allowed to park their cars here, ideal for nights out in China Town and the West End.

George led the way through the impeccably painted black gloss door and spoke to the elderly uniformed messenger on the front desk.

'Messrs Craig and McArthur to see Mr Allonby. We do have an appointment.'

'Yes, sir, one moment.'

The messenger reached for the black Bakelite telephone on the desk before him. The dial rattled as a three-digit number reached an anonymous destination for the announcement of their arrival.

'Somebody will be down for you shortly. Please take a seat.'

In a tick, another ancient messenger appeared and beckoned them towards the steep wooden stairs to the upper floors. As they followed their guide along to Allonby's office, the corridors exuded a subtle blend of vellum, Quink and aftershave. The door was already open and sitting behind a sturdy oak-panelled desk lurked their inquisitor.

'Hello, George, good to see you.' Allonby stood up and extended his hand in greeting. 'Ah, you must be young McArthur; I've heard all about you. I'm Grenville Allonby.'

It was clear that Allonby hadn't previously registered Tubal's presence at briefings and office functions, but that was fine. True, they had never spoken before, but Tubal figured that he now had Allonby's full attention as, spread out on the inlaid wine-leather tabletop was a faxed copy of his report.

'Now, George, thanks for this. Can you just run me through the highlights?' As expected, Allonby maintained protocol by leaving Tubal's boss to brief him.

As George spoke, Tubal fixed his gaze on Allonby and waited to reinforce his presence if the chance came. Up close, Allonby somehow looked different. When spied across a room, tics and finer contours of face and movement are lost on the casual observer. Allonby was probably in his early forties. His hair was slicked back, sandy brown fused with a slightly glistening pomade that caught the light as he silently listened to George's address. Although slightly built, a noticeable paunch extended below his chest, leading him to subconsciously tug at his shirt, leaving thumb indentations in the laundered blue stripes of the cloth. Every now and then, Allonby pinched the bridge of his bulbous nose and blew air down onto a caterpillar moustache nesting atop his anaemic upper lip. Maybe the self-perceived Lothario attributes the nasal muff to virility and masculine exudation when hunting prey from the clickety-clack harem of fleet-fingered subalterns. In Tubal's ruminations, moustaches belie cocksure, pedantic individuals with a misguided sense of achievement; the sort who go caravanning at the weekend.

'Do you have anything to add, McArthur?' Allonby turned to Tubal.

'Not unless you have any questions, Mr Allonby,' he replied.

'I do.' Allonby paused for a moment. 'How do you know that that the Pilgrims Pyramid developers are involved in this fraud that you suspect?'

'I don't at this stage. That's why I want to follow the money into and out of the Gilmore Angell bank account.'

Allonby cupped his chin in his right hand and leant back in his chair.

'This is a high-profile, multimillion-pound development. The rejuvenation of the docks is of great interest to the Government. I really don't think that BUR would be involved in anything criminal, do you?' Allonby smirked as he spoke.

'Grenville, a lot of work has gone into this,' George cut in. 'Tubal is trying to find out which contractors are paying into the Gilmore Angell account and how those funds are distributed.'

'I understand that, but if cash is withdrawn from the bank, it can then be paid to anyone. Aren't they more likely to be Sweeney's men than the main contractors?' Allonby continued challenging.

'Well, that's what we are trying to find out, but we are in a catch-22 situation if we cannot obtain the means to follow the money.' Tubal sensed that George was getting a little tetchy now.

'But if BUR say that they dealt directly with Sweeney as the company secretary of Gilmore Angell, a legitimate company, and the directors have no direct connection with the men on site, how are you going to prove your case?' Allonby raised a pertinent point, but he didn't have the insight of the IOs on the ground.

'Well, we can't speculate on that,' Tubal curtly replied as he felt George nudge his arm.

A long pause ensued while Allonby fumbled around in one of his deep desk drawers. Tubal thought that he might pull out a bottle of Scotch and three crystal cut glasses but, alas, nothing.

'OK. I will seek a Production Order on Gilmore Angell Limited and get back to you,' he said, 'but I don't want you to approach the BUR directors without speaking to me first.'

Allonby rose from his seat, signalling that their time was up. As they left his room, the door was shut firmly behind them, and they duly made their way back to the exit.

'What a prick,' George muttered. 'Come on, I'll buy you a drink up the Nell of Old Drury.'

'Sounds good to me, guv'nor.'

Another working day was coming to an end. Another piece of the jigsaw will hopefully follow. Tubal's evolution has grasped the next eon in his metamorphosis.

Chapter Nine

Tubal was still waiting for the Midland Bank account information. As anticipated, there was no problem getting the Production Order signed once he had Allonby on side to support his case. In the interim, the team had been busy on a referral sent over by the City of London Police. A number of financial companies and universities had received Inland Revenue letters telling them to forward their outstanding PAYE tax deductions to a new Inland Revenue office; the incredulously entitled HM Collector of Taxes (Neville Brown Division). Checks had shown this 'division' to operate from a run-down basement flat in Notting Hill Gate, so it was off over there to spend their time operating round-the-clock surveillance to identify who collected the post. These scams were not unusual, but the bogus letters included references and financial information that could only have come from an inside source. Luckily, the office had a tip-off that a bent tax officer in North London was taking PAYE cheques from the post room. They tailed her after work and identified an accomplice who, it was ascertained, was extracting all relevant details before the lady returned the cheque into the system the next morning. After what seemed like countless days and nights in an OP overlooking the basement mail drop, the recipient of the

'Neville Brown' post was arrested early one morning. The tax officer was detained later that day at her work. Unluckily for her, she was in the process of running off with a £2 million utility company tax cheque in her handbag: a great bargaining tool when faced with a charge of stealing the £2 million if she didn't cooperate. So, for her, an abrupt end of career and facing conspiracy charges with her little gang of scammers. For Tubal, another credit in the experience bank and satisfaction that another corrupt member of staff was exposed.

Today is going to be a bit of a piss-up, Tubal thought. Marty had arranged for him and Flick to meet up with one of his Special Branch contacts at New Scotland Yard to talk about the Pilgrims Pyramid development. Tubal still didn't know why SB had flagged it but would hopefully find out when they reached their bolthole within the granite and polished-steel structure that stood guarding the metropolis. As they walked into the sunlight from Broadway Underground Station, the iconic revolving sign drew them towards their destination. Tubal had not been there before, but by then he was well attuned to the parlance and expectations of what was to come. As they walked into the reception area, the flickering eternal flame memorialising fallen officers caught Tubal's gaze; a solemn reminder of the unpredictable road they all travelled. He paused in recognition that life was precious and that he or any one of his colleagues might also one day face the ultimate sacrifice.

After checking in and picking up their visitor passes, they were directed to a small waiting area. Tubal hooked the leather flap of his deputation over the breast pocket of his suit in response to the sign that read 'all warrant cards must be displayed'. Anyone looking from a distance might deduce he was a plain-clothes milkman displaying a silver top from his homogenised wares. A closer look would reveal the raised

Inland Revenue crest denoting Tubal's business. Flick looked across at him, pursed her lips and slowly shook her head. Tubal took the hint as he flipped the badge back over and returned the ID to his inside suit pocket.

'Who do you think you are? The sheriff of Hinchley Wood?' Flick quipped as a uniformed security guard ushered them towards him.

They followed Mr Security into the lift and began their ascent to whatever of the twenty floors available to them SB were stationed on. As the lift doors slid open, a figure emerged into the lobby area in front of them.

'Welcome to the Yard. I'm Berwyn Jones. How do you do?' The baritone voice conveyed the unambiguous tone of a Welsh accent.

Stood before them was a thin, middle-aged man in a dark three-piece brown herringbone tweed suit, looking more like a country gentleman than a cop. His slightly wavy black unkempt hair fell towards wild, bushy eyebrows mounted on a face of lined, weathered skin. Berwyn's right arm angled in front of him, holding a cigarette 'twixt thumb and finger as if lining up to throw a dart. As Tubal approached, the cigarette was pushed back between his lips. A nicotine-stained hand shot out in greeting.

'Hello, Berwyn, I'm Tubal McArthur, but everyone calls me Mac. This is my colleague Flick.'

'Nice to meet you, Flick. We don't get many girls up here.'

'Oh, I'm all woman, Berwyn,' Flick countered as she loosely placed her hand in his.

'Touché. Now let's go somewhere to discuss what we can do for each other.' Berwyn led them back along a narrow corridor towards another lift lobby.

When the lift arrived, all went quiet as they entered the cramped transporter. No matter where people roam, travelling in a lift follows the same pattern: mute passengers either stand facing the floor or stare up at the illuminated numbers as each level passed. Conversation was always suppressed in these environs to keep others from hearing your secrets and you theirs. They descended onwards below ground level and into in the bowels of the building. Tubal's imagination began to run away with him: where were they going? Had he identified a national security threat and was to be debriefed? Have the family connections caught up with him? As the doors opened, Tubal jolted back to reality. Berwyn beckoned them to follow him along a nondescript corridor and through a dark, varnished door that discharged the whiff of cigarettes and alcohol as it swung inwards. Chatter and laughter filled the room.

'Welcome to the Tank. Let me get you a drink.' Berwyn pointed out a table where they could discretely discuss what they'd come for and set about ordering a couple of lagers and Flick's Guinness.

As they moved across the room, Flick grabbed Tubal's arm and pulled him towards her. 'Be careful who we get too close to in here,' she whispered. 'Not everyone here is on our side.'

'What do you mean?' Tubal asked.

'Journos, reporters. This is where a lot of trading goes on from both sides, not least enterprising coppers earning a few bob for tipping the press off about jobs. Just be careful.' Flick jostled Tubal towards the table Berwyn had directed them to.

They had just sat down when the drinks arrived, and a few bags of snacks were tossed down in front of them.

'Don't you just love pork scratchings, Mac?' Berwyn's voice strained over the noise. 'I've mixed it up a bit so take what you want. It'll quieten down in a bit so let's have a few drinks and we'll see if there's anything we can do for each other.'

Over the next hour or so, they chatted about all sorts of trivia fragmented by sections where Tubal's knowledge of Pilgrims Pyramid and BUR was slowly sucked from him without comment from Berwyn. Perhaps the day was a test allowing introductions to be made and a mutual assessment of each other's character? Tubal guessed that these guys skulked in the shadows and intelligence was a commodity traded on trust. He didn't really expect anything else and was fully aware that he was an unknown quantity, but Tubal had gone there to find out why SB had the Pilgrims Pyramid development flagged so had to stick with it, the plus side being that they seemed to be getting on well and any excuse for a few drinks was welcome. Either that or Tubal had fallen into some not-too-sophisticated alcohol-fuelled trap. Flick seemed to take it all in her stride, but she was the old hand here. The only written note Berwyn made was in relation to Joseph Patrick Sweeney before abruptly changing tack.

'Right, you guys, I've got to pop back up to the office for a bit.' Berwyn rose to his feet. 'I've arranged for you to be shown round the Black Museum as an interlude and I'll meet you down in reception afterwards.'

'I was hoping for a bit of a steer on your interest in my case,' Tubal chipped in.

'All in good time, boyo. All in good time. I'll see you in a bit.'

As he walked away, Berwyn signalled over to a uniformed messenger who had materialised in the corner of the bar seconds earlier. It was as if they were scheduled to a cryptic timetable known only to Berwyn and his cohort. The messenger signalled for them to follow her as they headed back to the lift, up to the first floor and into the rooms housing the grizzly display of murder, mayhem and anarchy. Flick had been there before and had tipped Tubal the wink that SB use a tour round the museum as breathing space whilst they check you out. For Tubal, this was a bonus to their day as he was genuinely fascinated by seeing the exhibits, albeit that some graphically illustrate how depravity evolves and consumes some of those amongst humanity. It was a discernible truth that crime and criminals held an allure to some people; notoriety was often built upon reputation and established folklore within communities. Tubal in particular, spawned in South London and weaned on dodgy dealing and loyalty, had loitered on the margins, protected by name, self-preservation and a latent introduction to honest living. He wasn't convinced that the curator saw any merit in two fraud wallahs taking up his time at the behest of his clandestine colleagues. Any attempts by Tubal at humorous banter were swiftly countered by a curt repost and being moved swiftly onwards. Tubal wondered if he was perceived as not displaying the reverence demanded by some of the items on display. That perception was wrong. Even Tubal accepted that, faced with the machete-shredded uniform of Police Constable Keith Blakelock or the cooking pots and stove used to de-flesh dismembered body parts by serial killer Dennis Nilsen, humour had no place. Or it might just be that any delay in getting them both back to reception on time would make their host persona non grata.

Their visit over, a chaperone arrived and escorted them back down to reception where Berwyn waited with a small group of men.

'Thought you might like a drink to get all that blood and guts out of your system,' he called towards them. 'Then I might have a bit of information for you.'

They all ventured from New Scotland Yard and walked along to Petty France where Berwyn diverted them into the Duke of Buckingham pub. The trailing ensemble followed and clustered at the curvature of the bar leading towards a small annex to the left of the building. Tubal's new Welsh friend spoke first.

'You can speak openly in here. The barman is one of us.'

Tubal wasn't exactly sure what Berwyn meant. He could guess. The pub nestled strategically. Opposite to Wellington Barracks and its close proximity to military, police and governmental buildings begged the prospect that the barman is an intelligence service asset. This would make sense given recent IRA activity on the mainland and the need for eyes on the ground in the capitals hostelries. But Tubal was a novice in this area and his experience of the Secret Intelligence Service came from James Bond films and Stevie's surveillance war stories. Tubal pushed Berwyn's comment to the back of his mind to concentrate on more pressing matters.

'It must be my round,' he offered, pulling a crisp £20 note from his pocket.

Flick had already perched herself on a vacant bar stool and Tubal moved protectively behind her as he waved the note to attract the barman's attention. Berwyn's companions had congregated at the tables at the rear of the pub, leaving the three of them to speak at the bar. It was quieter there, the dead interlude between extended lunch break termination and end-of-day livener.

'As I say, Mac. We are in safe company here,' Berwyn reinforced as Tubal ordered up the drinks. 'Let's get the business out of the way so we can enjoy the rest of the afternoon.'

A slight lull followed as the drinks were served into the warmth of their hands and Tubal savoured his next refreshingly cold sip of lager. Berwyn sidled in closer and placed his hand gently on Tubal's shoulder as he spoke.

'We have a conundrum here. Your hypothesis being that your fraud is Irish-driven. Correct?'

'Well, all enquiries are leading me towards Pat Sweeney,' Tubal replied.

'Ah yes, Sweeney. I've passed his details on to the Irish

desk, but I think he's diversifying away from his kith and kin.' Berwyn paused briefly.

'He'd have to be a brave man to do that,' Flick cut in.

'Well, it all depends on your perspective,' Berwyn countered, 'and the opportunities that his new friends can open up to any patron with nationalistic ideals contrary to our own.'

This had all become a bit too cryptic for Tubal, and he wasn't sure where Berwyn was heading. Another gulp of lager might assist.

'Let me put a scenario to you,' Berwyn continued. 'Some of our adversaries, and indeed allies, have a few self-serving entrepreneurs amongst their elite who are looking to move recently acquired wealth away from State scrutiny. Shadow economies are flourishing in the new Russian Federation and, thanks to the more-than-generous incentives being paid to buy British armaments and vehicles, well-placed fixers in the Middle East.'

'So where does Pilgrims Pyramid fit into this?' Tubal asked.

'Well, dear boy, I don't think that you really need to worry about that. Just be mindful that somebody is going to great lengths to hide the source of the money funding that development.'

'So where does that leave me?'

'Exactly where you are. All I'm saying is, keep up the work on Sweeney if you must but be mindful of the powers behind Pilgrims Pyramid.'

As far as Tubal was concerned, this new information held little significance. He was only interested in the lump fraud and prosecuting those behind it. Who owned the development and how they financed it was more up Grenville Allonby's street: not that Tubal intended speaking to him anytime soon.

'So, who is behind Pilgrims Pyramid and where does the developer Boteler Urban Regeneration Limited fit in?' Tubal felt obliged to dig a bit further.

'These are matters that we are researching.' Berwyn closed his question down. 'Now that you've exhausted my knowledge, let's drink up and get another one in.'

The afternoon did not look like it was heading to a natural conclusion. Berwyn sank back in with the rest of his colleagues, and Flick and Tubal perched as observers on the peripheral of the group. Every now and then, someone would break rank and include them in the drinks round. They were clearly in there for the long haul, and the pair needed to get back to Surbiton. By now, Tubal was feeling decidedly woozy, not least because he'd only eaten a handful of pork scratchings. He didn't want to seem like a lightweight, but one of them needed to take the initiative.

'What time do you want to head back, Flick?' Tubal quietly spoke in her ear.

'Come on, let's go,' she answered, grabbing her bag from the floor.

Tubal did not expect such a quick response but he was glad that Flick was ready to leave. As they said their goodbyes to the now blossoming crowd, Berwyn pulled Tubal to one side and clasped his hand.

'Nice to meet you, Mac. I'll keep in touch.'

Chapter Ten

The morning's drive into the office was fragmented by remnants of the bank holiday weekend encroaching on Tubal's inner thoughts. There had been a bit of a family get-together down on the South Coast, with great-uncles and -aunts thrown in for good measure. Twenty-seven for Sunday dinner stretched on commandeered pasting tables across the floor of the family's Bognor betting shop, like a Cockney mafia council of war. Being a Sunday, the shop door could stay open to purge the accumulated smell of body odour and cigarette smoke from the week's punters. Tubal had done his bit on the Saturday, having earned a fiver sweeping up endless cigarette ends after racing. His grandad's idea of pocket money, thinking that he was still fourteen years old but trapped in a man's body. Still, it bought him a couple of drinks during the night's one-off cabaret with Marty Wilde. It was great to spend the weekend there. The place held special memories for Tubal. Since joining BIO, he no longer had time to holiday at Sandy Acres. The betting shop sat at the heart of the holiday camp near the reception office and the clubhouse. Despite Tubal's views on caravanning pedants, he had a confession to make. His family owned a large three-bedroom caravan on site there, singled out by being the only one in its own private grounds with mains drainage and a bathroom; great for showing off to family and friends but not big enough for twenty-seven dinner guests! For Tubal though, it was off limits to women that his grandparents thought would take advantage of him, particularly if they were 'gold-digging' barmaids. Mind you, with Tubal's proclivity towards alcohol, £5 in his pocket and a wanton desire to be ravaged, the match seemed ideal to him. We digress slightly, but it was a woman that troubled his thoughts on a sober Tuesday morning.

Time spent at Sandy Acres during Tubal's pubertal summer holidays fed his introversion. Rarely was he absent from his grandparents' gaze unless his Glaswegian minder, Auntie Lottie, organised an escape party for them both down at the seafront pubs and bingo halls. If he was lucky, Lottie would matchmake him with people she met, although things never seemed to work out. As soon as anything clicked, Tubal was whipped off home again until the next summer. The same worked in reverse for pets. Tubal was given a pet rabbit once but, on the eve of being deported to Sandy Acres for the summer, he returned home from school to find it had been gifted to a local Romani family. Allegedly as a pet. Moral of the story? Don't get close to anyone or anything. Tubal did have an admirer though: the granddaughter of one of his grandmother's friends from the old days in Lambeth who holidayed at Sandy Acres. Bethany was always hanging around. A pleasant girl to talk to with pretty hazel eyes, but her sallow, make-up-free face conveyed a sadness that remained buried. The only time Tubal saw her smile was around him, but he let her outmoded clothes and unkempt hair feed a shallowness in him totally alien to his nature. In hindsight, Tubal felt that he should have cut through this. He felt shame that he did not. They did go on one date back in London after Tubal felt guilty about surrendering to a drunken fumble in a dustbin compound. A one-off and never repeated. The last he heard, she had run away from home and taken up with a Maltese pimp in Soho. Then, on Saturday night, he saw her again, entrenched with her new family by the stage mouthing rock 'n' roll songs. Totally untouchable, physically and metaphorically, without retribution; the plain, unfashionable wallflower had morphed into a sophisticated, mannered courtesan that would bless any man's dreams. Tubal had tried to catch her eye, but it was no use. It was too late.

Tubal was the first one into the office. He had picked up the post on his desk and taken a deep breath. There it was: the information from Midland Bank about the Gilmore Angell Limited account. Thoughts of love lost quickly passed as Tubal carefully slit the envelope open and poured out the contents. Immediately, he realised the amounts of money that were involved. Weekly credited cheque payments of somewhere between £41,000 and £42,000. The payments were made on various days of the week, but one consistent entry stood out; every Thursday, cash of around £37,500 was withdrawn. What's more, the bulk of the remainder was subsequently transferred to another account. This had all the classic signs of money laundering. *Pity that the bank doesn't have the wherewithal to query it*, Tubal thought, *but that would scupper such a prosperous little account for the manager.* Just then, George poked his head around the door.

'Got the Midland Bank stuff then?' he enquired. 'Anything interesting?'

'More than I reckoned, gov,' Tubal excitedly spluttered. 'Thirty-seven grand a week taken out in cash.'

'Fuck, we'd better put some eyes on this,' George responded with his customary pragmatism. 'What branch is the account held at?'

Tubal searched back through the statements. It was most likely, he guessed, that this amount of cash would require the account holding branch to apply special collection arrangements with Sweeney. As a rule, on such investigations, IOs do not contact individual branches about their findings; some managers tended to be a little loose-lipped with favoured clients. Tubal would need to go back to the bank's fraud department to check the branch's daily diaries and ascertain the time that Sweeney or his courier generally visited.

'It's at Harlesden. The money comes out every Thursday,' Tubal informed George.

'OK, Mac, put the job together and I'll pencil in this Thursday.' With that, George was off.

He still hadn't checked all of the statements. As Tubal worked through, it became clear that at least another million pounds had been paid by BUR; the Exchequer stood to lose a quarter of this. Tubal had no indication of where the cash was going, but he thought it a good guess that BUR were receiving it back.

'Morning, Mac.' Flick appeared through the door, threw her handbag down and headed for the kettle.

Gradually, the whole team were in, and George gave them the news that they had a day trip booked for the coming Thursday. Tubal telephoned his Midland Bank fraud contact who disclosed that the cash was regularly collected from Harlesden branch's enquiry window around ten minutes before noon. This was just inside the entrance. By Tubal's estimation, he had about a day and a half to plan the job, book vehicles, plus equipment, and hold a briefing for the team. Such things were now taken in his stride. A new confidence oozed from Tubal. If only Bethany could see him now.

Wednesday went by in a bit of a blur, checking and double-checking, running queries past George and making sure the batteries for the covert radio sets were fully charged. The office had been allocated a couple of triangular sling-type sports bags that fixed around your waist and extended across your chest. Each had a microphone and a transmit button built into the shoulder strap, saving at least one of them the need to wear a radio in the bulky shoulder holster. These bags were fashionable apparently, although Tubal didn't know on what planet. Predictably, for the purveyors of the office's surveillance equipment, they had been procured in a fetching hue of fluorescent red. At least they were not as bad as the tie with a built-in camera that BIO had in their arsenal; excellent bit of kit if you exclude the tie, which might just have been fashionable in Allonby's great-grandfather's day. Not even Terry Two Sheds would wear it. Anyway, Tubal allocated just one of the bags. He thought that more than one would stretch credulity that two fashionistas with the same taste in accessories were present in Harlesden High Street on a Thursday lunchtime.

As Tubal collated the briefing packs, he realised that he needed an extra body to build a viable team. At this stage, he had no idea what would happen at the bank, so it was imperative that he had the appropriate number of vehicles and footmen available for any eventuality. George directed that Tubal bring over Nutty Nat to capitalise on his refined driving skills. Tubal couldn't do anything about his unrefined personality, but Nat was eager to rejoin the fray after his enforced absences. So, they were now set for Thursday morning's 6am briefing. Tubal appreciated that this was a bit early, but they needed to drive up to Harlesden and make sure that the vehicle plotting positions were viable.

In a whisker, Wednesday departed and Thursday was upon him. Tubal's big day. A quick bowl of porridge for breakfast and it was back into the office.

'Good morning, all, thanks for turning out today.' George hadn't given them a choice, but Tubal said it anyway. 'As you can see from the Operational Order, the pairings today are, drivers first: Hawk One, Flick and yours truly; Hawk Two, Nat and Sid; Hawk Three, Paddy and Paul; Hawk Four, Terry and George, with Stevie's Hawk Five backing us up on the bike.'

The briefing didn't take Tubal too long as the only objective was to identify the person collecting the money and see where they went. Sounded simple, but it would all depend on whether it was Sweeney or a runner that turned up. Paddy had a case last year where £1.5 million went through a bogus 714C company bank account in only three months. When the frontman was arrested, he was just a stooge running the account for a miserly £100 a week. He admitted being a 'complete mug', or words to that effect, before being transported off to chokey for a twelve-month stretch. The people behind him had disappeared by then into the Eirean ether.

They all made their way across to North West London and plotted where they could cover one-way streets and dead ends. Harlesden was a melting pot of ethnicities and culture; London's reggae capital blended with Irish charm and opportunity. A mishmash of fresh food emporiums and barber shops infusing the air with spices, pungent fruit and ganja. The Midland Bank sat on a corner opposite an ornate Victorian clock that stood proud atop its black-and-gold plinth. The bank entrance was observable from all angles, permitting the team's judicious voyeurism of the entrance and egress of the unsuspecting clientele. At a quarter to noon, they would blitz the street outside in the hope of snaring their mark. For the time being, they could relax, stretch their legs and reconnoitre toilets and bacon rolls until the adrenaline of the much-anticipated pre-noon rendezvous kicked in.

Flick drove the replacement Cavalier SRi procured following Nat's carpet shop escapade. All shiny and new with no trace of Wilton weave garnishing the bodywork. They found a parking spot in a public car park to the left of the bank's entrance. Here they could avoid the unwelcome gaze of prying traffic wardens. Terry and George were not so lucky and were perched on the yellow lines of Harlesden High Street. Stevie was covering the eyeball position from the bike, religiously checking all Hawk locations every fifteen minutes. By 11.30am Tubal could feel his senses heighten. Moisture seeped lightly from his palms as he grasped the handset to await the off. Flick sat in silence as he stepped out of the car, placed the sling bag over his head and fastened it behind his back. Tubal pushed the moulded plug of his covert radio receiver into his left ear and started making his way towards the bank. As he approached the high street, Tubal spied Sid across the road by the clock tower and Paul looking pensive at the bank's ATM machine. Stevie was parked in a loading bay astride the bike. His helmet visor raised as he posted chips into his mouth through the cavity. There were still a few minutes to go but no sign of George. Tubal was not concerned, invisibility was, after all, the aim. He paused at a newsagent's shop and studied the postcards in the window.

'Hawk Five to all Hawks. Radio check,' Stevie kicked off proceedings.

Each one responded and awaited the next move. At ten minutes to noon, Tubal took control.

'Hawk One Foot, permission.'

'Permission granted One Foot,' Stevie replied. 'Eyeball to you.'

This was Tubal's cue. He walked slowly through the bank's entrance, sidled up to one of the worn wooden shelves and collected a couple of deposit slips from a pigeonhole. Taking a pen from his pocket, Tubal made spurious entries onto the forms for imaginary payments. The enquiry desk was located behind him, but he could see the cashier's reflection in the window facing him. It was getting busy in the bank as the lunch period started and people emerged through the entrance.

Tubal was happy with his cover but no potential candidates for the money had arrived. He turned round to survey the scene. All of the cashiers were busy. Customers chattered about the weather as they moved slowly along the waiting queue. Tubal bided his time, mouthing imaginary figures to himself as he calculated an imaginary windfall on his bejewelled digits.

'Hawk One permission.' It's Flick.

Tubal depressed the secreted transmitter button on the shoulder strap once for 'yes'.

'One click heard. Man walking across car park towards bank. Approx. six feet tall, white shirt, black trousers, large build with glasses and a scruffy beard, aged fifty to sixty years,' Flick relayed. 'I think he's the man I saw with Shauna Brady at Greenwich.'

Tubal could not respond to this information without showing out. It was either ignore for the moment or leave the bank to find out more. When Tubal had previously asked Flick about the man Shauna met, she couldn't recall him. Now, seeing the man again, it had obviously triggered her memory.

'Hawk Five has him.' Stevie saved him. 'He's walking towards the bank.'

Could this be Pat Sweeney? Tubal thought to himself. If so, things were starting to click into place.

'Hawk Four Foot is closing in.' George had emerged from his hiding place. 'Hawk Four has subject in camera view.'

Tubal braced himself ready to react.

'Stand by, stand by. Subject has entered the bank,' Stevie spoke hurriedly. 'He's holding a khaki rucksack.'

They had him, whoever he was. George followed in on the man's tail. Tubal repositioned himself at the end of the longest queue and observed the man as George shouldered the mantle for composing fictional deposit slips. The man went straight to the enquiry desk and opened up his rucksack. Tubal could just about see him slipping a piece of paper through the security screen to the cashier.

Stevie continued to relay from his position.

'Hawk Five to Hawk One Foot. Do you have eyeball… one click heard.'

Tubal could just about make out the man's face as his head swung from side to side in banter with the cashier. His accent was definitely Irish, from the South, and as he conversed, stubby fingers intermittently pushed his glasses back along their skewed perch on a large, red-veined, pockmarked nose. He must be over six feet tall, his large frame topped with scruffy, sandy hair joined to a bushy grey beard. A pronounced midriff hangs over his trouser belt, partly liberating an off-white casual shirt from his trousers. Tubal doesn't yet know if this is Sweeney, but he could fit the description given as the buyer by the booksellers Thomas Cole and Robbie Quinn. At the morning briefing, Tubal did cover such a possibility as Quinn had mentioned a 'Patrick' and there was the link with BUR through the 715s. The queue in front of him was reducing now, and after the next person, Tubal would be forced to withdraw. George was still the wingman. As Tubal glanced at the man, the cashier pushed two plastic-wrapped bundles across the counter towards him. Each was about ten centimetres high, and they were swiftly placed into the rucksack, which he then buckled shut. Tubal slowly made his way towards the exit before the man turned round. As he passed him, he could just make out the cashier's words.

'Until next week then, Mr Sweeney.'

A series of rapid clicks filled their earpieces as George signalled the standby. They had their man, Joseph Patrick Sweeney.

Back on the street, Tubal pressed the transmit button and quietly updated the team.

'Hawk One Foot to all units, it's an off, off, off. Confirm Target One is leaving. Description as given by Hawk One.'

Sweeney exited and walked slowly back towards the car park. Tubal noted a pronounced limp. His gait was that of someone being ravaged slowly by illness or excess. The rucksack swung from his left side, the strap firmly wound around his hand.

'One Foot to Hawk One. Did you identify a vehicle in the car park?'

'Negative, One Foot.'

'Hawk Four permission.'

'Go ahead, Hawk Four.'

'I've got some cracking pictures of target leaving the bank.' Terry had sprung into life.

'Roger Hawk Four.'

Tubal followed at a distance with George behind him. If Sweeney climbed into a vehicle, the footmen might struggle to get back to their partners, but Tubal needed all the backup he could get.

'One Foot to Hawk One. Entering car park. Do you have eyeball?'

'Yes, yes, One Foot. It's Wendover Road Car Park.'

'Roger Hawk One. Eyeball to you.'

As Flick's commentary guided the team through the car park, Tubal prepared to rejoin her. He spotted the other Hawk units moving into position to pick up their footmen and watched Stevie as he positioned himself opposite the exit. Tubal did not expect any drama once Sweeney left. Wendover Road was a one-way street, so they would easily be able to contain him.

'Stand by, stand by. Target entering a grey Jeep-type vehicle by the ticket machine at the rear of the car park. One Foot, can you confirm the number plate?'

'Roger, Hawk One. It's a grey Toyota Landcruiser registration number Golf Alpha Lima Eight Three Whisky. Target is alone in the driver's seat. I'm returning to vehicle.'

Everything was slotting into place. Judging by the registration number, it even looked like the Gilmore Angell Limited vehicle Sweeney had purloined. Tubal would get Marty to run a vehicle check back at the office.

'Manoeuvring, manoeuvring… it's an off, off, off towards car park exit. Eyeball to you, Hawk Three.' Flick handed the reins over to Paddy and Paul, who were parked southbound of the car park along Wendover Road. Sweeney would have to pass them to go anywhere.

Once Sweeney had left the car park, Tubal sprinted towards Flick as she manoeuvred to meet him. Just before he reached the car, a voice called out beside him.

'This is your lucky day, mate.'

Tubal looked across at the source. Four heavily built men occupying the seats of a Ford Granada Scorpio. The driver had his arm out the window clasping a spent cigarette, which he flicked to the ground.

'Definitely your lucky day. We had a tip-off that the Midland was going to be turned over,' the driver continued. 'If you had reached inside that bag round your neck, you might have been taken out. No worries now. We know who you are.'

As he spoke, his passenger drew back the lapel of his leather jacket to reveal the black grip of a revolver peeking out from a shoulder holster. *Obviously, there's more than one Sweeney in town today*, thought Tubal.

'Yeah, thanks, mate. Can't stop now,' Tubal shouted as he leapt in beside Flick.

They were now late to the party. Sweeney was moving quickly and had already driven around the side roads, leading him back onto the main drag into Central London.

'Southbound on Harrow Road. No deviation,' Paul's laidback voice was heard. 'Convoy check.'

The other Hawk units each signalled their location. Flick hit the car park exit at speed, glanced right and sped the wrong way up Wendover Road.

'What about the Old Bill?'

'Fuck 'em,' she spluttered as she slammed on the brakes to avoid a car turning left towards them.

Tubal just caught sight of the shaken driver. Instinctively, his hands had shot up from the steering wheel to cover his eyes. Flick veered left and swerved past the now motionless vehicle.

'Hawk One making ground,' Tubal transmitted as Flick blasted the horn to force their way back through the traffic and out onto the A404 into Central London.

'Odd that the police show up at the same bank as us,' Tubal reflected during a gap in the commentary.

'Yeah. Could be coincidence, or the cynic in me thinks that someone's trying to spoil our party.'

Tubal banked Flick's comment. The only people who knew the day's plans were there with them on the job. The immediate priority was catching up and playing their part. They pushed on through the traffic, Flick concentrating hard on making ground and Tubal tracing the *A to Z* as the commentary rolled on. Soon they were within spitting distance of Hawk Two on the approach to the A40 flyover. As the road widened, Nat pulled over to let them pass. It made sense for them to press on with a chance to assume the backup position.

'Target is taking a right, right. Committed Edgware Road, southbound towards Marble Arch.' Hawk Four was currently on Sweeney with Hawk Three backing them up.

'Hawk One permission,' Tubal quickly spoke, to keep the commentary rolling.

'Go ahead, Hawk One.'

'Roger Hawk Four. We're now two for cover behind Hawk Three.'

George acknowledged as Flick settled the SRi into the traffic queue heading towards the West End. Tubal hoped that Sweeney was heading for the BUR offices, but at that stage, he was still an unknown quantity. They had no idea where he lived or what his daily movements were. There was no room for complacency; too much was at stake.

The journey through Central London was uneventful as Sweeney ambled along Park Lane and headed towards Victoria. By the time he reached the Thames at Vauxhall, Tubal was eyeball a few cars behind him. Stevie hung back at the rear, his services not needed on the journey so far.

'Eastbound on Kennington Lane. Direction of Elephant and Castle,' Tubal updated.

He knew the Elephant and Castle well from growing up and working around South London. The iconic pink elephant lording over the 1960s homage to the American mall. The first such shopping centre in Europe.

'Left, left, left onto Newington Butts… approaching roundabout… first exit, first exit. Shopping centre on offside,' Tubal continued. 'Hawk Four, are you in a position to take eyeball at next junction?'

'Roger Hawk One.'

Sweeney had moved to the outside lane on the approach to a further roundabout. Flick moved up his inside and held back as the target blended into the traffic. Hawk Four followed behind him.

'Eyeball to you, Hawk Four.'

'Roger Hawk One. Not one… not two… not three… fourth exit. Fourth exit, New Kent Road. Speed three zero,' George's Celtic brogue reported.

Flick quickly cut across the traffic and spun them full circle round the roundabout before joining New Kent Road at the convoy rear. Hawk Two was now backing up Terry and George as they all headed in the direction of Surrey Docks. Sweeney ploughed on, over the flyover heading south on the Old Kent Road before swinging left towards Rotherhithe. Tubal felt the adrenalin flowing in anticipation that they would soon be on the approach to the Pilgrims Pyramid site.

'Approaching junction with Rotherhithe New Road... at roundabout. It's straight on. Second exit,' George spluttered.

They had expected Sweeney to turn right. He might just be ultra-careful, or he knew a scenic route to the site and BUR office.

'It's a left, left. Northbound Lower Road.'

Sweeney was now heading in the opposite direction.

George continued, 'Nearside indicator... slowing... slowing. Hawk Five, make ground. It's a left, left into Southwark Park.'

In the wing mirror, Tubal watched Stevie in the distance tearing down the tarmac towards them as Hawk Four's backup. Terry continued along Lower Road as Stevie turned left to provide eyeball in the park. The remaining three Hawks slowly filtered behind him to await further commentary. The *A to Z* showed Tubal that the park was dissected by an avenue that emerged back into Bermondsey. As they were tail-end Charlie, Flick manoeuvred them into a parking space near the entrance ready for the next standby.

'Moving slowly, speed zero five... target looking around.' Stevie paused momentarily. 'It's a stop, stop, stop near sign marked "café". I'm going past.'

'Roger, Hawk Five. Hawk Three is now eyeball. Footmen, standby.'

Tubal popped in his covert earpiece. Having now decided to ditch the shoulder bag, he clicked on the radio handset holstered beneath his armpit and emerged slowly from the SRi. It was a lovely day for a walk in the park.

'Hawk Three Foot is out. Target is walking in the direction of a building. Looks like he's heading towards the café.' This was the first time Tubal had heard Paddy's screech during the surveillance.

Paul followed up soon after. 'Three Foot has eyeball. Target is standing outside a building marked "Café Gallery". He is carrying the rucksack in his left hand.'

'Two Foot also has eyes on.' Sid is backup.

'Hawk Four is covering Bermondsey exit.' Terry and George had worked their way back to them.

Tubal had an idea but didn't know if he had the balls to do it. Sweeney was contained, and they were better served by keeping tabs on his vehicle. He leant back into the SRi.

'Flick, I'm going up to Sweeney's car. Pass me the camera. If you see me running, get ready for a quick getaway.' Before she could answer, Tubal was away and strolling along the line of parked vehicles.

'Stand by. Target is approaching a smartly dressed man. Black suit, glasses, balding, carrying a brown briefcase.' Paddy broke the silence. 'Both men shaking hands. Walking towards table and chairs... both now sitting down.'

Tubal reached Sweeney's Landcruiser, paused and stooped down as if to check his shoelaces. As he slowly rose back up, he stared pensively in the direction Sweeney had walked. Tubal could not see him, so he guessed that Sweeney would not be able to see him either. He peered through the Toyota's windows to spy an untidy mass of dirty cast-off site clothing, grubby newspapers and assorted rubbish. As he moved to the rear of the vehicle, Tubal took a sharp intake of breath and tugged at the tailgate door catch. Nothing. It was locked. Not sure what else he expected. He stood momentarily, psyching himself up, beads of sweat were building along his brow. It was then or never, an opportunity too good to miss. Ditch the reticent Tubal and galvanise the new brave. Reaching into the zip pocket of his coat, Tubal pulled out the key given to him by Devereaux Angell. He knew that he would find a use for it and had carried it around ever since.

'Target reaching into rucksack, taking out package and handing to black suit man... man puts package into briefcase. Handing target white envelope,' Paddy continued. 'Waitress approaching with one cup.'

Tubal pushed the key into the lock and turned. It worked. Guess he won't need the registration number check from Marty after all. Slowly, he raised the tailgate enough for him to reach in and grab a cardboard box that's nestled amongst the miscellany of tools and discarded, mud-sodden footwear.

'Stand by, stand by. Both men standing up.'

Shit! Tubal's heart pounded as he pulled the box towards him. Peering inside, he saw the unmistakable logo and bold notation 'Inland Revenue Property' on the manila-wrapped books inside. He fumbled nervously and grabbed the nearest to hand. Opening the cover, Tubal could see the name R. Quinn embossed on each of the green-coloured vouchers. It was the missing book of 715 vouchers sold by Robbie Quinn. He hastily peeled open another and spotted Thomas Cole's name staring back at him. Grubby photocopies of his 714 were tucked under the back cover. There were more books underneath and a wad of virgin Gilmore Angell Limited invoices awaiting completion.

'Target shaking hands with man. All footmen stand by.'

With one hand on the tailgate, Tubal swung the camera into the boot. There was no time to be a budding David Bailey. He blindly hit the shutter button and hoped that he had captured the evidence. Doubt if it would stand up in court, but at least it proved that he was on the right track. Tubal eased the box back and let the tailgate fall with a clunk. Turning the lock, he snatched the key back and pocketed it before moving towards the café footpath.

'One Foot permission,' he called.

'Go ahead, One Foot.'

'Making ground to join you.'

'Roger that, One Foot. Target is sitting back down. Other man is walking away towards park exit, Lower Road,' Paddy continued.

The excitement pumped through Tubal. He had Sweeney bang to rights in possession of everything he had hoped for but all he could do, in the interim, was note the information. This case had far bigger fish, and he needed all the pieces in place before they could make their move. Tubal had no time for hesitation. He hit the transmit button.

'Hawk One Foot to all units. Stand down, stand down from Target One. Follow the money with Target Two. All units acknowledge.'

Each of the footmen responded in turn. Tubal hoped that George wouldn't have his balls for cufflinks if the call was wrong.

'Roger, One Foot. Hawk Two Foot can now take eyeball.' Sid had taken the initiative, allowing Tubal to gain ground and fix Target Two in his sights ahead.

'Roger, Two Foot. One Foot is your backup.'

Tubal headed across the grass to get into a position where he could clearly track their new mark. Sid kept the commentary going as the cars scooted back to Lower Road. As Tubal looked over his shoulder, he saw George emerge onto the street via the roadway through the park. All four of them had black suit covered. Tubal crossed the road to keep himself out of his eyeline and to keep tabs on Sid, the street furniture providing any cover that he needed. The cars were about somewhere. Tubal could not see them. Stevie passed by to find an OP ahead.

'Target Two is still eastbound on Lower Road. No deviation,' Sid updated.

Tubal did not know who this man was but would bet his last farthing that he was connected to BUR.

'It's a stop, stop, stop. Target entering Mo's Sandwich Shop on the offside. I'm going past. One Foot, eyeball to you.'

'Roger, Two Foot.' Tubal positioned himself opposite the sandwich shop so that he could see the man. 'Target Two is stood at the counter.'

Nobody had queried why Tubal let Sweeney go. His only hope, as case officer, was that they respected his decision. He moved a bit closer to get a better description.

'Stand by, stand by. Target Two is walking back towards the exit. White paper bag in hand.'

Tubal crossed the road to meet the man full on as he exited the shop. As he sent a series of rapid clicks to signal his departure, Tubal's eyes caught sight of an unshaven, bespectacled, puffy-cheeked, middle-aged man. His shirt, the brown check of rural dwellers, lurked beneath a faded black suit, wearing thin at its extremities and markedly stained. Who said smartly dressed man? A brown tie loosely knotted at three quarter mast lay beneath a double chin. There was an air of unpleasantness about this individual as he continued his walk, his briefcase clenched tight beneath white shiny knuckles.

'Continuing along Lower Road,' Tubal updated. 'Who's my backup?'

'Four Foot is backup.' George had caught up.

Tubal fell back to let the man go on his way. There was a clear route between the two of them and, thankfully, he was still heading in the direction of Pilgrims Pyramid and BUR's office. Wherever he went, they would have it covered. Within minutes, the property Shauna Brady visited emerged. The man reached the steps of BUR's office and paused before looking both ways. *For a man potentially carrying up to forty grand in his briefcase, it's a bit late now to be cautious*, Tubal said to himself.

'It's a stop, stop at known office. Target Two is climbing steps to entrance… entering building. All stand down. Stand down.' Tubal brought the day to an abrupt end and walked towards the SRi that had just passed him and pulled into a turning further along the road.

The day couldn't have gone better. Sweeney was confirmed as running the bank account, and they had witnessed the handover to what surely must be BUR's man. Not only that, Tubal had evidence that Sweeney was in possession of stolen tax exemption documents. It was certainly atypical to get so much intelligence in one day. Infinitely more exciting than sitting around all day with nothing going on. Tubal was on a high and, as they headed back to base, verbal overdrive kicked in as he regaled Flick with his thoughts on the day and life in general. She looked ahead at the road, smiled knowingly but said nothing.

Chapter Eleven

Friday again. Time for tidying up diaries, updating overtime claims and completing expenses before heading off down the Orleans. This Friday though was a bit different. Tubal would have to debrief the team whilst Sweeney's surveillance lingered fresh in the hippocampi of their collective brains. Doctors claim that the memory can hold limitless amounts of data. With the Friday afternoon plans, followed by the weekend, Tubal wasn't so sure that assertion would apply to all of them. What's more, it was Sid's birthday, meaning that the normal extended lunchtime session would morph into 'last man standing'. First, Tubal felt that he better sort out the boss. Flick knew about his unofficial incursion, but the others had shot off home once they had arrived back to the office. As soon as he heard George's car keys clunk down on his desk, Tubal nervously sidled into his office and gave him the news. His reaction, the predictable decibel level in these situations:

'*What the fuck. You did what? Shit, Mac.*'

I just about got away with it, Tubal thought to himself. George reacted like this to most events first thing in the morning. After a bit of arm waving and pacing, he sat back down, lit a cigarette and waited for Tubal's explanation.

'The thing is, boss, the way I look at it is that the Landcruiser

is an asset of Gilmore Angell Limited, the true 714C holder.'
He only had one shot at this. 'The key was given to me by
the company secretary, and, by inference, I have permission to
use it. Sweeney is not the owner of the vehicle, so I'm doing
nothing illegal.'

George silently stared back at him. Tubal felt that he
needed to fill the void.

'By looking inside the vehicle, I now know that Sweeney
is carrying around stolen 715 vouchers and seems to use the
Landcruiser as his office.'

Still nothing. Tubal paused before some other gems of
speculative wisdom spurted from his mouth.

'Shut up a minute, Mac. I'm thinking.' George closed
Tubal's justification down, drew on his cigarette and raised
himself off his chair. 'OK, I get it. I suppose you expect a slap
on the back for initiative. Well, for now I need a coffee.'

George handed Tubal his Hearts FC mug containing the
curdled remnants of a long-forgotten beverage, tinged with a
light-green crust of penicillin. *Surely it hasn't got like this since
Wednesday*, he thought. *This must be the special mug for atoning
IOs.*

'OK. I'll wash your mug first,' Tubal said sarcastically as he
walked towards the door.

'Don't push it, Mac. Debrief at ten o'clock.'

Coffee duly made, Tubal returned to his desk and waited
for the others to drift in. In the meantime, he updated the
intelligence database with the latest on 'Patrick' and his likely
identity as Joseph Patrick Sweeney. This might click with other
IOs and identify him as the dealer in further cases. Tubal
regretted not having the time to sort through the other 715
books in Sweeney's boot. Just to cover his arse with George,
Tubal hastily phoned the Registry to run a licence plate check
on Sweeney's car. Thankfully, it was still registered to Gilmore

Angell Limited. Tubal would require Devereaux Angell's retrospective written permission for use of the key, but that can wait for now.

Earlier that morning, he dropped the camera film off at the photographers used by the office to develop surveillance photographs. Pictures of Sweeney's illegal horde would be ready in a few days; fingers crossed. So, everything was set for the weekend. The debrief took up little time, just tidying up the surveillance logs and Tubal updating the team on his discovery in the boot of Sweeney's vehicle. Nat was back to his old self and sat with that inane grin on his face as he referred to Flick and Tubal as the new 'Dempsey and Makepeace' after the detective duo on TV. Tubal convinced himself that the novelty would wear off with him in time, maybe a few years. Thankfully, Nat will return to Group Two and his new hook-up with Debbie. Tubal doubted if he would be around lunchtime. It'll be a pie and a pint for £1 and 50p in the stripper's beer glass for a quick thrill. That or a salad round at Debbie's place.

'Right, I'm off home for a bit, domestic issue,' Terry piped up to make his excuse before lunch. 'I'll be passing the Orleans if anybody wants a lift.'

'Not buying me a birthday drink then?' Sid countered half-heartedly.

'I'll pop in for a half on the way back,' Terry replied.

The betting man in Tubal foresaw long odds on this happening. A gift horse stood before them with the challenge of how many IOs you could fit in Terry's Volvo Estate. The clamour for jackets and drinking boots spontaneously erupted as the office bled out. Sid's birthday was a great excuse, but chances are this would be a typical Friday at the Orleans.

'Afternoon, lads, what can I get you?' Marie was waiting at the bar.

She must have seen Terry shoehorn them out of the Volvo. Pints were already lined up behind the counter.

Gradually, the Orleans filled up as the five London teams spilt into the bar. The regulars kept their distance as they jockeyed for position around the bar to catch up on news, share gossip and celebrate successes. Sid bought the first round as Marty pre-emptied the next drink by starting a whip-round three sips into Tubal's lager. The rounds come thick and fast, directing the rate of drinking. Tubal had always been a fast drinker, but this was Olympic standard. Nobody, other than Paul, sat down, and Tubal moved from huddle to huddle of IOs, only breaking out for the sustenance of a sausage in French bread. Sid was looking a bit worse for wear after a couple of hours. Everyone who came through the door bought him a drink and Sid had adopted the Tubal McArthur mantra, 'it would be rude to refuse'. And him being a good Muslim. Well, they thought he was. Nobody ever mentioned it. As they say, people's private lives stay private. Sid did mention once that he had been in an arranged marriage since the end of puberty. Nobody had ever met his wife, which might explain the Lithuanian student draped around him that he 'sponsored'. Still, it was of no concern of theirs. When you work hard and spend a disproportionate time away from home, relationships blossom where you find them. Tubal's garden, by comparison, was barren; a haven of gymnosperm with pine nuts trodden underfoot. It must be the drink getting to him. Time to buy himself a cigar. As Tubal smoked, the long draws compared favourably against the involuntarily inhaled discharge of betting punters' cheap baccy. Smoking provided him with a momentary antidote to intoxication. It didn't deter his alcohol-fuelled imagination from overflowing with premonitory events though. *I don't like him; if he starts on me, I'll have him. I quite fancy her; if I get the chance, I'll kiss her.* The first thought never materialised, but the second scenario occasionally got Tubal into trouble. At his twenty-first birthday party, he invited his next-door neighbour in, only to fall out with him after he was caught snogging his soon-to-be ex-girlfriend. By the time it came to cake cutting time, a search party nearly caught him in flagrante with a distant cousin. Luckily, all was accepted with good humour after the event. After all, it was his party. Sobering up always brought Tubal dramatically to his senses. Sobriety restored the shy carnal coward within him.

'You alright, Mac?' George put his hand on Tubal's shoulder and quietly enquired, 'I didn't know you smoked.'

'I don't,' is all he could muster. 'It's medicinal.'

'Yeah, alright. Listen, you did great yesterday and full marks for bottle,' George replied. 'You've just got to tidy up the loose ends to make sure any evidence is not thrown out of court. Don't give Allonby any reason to cause us problems.'

'Thanks, boss. It was a spontaneous decision,' Tubal slurred. 'I had the key so thought I'd try my luck.'

He left out the bit where he was shitting himself. Two things Tubal has learnt since starting work: never admit you've had too much to drink and never show you're outside of your comfort zone.

'Well done anyway. Have a think about the next move and speak to me next week.' With that, George sidled over to his fellow SIOs and Tubal returned to the reprobates hugging the bar.

'No sign of Terry yet,' Tubal joked. 'Probably lost in one of his two sheds.'

Tubal always found that great conversation with amicable company burned the hours away. As he looked out of the pub window, he saw the sun departing with the light fading fast. There was still a small enclave of them steadying themselves against the bar. The usual suspects. Regardless of how Tubal thought he was presenting, maintaining the charade of clear-headedness was impossible, and he needed to get off home.

'Right, I'm off,' he spluttered as the last mouthful of lager sank down his throat and he turned tail to the door.

Emerging into the fresh evening air, Tubal took a deep breath and relied upon autopilot to direct him towards Esher station. There was a decidedly inert feeling in his legs but he forced himself forward, left leg swinging over right, torso swerving side to side, eyes locked on the horizon. As Tubal reached the stairs up to the booking hall, he felt a presence behind him, then a hand clasping his upper arm.

'Hang on, Mac, I'm coming with you.' Flick's voice was unmistakeable.

There wasn't long to wait for a Surbiton train, and Flick's presence rejuvenated him. A compulsion to ask the simple questions that ordinarily felt taboo niggled inside him. Since the day when he collected her from home, he wondered who the 'arsehole' she referred to was. On the train, Tubal thought about asking, but the short journey lapsed in mutual silence. As they alighted at Surbiton, the town buzzed with late-night shoppers and couples out visiting the few restaurants and even fewer pubs. He still had the walk home down towards the river, so it was time for them to part.

'I'll see you Monday then, Flick. Have a good weekend.' Tubal lifted his hand in a half wave and turned on his heels to leave.

'Well, I don't know about you, Mac, but I'm starving, and it's only early,' Flick replied. 'What you going to do when you get home?'

'Well, nothing,' was all he could say.

'Come on then, let's go down to The Old Ferryman. We can get a bite and have a nightcap.'

Tubal didn't take much persuading. The thought of going

home alone wasn't too daunting, but spending time with Flick trumped it anytime. They had become good work buddies and shared a similar sense of humour most of the time. Other times, things would be better left unsaid; an inevitable trait borne of familiarity around those Tubal became comfortable with.

On the walk down to The Old Ferryman, they chattered about the day's revelries and speculated about Sid's Lithuanian. Tubal found it cathartic sharing his discussion with George with Flick. They laughed about the Flying Squad being at the bank and drummed up imaginary consequences, each embellishing the story for greater comic effect. The air was quite crisp and the cold atmosphere, laughter and companionship had revitalised the wearied, sozzled sole in Tubal. It was not long before the pub's oak gateway swung inwards and they settled down, pints before them, in one of the booths. Tubal sipped slowly as the day had taken its toll on him. The lunchtime hare had transformed into a lame tortoise supping as if it was his last. He really should get something to eat. The menu was pretty standard pub fare but it was stodge that he was after to mop up the booze. Steak and kidney pudding with chips. Magic. Flick opted for a burger, and they sat back and soaked up the Friday-night atmosphere. Tubal even took his tie off. Neither one of them were dressed for a night out.

'So, what do you like doing outside of work?' Tubal asked, knowing that was not really what he wanted to find out.

'Oh, this and that. Depends on who I'm with.' Flick's reply was of no help. 'What about you?'

Now that he had crossed the line to personal questions, there was no going back.

'Mainly meeting up with family and friends,' Tubal replied.

In truth, the friends were limited to a few school friends Tubal played rugby with and the odd mate from the old office.

Odd being the operative word, although he did have his first overseas holiday with him.

'What are you up to this weekend?' he continued.

'Nothing much.'

The conversation was going nowhere unless Tubal upped the ante.

'Just a quiet weekend with your significant other then,' he teased.

'Significant other? That's funny, Mac. No, just me and the cat.'

'It's just that day I picked you up to go to Mrs Angell's—'

'I know what you are going to say,' Flick cut him off mid-sentence. 'That's Ross. We're having a bit of a break. He can't cope with the demands of this job.'

Tubal saw his point. It couldn't be easy having a girlfriend that regularly disappeared early morning with no idea when she would return. It must be draining, particularly if they have a penchant for after-work curries and drinks with tubby, fledgling investigators.

'Anyway, Mac. You keep your love life well hidden.'

There was no point in telling the truth. He wasn't looking for sympathy.

'Well, let's just say I've too much Quink in my Parker and no inkwell to squirt it.'

Flick was halfway to the bar as the metaphor left his lips.

'What's that, sir?' said the comely young waitress stood behind Tubal with their food. 'Would you like anything else?'

He resisted asking for blotting paper.

'No, that's great thanks,' Tubal replied as she placed his meat pudding in front of him. 'Nothing else.'

'Got any ketchup?' Flick called over from the bar. 'He forgot about me, love.'

As if he could.

Chapter Twelve

'Swear on your mother's life that you are telling the truth?' Paul cranked up the pressure.

They had already been there two hours and were getting nowhere.

'Don't talk about me mother, yer bastard.' The man lunged forward at Paul, grabbed him around the neck and knocked him backwards onto the grungy duvet draped across the steel-framed divan.

Tubal momentarily froze, shock stalling any reaction, then flung his notepad to one side and wrestled away the man's left arm. Paul grabbed the right and pushed himself back upright. Outnumbered by two to one, the man quickly desisted; the tension in his body receded in seconds.

'Sorry, Mr Ramell, I don't like talking about my mother,' Paul's assailant spoke quietly and sank back into his grubby armchair as if nothing had happened.

Paul paused, lit a cigarette and ran his hands through his hair before raising his voice to reassert some authority.

'Well don't you ever attack a member of Her Majesty's Inland Revenue again.'

Tubal had to suppress a smile. Paul's words appeared crass in the circumstances. They could have ended up in a fight, but where would that leave them? Tubal already suspected from his demeanour that the man might have some ongoing mental health issues. Nevertheless, throughout their time with him, he insisted that every penny of the tens of thousands on his 715s had been earned by him alone. Given the known information they had, this would have been impossible. He had been off radar for a while; the address on his vouchers was false; and it took some finding to pinpoint his current location. So, here they were, sat in one pokey room: a thin mattress of a bed, a tip-salvaged armchair and a kettle. No tools, no car and surrounded by spent cider bottles. Paul did know that the man had disappeared into a psychiatric hospital for a while; gauging by his reaction, maybe for killing his mother. Still, they had a job to do, and their questions highlighted the ambiguity between reality and what's written down on paper. The fact is, he couldn't have done the work, but rather than be seen as a grass, he would brazen it out and disappear back over the water before the heavy tax demand lands on his mat.

There was no point labouring the issue any longer. Time to leave. Paul issued a notice cancelling the man's 714 certificate and they swiftly departed. Hopefully, the visit did not trigger any inner demons. If any harm did come to him, any neighbours passing the bedsit's garden-facing window may have witnessed two suited strangers pinning their man down in his armchair. Chances are though, nobody cared.

The journey back to base was filled with excited banter between the two of them. Paul laughed off the encounter as befits his imperturbable nature, and Tubal felt a glow of excitement as if grappling with the punter was a figurative badge of honour. After a few pints, they finished the day with a curry and a catch-up with other late-finishing colleagues.

'Yeah, there he was, strangling me with his bare hands. I'm trying to fight him off and Mac's grabbed him with one hand whilst still taking notes with the other,' Paul regaled the assembled IOs in the Akash. 'Mac never even looked up and left me to it.'

'Well, I was keeping contemporaneous notes as instructed,' Tubal answered, not wishing to spoil the illusion.

No one's likely to listen to the truth, and at least these two fledgling IOs might gain a place in BIO folklore. There was bound to be a bit of ribbing in the Tea Club. That's how things worked around the office. Tubal decided that he would rather be known for his casework than tomfoolery, but any form of recognition aided acceptance within the ranks of the old warhorses who've spent the best part of their career ensconced within Technical Division T2/A4.

And so, the regular work ground on. Thursdays were pencilled in for discovering more about Sweeney's movements and his dealings with the mystery man in the black suit. Nutty Nat was seconded to provide an extra driver and amuse them with his acerbic wit. Tubal had the financial side covered; the bank had supplied all of the account updates, and any BUR-submitted 715s came straight to him to check if they were kosher. Thankfully, the photos he took in the back of Sweeney's Landcruiser came up trumps and his actions were forgiven. The boss had been up to see Allonby again and wrestled a Production Order from him covering the account used to siphon regular debits from Gilmore Angell Limited's income. Slowly, the pieces of the jigsaw revealed the wider vista to Tubal, despite having no idea what Sweeney was doing with Shauna Brady that time in Greenwich or why she went to BUR's office. Likelihood was, Shauna was seen as a bad omen since Gerry Murphy got his comeuppance and any devotees were keeping away. Whenever a passing IO had looked, there was no sign of life around her Kilburn love nest, so it was anybody's guess what she was up to.

Another Thursday soon arrived and Flick and Tubal set out for another early morning in North West London ready for the team to plot up around the Harlesden bank. As expected, Sweeney collected the money and drove down to Southwark Park to meet his BUR contact. Same old story: money handed over, manly handshake and the two diverged their separate way. That week the team agreed to stick with Mr Black Suit to observe his movements. Hopefully, they would find out if and how the money filtered out from BUR's office to the Pilgrims Pyramid site. That would not be easy, as anyone exiting the building might work for the people on the ground floor. Sid and Tubal were this time wading through the dog shit, wind-blown takeaway boxes and kamikaze pigeons along Rotherhithe's Lower Road to keep tabs on the man; bus shelters, postboxes and parked vehicles providing enough concealment to keep these watchers from prying eyes. They believed that they knew where he was going, but once he had mounted the steps into the building, everything was supposition unless they could get somebody inside. Tubal had already used up one life and he doubted if the little-boy-lost routine would work a second time. No, the plan was for Stevie to conjure up his best motorcycle courier act. Tubal could already see the bike perched on the pavement and Stevie unstrapping something from the pannier. He didn't even need to show the face behind the helmet, just carry a document pouch and follow a few steps behind the faded black suit into the building. If he got the opportunity, Stevie might even be able to shadow him up to the first floor.

'Hawk 5 has eyeball, target walking towards me… stand by.' Stevie paused as the man made his way towards the target address. 'It's a stop, stop, stop… up into the building. I'm going in behind.'

Well, so far, so good, Tubal thought to himself as he and

Sid continued on past BUR's office and met back with their vehicles ensconced off the main drag. Flick was waiting for Tubal with a tepid coffee drawn from the Thermos she kept for these jobs.

'Fancy a change around, Mac?' She'd already shifted to the passenger seat. 'If you spin us back round the block we can cover the eyeball on the front of the building.'

Tubal didn't need much persuading. These days were normally draining, and the chance of a sit-down came as welcome news. Besides, they were still waiting for an update from Stevie, so whilst not much was happening, they had the chance to regroup. Tubal found a good spot further along Lower Road, close enough to see if anybody left the building but out of the eyeline of anyone peering out the window. Flick organised a quick update on the positions of the rest of the team and they readied themselves for the next move.

'Stevie's been in there a long time.' Tubal checked his watch and looked across at Flick. 'Do you think he's alright?'

'I'm sure he is, licensed to kill and all that.' Flick giggled. 'I'll try him on the blower.'

Flick sent Stevie her message, slurped her coffee and waited for the radio squelch when he clicked his reply. Nothing was heard. After thirty seconds or so, she tried again. No response. Tubal's mind started running away. The banter about his indifference to Paul's attempted murder was one thing, but now he had mislaid a former asset of Her Majesty's Security Service. At least the motorbike was where Stevie left it, so the bean counters would be happy.

'Hang on a minute. There he is over there.' Tubal nodded towards the leather-clad figure appearing from a gap between the houses further up the road.

'Five permission.'

'Go ahead, Five, thought we'd lost you,' Flick responded.

130

'Cheers, One Foot, are you sitting on your crown jewels?' Stevie teased. 'You've gone up a few octaves.'

'Mac's shedding a few tears thinking you'd been kidnapped so you're stuck with me.'

'Fair do's, One,' Stevie countered. 'Quick sit rep. Target has office on first floor. He entered with the package and locked the door behind him. There is a rear exit leading down the fire escape into a small car park. So far.'

'So far, Five.'

'Three vehicles parked and egress via private lane back onto Lower Road. Over,' Stevie tailed off.

'Roger, Hawk Five, thought you'd teleported out of there,' Flick quipped.

'I have many talents, but mastering quantum mechanics is not yet one of them, darling. Eyeball to you, One.' Stevie kicked the bike off its stand, revved the throttle and retreated out of sight.

'I'll give him darling, cheeky sod,' Flick spoke to no one in particular as she rested the radio handset on her knee.

They were to maintain eyeball on the building from that point. Flick and Tubal needed to cover any exit from the building and from the slip road leading from the rear car park. Nobody knew if their man would go to the site, or if the wages were collected from the office. At least they had confirmed that Sweeney did return the cash to Boteler Urban Regeneration Limited, and the man had an office there. It didn't really matter what else might happen as Tubal only required reasonable suspicion to arrest the BUR operatives and Sweeney. His remaining problem being, that he had to know where the main players lived in order to search for evidence. It was one thing catching Sweeney red-handed with stolen 715s on him, but what if the day they nick him he's clean? No, there was still a lot more work to be done. Tubal still didn't know who the man in the black suit was, but if they could link him to one of the cars parked out back, the registration number might give them a clue. Tubal concluded that he was a bit too scruffy to be a likely big shot in the company, particularly given what little information Berwyn imparted about the suspected surreptitious financing of Pilgrims Pyramid. He also didn't look very Middle Eastern to Tubal.

'The bloke in the black suit,' he asked Flick, 'does he look Russian to you?'

'Why? Do you think he's carrying a bottle of vodka in the lining of his jacket?' she replied. 'I've met Russians on an exchange visit to Somerset House. They wear suits that look like they're made of corrugated cardboard and are all called Boris.'

'I'll take that as a "no" then,' Tubal answered, realising too late that a stupid question deserved a stupid answer.

Flick checked back with Stevie to confirm that he had noted the car registration numbers. He had, so they settled down but could not relax their guard.

The afternoon dragged on, Tubal's only excitement drawn from watching curvy pedestrians ambling past or waiting for fast approaching police cars to roar past them to some misdemeanour on South London's streets. Flick was too focused for small talk. Her eyes were glued on the target address, trance-like, dreading that anyone or anything was missed. Each event was logged in her neat, stylistic handwriting. Tubal also watched, but he had acquired the ability to stave off long periods of inactivity by retreating within the closeted inner sanctum of his mind. His imagination was fed by sporadic daydreams as he pondered hypothetical presentiments about life and relationships, each scenario burning down the passing minutes as they anticipated the next move.

'Mac, wake up!' Flick pulled on his jacket sleeve. 'Stand by, stand by. Grey car held at junction with Lower Road.'

'It's a "T" registration Vauxhall Viva,' Stevie cut in. 'I'll check on driver ID.'

'Roger that, Hawk Five,' Flick continued.

Stevie passed them at snail's pace and pulled onto the kerb parallel with the Viva. Tubal had started the engine in their vehicle but wouldn't move until the direction of travel was known. Therefore, eyes on the vehicle remained with Stevie.

'Confirmed ID, black suit target. Nearside indicator. Still held. Still held. It's a left, left, left. Northbound towards the City,' Stevie updated the team.

Once clear of the BUR office on his offside, Tubal accelerated fast to find a side road to spin round in and join the convoy. Stevie was already out of sight and Sid's brusque tones filled the airwaves from Hawk Three, already set up for a northbound exit but now looking for backup. It was not long before the convoy was complete, and the Viva was shadowed westbound through Kennington and onto the A23 towards Brixton. It was clear to all that he was not going to the Pilgrims Pyramid site but Tubal, at the morning's sunrise briefing, instructed the team to stick with it until the death; figuratively, that is.

The man was oblivious as they chopped and changed eyeball as roundabouts and junctions passed by. Unsuspecting motorists were used for cover. The motorbike provided their lifeline when trapped at roadworks or the occasional miscalculated junction. But on he plodded, at each stop his head bobbing along like a nodding dog, his car emitting the *thud thud* bass of an indistinguishable tune. They were clear of Central London and heading out towards Surrey's semi-rural spaces past Hooley. The clogged capillaries of London's lungs opened out into dual-lane arteries feeding the South Coast and orbital motorway network. As they approached the junction with the new M25, the team held back, knowing that whatever way he went, there would be enough available road to catch him before he had the chance to stray anywhere.

'No deviation, no deviation. Committed A23 towards the M23,' Hawk Four reported as they maintained their distance and watched the Viva glide past the M25 junction.

'Perhaps he's going to Brighton for a paddle,' Flick quips, 'or picking up a rent boy.'

Tubal was too absorbed to reply, his eyes locked onto Hawks Two and Three up ahead. The Viva had already scooted off beyond their vision, but as long as he could see other Hawks, they were less conspicuous. They held back as far as they could. If summoned forward, Tubal could ram on the gas to whip up the horsepower to make ground. Stevie was cruising in the offside lane beside them, hovering in anticipation.

'Nearside indicator, moving to lane one of three on approach to services,' Paul broke in from Hawk Four. 'Count down markers, three… two… one… it's a left, left, left into services. All Hawks acknowledge.'

'Roger, Hawk Four, making ground,' Flick chipped in as Tubal hit the gas.

All units headed for the services. Paul updated them as the Viva manoeuvred into a parking spot and their man readied to leave the vehicle. As Tubal glided into the car park, George and Paddy were already out on foot and ambling towards the food hall from different directions. Tubal drove through the main parking area and waited on the petrol station forecourt just before the exit back onto the motorway. Stevie pulled in behind them. As he dismounted, Flick and Tubal eased their way out of the car into the evening sunshine to meet him.

'Looks like we are in for a long day, campers.' Stevie stated the obvious but small talk kept the focus going and the world could be put to rights later in the pub. 'You know, Mac, when I was in the BUR office, I got the impression that your man works independently from the rest. More a ledger jockey than a site man, I'd say.'

'Yeah, I'll be happier when we ID him,' Tubal replied. 'With any luck, he's in the intel system somewhere.'

As they stretched their legs, grabbing a comfort break and snacks from the petrol station, their earpieces rattled with the commentary emitting across the airwaves. Nothing exciting had happened, just black suit having a leak before plodding through the services stuffing a Cornish pasty in his mouth. Stevie was stretched out in the back seat of their car whilst Flick closed her eyes in quiet contemplation. Tubal stifled a yawn, hands hanging on the steering wheel at ten to two poised for the next move.

'Target is at the cash machine,' Sid reported. 'Two Foot is behind him. Time check to follow.'

Flick stretched out to update the surveillance log. If they could get a time stamp on the cash machine use, they might be able to link back the transaction to a bank account.

'Two Foot permission.'

'Go ahead, Two Foot.'

'Cash withdrawn at 4.58pm, Sid,' George updated. 'He threw the receipt away. I've now got it.'

'Roger, Two Foot,' Sid replied. 'Log to be noted as 1658 hours.'

Flick acknowledged, scribed the detail and replaced the log away from prying eyes under her seat. Tubal started the engine prepared for an 'off'. Sid had called a 'stand by'; Stevie slid off the back seat, helmet in hand as the footmen reported their scramble back to the vehicles.

Tubal and Flick were ideally placed for the eyeball as they could blend in behind the target as he exited onto the M23. Tubal carefully manoeuvred as Flick relayed this to Paul in Hawk Four. The Viva was within his view after taking back visual control from Sid. Within minutes the standby was over, and the target was moving again. As he came into sight, the eyeball was theirs and Tubal eased out into the traffic behind him. Stevie hung back in the service station to take up tail-end Charlie once the rest of the team had passed him. There was no hanging back for Tubal. The man accelerated away in a pasty-fuelled desire to get to wherever he was going. They remained two for cover behind him but he was pushing eighty-five as he weaved from lane to lane, seemingly oblivious to their interest. The motorway was coming to an end and the verdant landscape of the South Downs loomed peacefully in the distance. Soon, after they emerged into the countryside, the Viva diverted off across country into the villages of East Sussex. A regular change of eyeball was required with enough distance kept between them to allay suspicion. Finally, they reached a small row of Victorian cottages nestled within a rustic tapestry of windmills, grapevines and fluffy sheep. The Viva parked up and the man emerged into the fading light. Tubal drove past and, anticipating their vulnerability to showing out, all except Hawk Two held back. As Tubal spun back round, he could see George at the top of the hill leading down to the row of houses. He was parked outside the village pub.

'Two Foot has eyeball. Target entering property. I'll get address once he's in.'

It was a waiting game. They had arrived there, wherever there was, but could not relax until they knew what was going on. Was this black suit's home? Was he just visiting? Tubal could check out the Viva's registration number back at the office to see if it matched the address, but the most prudent option was to stay where they were.

As the clock ticked, the evening started to draw in and darkness was descending. Terry had parked Hawk Two facing down the hill with eyes on the Viva. The others could be anywhere. There was only one road through the village, so it was just a question of finding a quiet hidey-hole away from nosy neighbours. It wouldn't be long in a place like this before curtains started twitching; not that anyone would actually guess who they were. Worst case scenario, the police were called, but they wouldn't bother once the vehicles were checked. Different case up North. Tubal remembered a job with the team near Manchester. There were four of them, wrapped up in their cold-busting winter coats, ripe to conceal all sorts of weaponry, sat in a fast motor, engine running for a quick getaway. Stevie poised in the back, crash helmet on, visor down. Fans of *The Sweeney* would think, *gang of blaggers up from the smoke*, ready to take out Securicor with some across-the-pavement villainy rather than, *oh look, there's some stuffy civil servant types on a day's sabbatical from their manor*. Not in Oldham. Out of the blue, a local bobby appeared, tapped on the passenger window, removed his custodian helmet and squatted down beside them. As the tinted electric window whirred down, all eyes burned into their inquisitive visitor who had now unilaterally shone a beacon on their presence. His view inside the car jolted the realisation that he might have disturbed something he ought not to. Following a brief double take, he stood up, stepped back and uttered the only words that he felt would absolve himself from the potentially difficult situation he was now in.

'Hello, lads, you're not from round 'ere, are you?'

The reply from Terry, not an aficionado of *The Sweeney*, was exemplary in its politeness and failed to capitalise on the faux pas. They were burnt now, so he might even have said who they were.

But there in this sleepy unknown village, Tubal had found a quiet lane, sheltered by overhanging branches, to reverse into. To all intents and purposes, two perceived lovers seeking a little private fun time. In reality, two weary soles fatigued by an early morning start and no chance of getting home anytime soon.

'Two Foot to Hawk One.' It was George. 'Mac, can you meet me down by the pub?'

Tubal reached into his rucksack and pulled out an old black beanie hat to cover his head before slipping on a scarf and his spare jacket from the back seat. Best to try and change appearance just in case their man pops out for an evening stroll; not that Tubal thought he would recognise him. People generally do not pick out the faces of strangers in a crowd, maybe here but not in busy London streets. It's more likely that items of clothing are spotted. Hence, Tubal had learnt to pack a range of props when out on jobs. Having already swopped his contact lenses for glasses when they pulled up, Tubal handed Flick the car keys and quietly closed the car door before slipping into the dimly lit road leading down to the pub. It was not far to walk and he could see George lurking in the shadows. As Tubal approached him, George leaned in and whispered, 'He's in Berkeley Cottage. Still not sure where we are on the map.'

They didn't wait long for the answer. As Tubal moved to walk away from George, he glanced at the green-tiled pub frontage. A shallow, red-brick arch led into the public bar and his eyes fixed on the entrance doors. Each bore the image of a cricketer, one batsman and one bowler, both criss-crossed with a thin piping of black lead. An impressive sight forged in intricate stained-glass panels bordered by opaque flowers in red, yellow and cobalt blue. Over the arch, on a white panel adorned in black gothic lettering, Tubal saw the words 'The Cricketers at Stonepound Oldland'.

'There we go, guv'nor, riddle solved,' he informed George, pointing at the signage. 'I'll make my way back to Flick.'

Feeling pleased with himself, Tubal walked back towards the car. As he approached, a man appeared from the lane and walked away from him. They both kept their heads down but Tubal caught a whiff of Brut aftershave as he passed. Tubal turned into the lane and climbed back into the car beside Flick, who looked relieved to see him.

'Where did Henry Cooper come from?'

Flick shook her head in the indeterminable way Tubal had become accustomed to.

'The man, smelt of Brut,' he continued before lapsing into a woeful impression of Our 'Enry. 'You know, "splash it all over".'

'Oh him, I dunno. Just appeared from behind the car.' She remained unimpressed. 'Gave me a bit of a fright to be honest.'

'Well at least I know where we are now. Some hamlet called Stonepound Oldland. The pub looks inviting.'

They settled back into hibernation mode. The morning newspapers had been read cover to cover, the crosswords attempted and tonight's TV plans abandoned. Hours passed, but nothing was happening. Tubal took that as a good sign, as the likelihood was that they had located the BUR man's home address. Flick had her eyes closed again, and although she was probably not asleep, he did not want to disturb her. She looked so harmless and peaceful. Tubal just stared into space, reflecting upon the day's events. The time was dragging now, but they had to see this though to conclusion. Tubal felt sure that if George disagreed, he would have let him know before now.

Thump. Tubal sat back, startled. Our 'Enry had appeared round the corner and stumbled onto their bonnet. As he slid past Tubal's door and disappeared to the rear of the car, he seemed oblivious to his surroundings. Perhaps he was looking for a discrete place to piss. Flick barely stirred other than to mumble some likely profanity. It was 9.45pm and all Tubal could think about was getting home.

Ten minutes passed, and Tubal guessed that some higher being had read his thoughts. The radio crackled into life.

'Hawk Two. Sit rep.' George's voice sent Tubal's adrenaline racing back. 'All lights have gone out and house in darkness. Vehicle still in situ. Suggest we stand down, Hawk One.'

Tubal grabbed the handset resting on Flick's thigh and acknowledged.

'Affirmative, Hawk Two. Stand down all units. Debrief tomorrow morning at ten.'

Each Hawk radioed their response. Tubal passed the handset back to Flick who yawned, tapped his hand and murmured, 'Easy, tiger. You'll have to marry me if you're gonna touch my leg again.'

Tubal praised the blanket of darkness as he sensed his face flush. After opening the front windows to clear the windscreen and get some cool air, he turned the ignition. The engine purred back into life. Just as Tubal slotted the car into gear, a dark figure appeared from behind them and moved to Flick's side. It was the man from earlier, the aftershave now replaced by the stink of stale alcohol and tobacco. Tubal waited to let him pass safely, but the man stopped and leant in towards Flick. All they needed at that point was a drunken admirer.

'Excuse me,' the man slurred, 'are you going to be long?'

'No, why?' Tubal answered.

'Well, you've been parked on our drive for hours and my wife's a bit worried.'

Tubal reached for first gear, revved the engine and brusquely left the man standing. A late curry and a warm bed were waiting. Sadly, he had to face one of those luxuries alone.

Chapter Thirteen

The answers that Tubal needed trickled in over the course of the following week. Mr Black Suit was Tony Martindale, a self-appointed accountant registered on the national intelligence database as a fixer-cum-middleman, providing fabricated accounts for anyone that paid well. His professional body disowned him years ago, not that that worried those that engaged him. The records showed that Martindale had crossed swords with the BIO Bristol office on several occasions. His handiwork was linked to criminal activity, including overseeing the operation of phoenix companies; those that liquidate with substantial debts then rise from the ashes the next day with the same directors, assets and clients. The business carried on as normal, except that any taxes due from the liquidated company were written off. Martindale's grubby fingerprints featured in many pies; he had contempt for the taxman and served his latest prison sentence two years earlier. Since then, he'd been off the radar, but thanks to Group Five's efforts over the last few months, they had placed him operating in London and acting as the link between Sweeney and BUR. Stevie's hunch that he was working independently also rung true as there was no Tony Martindale registered on the Boteler Urban Regeneration Limited payroll.

Checks on the Vauxhall Viva and the Stonepound Oldland address confirmed that it was Martindale, and a mugshot sent over by the Bristol office planted the cherry firmly on the cake. His file also informed Tubal that Martindale had a reputation for courting sex workers, trading bookkeeping services for personal services. This was how he met his wife Eileen, who tolerated his indiscretions in exchange for Martindale allowing her three teenage children, of unknown paternity, and mother to live with them. Marty's background checks revealed that this ménage was still currently residing at Berkeley Cottage with Martindale.

The following Tuesday, George handed Tubal the bank statements for the account receiving regular payments from Gilmore Angell Limited. Grenville Allonby didn't waste much time getting these, so perhaps he was warming to Tubal's case. As suspected, most of the remaining funds filtered their way over to the Republic of Ireland and out of UK jurisdiction. What didn't evaporate there was taken out in irregular cash withdrawals from ATMs, and a monthly debit of £200 transferred to Wilson Scott Lettings in Dunstable. This glared at Tubal from the page. For the first time, he felt close to finding Sweeney's hideaway and recovering any booty held there. Tubal's metamorphosis from chrysalis IO to the emerging butterfly of a respected investigator was on track. Excitement bubbled within him. He knew that it would take a lot to impress the experienced hands. Their stoicism could drown overt recognition of any success by inexperienced investigators.

So, no time to slack. George was pressuring him to get the search and arrest operation set up, and there was a mountain of paperwork to do. First though, Dempsey and Makepeace were on their way to Dunstable. Since joining the team, Tubal had always felt more relaxed in Flick's company than the others'. She installed the confidence in him to push boundaries and challenge his own limitations. If he did overstep the mark, Flick reeled him back, quietly and without drama. They complemented each other's personalities, but Tubal believed that he still had a lot to learn from her.

The Wilson Scott Lettings office were located over a haberdashery shop in the old part of Dunstable near Priory Gardens. The entrance hall led into a bright, airy, open-plan office adorned with available commercial and private lets in the area. They were not expected. The element of surprise enforced the urgency of the visit and prevented leaking tongues. Tubal approached a group of three empty desks at the back of the room. A smiling woman, dressed for business in a tailored aquamarine trouser suit, emerged from a door leading from a sub-office. Her hand extended towards his, probably guessing by now that Flick and Tubal were not in the market for a two up, two down. Tubal felt her soft hand limply grasp his.

'Hello there,' she spoke confidently. 'I am Abbie Scott, one of the partners here. How can I help you?'

'I'm Tubal McArthur and this is my colleague, Felicity Francis from the Inland Revenue. We are looking into some payments that are being made to Wilson Scott Lettings.'

'Rental payments?' Abbie asked.

'Well, that's what we want to find out,' Flick chipped in.

Abbie invited them to sit down at one of the desks, put a floppy disc into the slot and tapped at the computer before her.

'Great things these, aren't they. When I think of the hours spent going through a card index before.'

Tubal nodded in agreement as he dug around in his briefcase for the papers that he needed. Abbie sat back in her chair and momentarily placed both hands flat on the desk. As she spoke, her hands rose back up and met as if in prayer.

'Now, what do you want to know?'

Tubal opened his notebook and scanned down the page.

Before he left the office he'd written an aide-memoire to remember the information that he needed to follow up. Yep, there it was.

'If I give you a bank account number, can you tell me what it relates to?' he asked.

'Well, I'll try. What's the number?'

He read the figures out slowly. Abbie typed them into the keyboard. There was a brief interlude before the computer clicked and whirred a response.

'Oh yes. These payments are rent for a property out in the countryside. Off the A6 near Barton-le-Clay. There are only a few weeks left to run on it as the tenant is moving abroad,' Abbie informed him. 'The tenant is a Mr Sweeney and, from letters we've had, the neighbours will be happy when he's gone.'

Tubal felt like fist-pumping the air. He remained straight-faced and professional.

'Why, what's the matter with the neighbours?' he asked.

Abbie looked pensive and paused a while. As she considered her answer, she gently squeezed her bottom lip before answering.

'Let's just say that we have had a few complaints about his nocturnal activities. The neighbours reckon he's an insomniac. Comes in at all hours of the night, then leaves early morning, waking the neighbours up with the noise of his car engine.'

'Are the neighbours tenants of yours?'

'Well, technically. We are the managing agents for a small development out there. The owners are based abroad in the British Virgin Islands.'

It's amazing how much information people give you once they start talking. Perhaps they felt that chatting about others would keep the taxman from their door. It would be a great lever but wasted on them. Eric made it very clear on day one of training that they only investigate criminal matters. Making a potential witness feel that they were under scrutiny from the taxman was not in their interest. There were other State puppets for that.

'We were asked to accommodate Mr Sweeney until the end of September via an intermediary of the owners,' Abbie continued.

'And do you have the details of the intermediary to hand?'

'I would have to check our files. The owners are quite secretive so I will need to write to them for permission to divulge the details.'

Looked like Tubal's luck had ran out. Abbie was willing to give up Sweeney because he was causing a nuisance to the other tenants. Anything further might risk Wilson Scott Lettings losing their Virgin Islands contract. Tubal felt that he wouldn't push it further. He still needed Sweeney's address from Abbie.

'OK,' he conceded. 'If you could just give me the address for Mr Sweeney.'

Abbie pulled out a compliments slip from the desk drawer, scribbled the address down and passed it to him.

'Number 10 Washing Meadow,' he read out. 'Thank you, you've been a great help, and we won't trouble you any more today.'

Tubal moved towards the exit behind Flick. She was already on her way out. As they exited back onto the street, they looked at each other, nodded acknowledgement and mouthed the word, 'yes' in unison. They were getting closer!

The next stop was Washing Meadow. As they drove over, Tubal started planning in his head. If Sweeney was to be nicked at home, it would have to be in the early hours of the morning. That would certainly upset the neighbours, but there was little that he could do about that. Any plan would depend on the layout of the development and how they accessed Sweeney's plot. Reconnaissance. in daylight, was imperative.

'What are you thinking, Mac?'

'Just hoping that I can get the timings right and that Sweeney's in when we call.'

For this to go to plan, there had to be a coordinated knock to take out Sweeney and Martindale first and hit BUR as soon as the site and head offices opened. The Pilgrims Pyramid site would be raided early to interview the workforce and identify who they believed to be their employer. Tubal realised that he could not be in more than one place at a time. Reluctantly, he would be forced to surrender control for some aspects of the case to others. Privately, he again felt vulnerable to the more experienced IOs getting all the credit.

'Cheer up and don't look so glum.'

Flick must have read his thoughts. Tubal snapped back to himself as he located Washing Meadow surrounded by woodland and positioned off a small feeder road to the A6. Before them was a small group of modern, chalet-type bungalows neatly placed around a cul-de-sac, somewhat out of place in this rural architype of chalk downland. *Must be someone with a bit of influence who built these here*, Tubal thought to himself. Flick drove to the end of the road and manoeuvred them slowly in a three-point turn, giving him time to note the door numbers. There it was, number 10. Nothing distinguishable other than the curtains were closed. There were no vehicles on the drive, and the rest of the road was peaceful and devoid of recognisable life. Everybody must either be out or dead. Perhaps it was the time of day. They parked up for a little while to observe and discuss their next move. If Sweeney was staying here, they needed some idea of his movements. Putting the van in with a time-lapse camera was not viable – it would stand out a mile. The only way would be to track Sweeney into the address either late at night or in the early hours of the morning. If the agent was right about him moving abroad within a few weeks, things had to move fast.

'Looks like I'll have to come back up here overnight,' Tubal subconsciously verbalised his thoughts. 'I can't see any other way to confirm that Sweeney's here.'

'I'll help you get the whole job set up if you like and we can agree a date with George to strike,' Flick replied. 'We can confirm Sweeney lives here in the next few days and go from there.'

Tubal didn't relish the idea of spending a late night on the A6, but the best way to spot Sweeney entering Washing Meadow was to sit up on the junction. At that stage, it would be superfluous following him for a full day and a drain on resources. He might even spot them and decide to move away early when all they required was confirmation of the address for a search warrant.

'Right, let's get back to the factory, Mac. I'll find us somewhere for a late lunch on the way back.'

In all of the excitement, they had not stopped for anything to eat. Tubal checked his watch and reckoned that the working day would be over by the time they arrived back to Hinchley Wood. There was no rush; they might as well use the rest of the day at their leisure.

Chapter Fourteen

The hotel oozed decadent parties, flappers flouncing on the lawn and penguin-suited bon vivant cads clutching cigars and whisky. Or so Tubal imagined as he focused on shards of light tumbling from the crystal chandeliers within. Closer look attested that these once salubrious beacons now shone friendless behind the distemper-painted frames of rot-pitted windows, the lost glory days only offered to him by fogged monochrome photographs hugging the entrance hall walls. This was what the office finances tolerated when they were not entrenched on one of Allonby's fool's errands: coach tour meccas bedding down weary pensioners for the night; coroner on speed dial, a pyramid of cold toast piled on the breakfast table for expediency. As he marched into the reception, Tubal's senses snared a cocktail of lavender soap, mildew and funereal lilies. He dropped his rucksack to the floor as the automaton-like receptionist pushed a pen and registration form at him. It was only 5pm. They had made good time from Surrey, so the whole evening was there for them; not that Tubal was expecting much fun.

'Just the one night is it, sir?' the automaton enquired, already knowing the answer as the room was pre-booked by the office.

'Yes, one night's bed and breakfast.' *I'll not have the toast,* thought Tubal.

Formalities concluded with no dissent on the likelihood of his personal address being Somerset House, London, he collected his room key and waited in the foyer for Flick. She was outside parking the Peugeot 309 GTi out in the grounds. Horses for courses. Notwithstanding its sporty looks, the Peugeot had the advantage of being fairly squat, giving some concealment to the nosey occupants. That would be useful when parked up on the A6 lay-by on the approach to Washing Meadow. They could stay nondescript for hours with passing traffic travelling at such speed they would be invisible unless a courting couple decided to join them in the dark.

Flick shortly followed and tossed the car key over. Plan was, they would meet in the lounge bar in thirty minutes. Tubal shot up to his room while Flick checked herself in. He just had time to freshen up and grab a quick cuppa of the hotel's finest tea dust before heading out. The room was basic but surprisingly fresh with a good-sized bed, TV and trouser press. His jeans could stay creased as far as Tubal's was concerned. He grabbed the mini pack of shortbread biscuits from the tea tray, tossed them in his rucksack and left to go back downstairs. They were about five miles from Sweeney's place, the closest their cheapskate budget could handle. Tubal hoped that Sweeney would get home for an early night so that he could catch up on his beauty sleep.

The lounge was empty as he walked through the open door from the hallway. Tubal sank down into a jaded oxblood leather armchair by the fireplace. Thirty minutes had gone by and no sign of Flick or anyone else for that matter. There was no rush. If Sweeney's neighbours were right, it would be some time before he got home. He might as well get himself a lager and savour the moment until his date appeared. As he eased himself to the bar, the receptionist abandoned her post and ambled over to serve him. No small talk was offered, and Tubal was happy with that. As he collected his lager and took the first gulp, Flick appeared.

'Do you want anything?' he called across.

'No, you're alright, if I drink anything now, I'll need a wee later. It's alright for you men. Just whip it out and go anywhere.'

Tubal felt sure that her comment could have been quieter and waited until she was nearer. Flick had a point, although he was not in the habit of whipping anything out, particularly on a main road in front of a work colleague.

'Fall asleep in the bath, did you.'

'If only, Mac.' Flick lowered her voice. 'No, I've been changing rooms.'

'Why, what's wrong with your room?'

'Well, nothing if you ignore the Aussie in his boxer shorts I found when I opened the door.'

'Really? Mine only has a trouser press.'

'Gave me the spare key for the wrong room.' Flick nodded towards the receptionist. 'That's all I need. I have palpitations thinking about it.'

'Come on then, let's hits the road before you choose your Australian over me.'

Tubal swigged back the rest of his drink and they made their way out to the car. Flick carried out the equipment that they needed. It wouldn't take long to get to Sweeney's place and set up. It would probably be livelier in the A6 lay-by as the evening dragged on than it was back at the hotel.

As they approached Washing Meadow from the A6, Flick leant over the back of her seat and pulled the camera case over into the front. Flipping up the metal catches, she lifted the lid and checked the contents. Inside, Tubal noted that she had packed their standard 35mm SLR camera and the night vision lens. Flick removed this and placed it on the floor in front of her. By now, Tubal was in a position to park at the junction with the cul-de-sac so that they could do a recce of the area. As he pulled up, Flick unbuckled her seat belt and slipped her jacket on.

'I'll have a walk up and see if there's any life at number 10.'

As soon as Flick was out of the car, Tubal drove further up the lane and onto a small industrial estate. The road was a dead end, randomly pitted with potholes like an asphalt bar billiards table. All of the factory units were locked up. There were no vehicles in the car park. If Sweeney was not home yet, they knew that he could only arrive from the direction of the A6. As Tubal turned the car around, Flick appeared back into view at the top of the lane. Slowly, he weaved along the roadway to meet her. The low-profile tyres wouldn't tolerate sinking into these craters, and a puncture was the last thing that they needed.

Tubal stopped just long enough for Flick to jump back into her seat before he accelerated away for the short drive to the A6 junction.

'There's no sign of life at the address,' Flick told him. 'Looks like we've got to wait after all.'

'Great. And there was me looking forward to nightclubbing in Dunstable. At least I've got a packet of Shorties to keep me going.'

'Always the Boy Scout, Mac.' Flick assumed wrong.

Tubal pulled into the lay-by they would call home for a while and reversed up to allow plenty of space ahead of them. This would give them cover should anyone else pull in front. Could be awkward though, Tubal surmised, if they find themselves parked in the rendezvous spot for the doyens of the Dunstable Dogger's nightly cabaret; if that's even a thing. He hoped not to find out.

As light faded to night, the woods coddling them morphed slowly away from the blaze of warm orange, red and yellow autumnal tones swaying in the breeze. The wind was more restless now, shuffling the trees; rain drops spat sparingly on the windscreen. As hurtling headlight beams pierced the canopy, dark ghosts appeared to dance in the clouds above them. Time was moving very slowly, but there was no sign of the Landcruiser. Nobody else had pulled in to join them; must be at home washing their thongs.

'Well, this is fun,' Tubal broke the silence. 'At least we've got the car. Wouldn't fancy being a CROPs man out in this.'

Covert Rural Observation Post, or CROP, surveillance was another of Stevie's specialities. Secreting himself down a hole enveloped in a ghillie suit to watch a target in isolated rural locations. Nerves of steel essential and no qualms about shitting in the woods like Yogi Bear and packaging it up nicely to take home. No, not for Tubal. Sitting in a cold, dark lay-by soundtracked by the unceasing whoosh of spray-emitting lorries already impinged upon his comfort zone. It was only made bearable by partnering the surreptitiously demure wicked Maid of Kent as opposed to the anal Terry Two Sheds. Or should that be wicked Kentish Maid? Tubal made a mental note to ask Flick which side of the Medway her bread's buttered. Perhaps now was a good time. Too late.

'Nearside indicator approaching.'

Tubal could just make out the pulsating amber light decelerating towards them. Flick rose slightly, pushing her right foot down to the floor to balance herself as she swung around onto her knees to face the direction of approaching traffic. Tubal watched in his wing mirror as the vehicle moved closer.

'Bingo. It's him,' Flick exclaimed as she moulded back into her seat and buckled up.

'Golf Alpha Lima Eight Three Whisky,' Tubal spurted out to nobody as the Landcruiser passed and exited left towards Washing Meadow. 'Did you see the driver?'

'Just about. It looked like Sweeney, but I can't be definite.'

'There was no passenger visible as he passed, but I couldn't make out the driver.'

Tubal started the engine and began the countdown, anticipating time to allow Sweeney to park up and settle in. It had just gone 10pm so better than expected. He gave it a few more minutes. Wait. Wait. OK, better go and have a look. He pulled out onto the A6 and readied himself for a slow drive back along the pockmarked roadway to Sweeney's abode. The excitement of putting Sweeney to bed and still having time for a curry and a few pints motivated them forward. As Tubal moved into Washing Meadow, the clues indicated that the incumbent denizens have resurrected. The landscape was illuminated by two solitary lamp posts squeezing out light into the street. A luminous hue emanated from behind the assorted flowery curtains. Sleeping cars hugged the driveways. The neighbourhood was restored. Number 10 was no exception, and the grey, sod-splattered Landcruiser sat waiting for its master. Tubal drove past and manoeuvred back round at the road's end.

'Pull over back at the junction, Mac. I think you can get round the back of the houses.'

'You think I can get round the back. I, me.'

'Well, you wouldn't want *me* to go on my own, would you?'

'Well, yeah!' He was less than convincing. 'I'm in charge of driving.'

Flick rolled her eyes, grinned and grabbed the camera from the floor as Tubal pulled the car into the kerb. She was right – they should seal the deal by scouting around the back to try and get a glimpse of Sweeney. The back of the bungalows were not overlooked if you discounted sleepless avian observers and curious nocturnal intruders. If they could get round there and see into the garden, they might just about get the camera shot they needed.

'And I'm in charge of kicking your arse if you don't come with me.' A mock scowl emerged briefly before evaporating from Flick's face. 'I'll drive back if you like.'

'Come on then. What happened to women's lib?'

They emerged into the dark, and as Tubal locked the car, Flick skirted across the road with the camera and disappeared into a break in the hedgerow. Tubal slowly walked after her, half expecting that she would pounce on him from behind. No time for games. He shone the thin ray of his ersatz Boy Scout torch at knee height. There she was, ten paces forward following a line of rough featheredge fence panels by touch, each section securing the rear of the bungalows from predators and interfering IOs. At random points, neat, rectangular doorways were cut out from the soil-level gravel board for transient hedgehogs to penetrate the outer perimeter. A consideration not supported by all. And yet further breeches do appear in the fence, not borne from man but panels warped by nature's response to inclement weather. Gaps contorted enough for Flick to see through without splintering an eye and identify the buildings along to number 10.

'What's that smell?' she whispered from the dark.

Tubal didn't have an answer. All he knew was that a hybrid odour of ammonia, musk and purification had invaded his nostrils. He scanned the ground with his torch. The narrow beam struck a decaying badger draped astride a fallen tree trunk; possible road half-kill vying to get home to its kinfolk without success. Now the remains of a carcass that had since imploded, spilling brock juice and maggots into the leaf mould. Tubal thought better of sharing his discovery.

'I thought it was your perfume,' he whispered back.

'Cheeky bastard. Come on, let's get away from that stink.'

As Flick led on, they quickly found the spot. Number 10's fence was pristine. No warps, slots or missing slats. To see into the property, one of them would need to climb a tree or give Flick a bunk-up. They were Tubal's options. Flick found a third and was standing on the beer crate seat of a strategically positioned rope swing that dangled from one arm of an oak tree.

'Pass me the camera, Mac. There's somebody in the kitchen. The lights are on.'

Tubal handed the night vision kit up to her. She hooked her arms round the ropes while he held the seat still. Her fingers slowly rotated the lens as her eye scanned the viewfinder.

'It's him.'

She depressed the shutter button, emitting a series of sharp clicks, before jumping down from her perch.

'Let's get back to the car.'

They moved out of the woods stealthily but quickly, the journey devoid of fence hugging and breath holding as they passed the proliferating post-mortem life within Tubal's badger. As they reached the car, Flick's offer to drive was forgotten as they jumped in for a quick getaway. Tubal headed back towards the hotel buzzing. Their job was done. Too late for a curry though.

The bar was still open as they walked in. It was a bit livelier than before with four wrinklies huddled around their dominoes tiles. They ignored these scruffy tykes with dried clay streaking their jeans and congealed mulch hibernating in the tread of their trainers. The barman was more receptive until Tubal asked for the menu.

'Restaurant closed at nine, sir. No, we don't serve bar meals.'

The emergency Shorties had long gone, so it was pork

scratchings and lager for Tubal. Flick had her Guinness, which she convinced herself had some sustenance to it. Tonight, the extent of their healthy living lay bare before them.

'You know, I'll be surprised if the photos I took come out.' Flick threw a spanner. 'Night vision lens might not tolerate the light from the bungalow.'

'But it was him.'

'Definitely.'

'So, you are witness to him being there. We don't really need the photos.'

'So, you are learning, Mac.'

Talk of the day's events didn't last long. The drinks flowed freely as befits a day where a plan had come together. Flick's Aussie didn't make an appearance, but the episode fuelled the banter for a while and saved any embarrassment for him. Here they were. Another bar. Another place. Each mutually giggling over nothing; workmates confined by unwritten protocols yet intimately seated. Teasing and jousting. Flick's hand fleetingly touching Tubal's wrist to enforce her point. An ocular pooling of olive and blue as eyes met words.

'Still got your cat?' Tubal filled a void as tiredness and alcohol conspired against them.

'Yes, she's at home with Ross.'

He wouldn't probe deeper as that was enough for now. Secretly, Tubal wondered if the cat is at Ross's place or Ross is at Flick's place. Was their break restored or terminal? No matter.

'I like your perfume.' He just caught the faint scent mixed with perspiration from the day's labours.

'That's not what you said earlier.'

'I've just noticed. What is it?'

'It's called Opium by Yves Saint Laurent.' Flick tilted her head to the left and swung her neck closer to Tubal for him to closely sample the aroma. 'I always wear it.'

Tubal knew that she always wore perfume but felt unable to ask what it was before. Perhaps this was a good time to put the day to rest.

'I've got to get some sleep,' he groaned. 'A man cannot live on biscuits and pork scratchings alone. Roll on breakfast.'

The bar was now empty. They left together and gingerly climbed the stairs to their rooms. There was no sign of life. As they moved, their footsteps aroused the creaking floorboards skulking beneath the sticky Axminster broadloom. The shadowy corridor blinked as night lights awakened to announce their presence. Before them, an assault course of discarded food trays from antisocial patrons challenged the dexterity of two beery souls. Tubal's room came first. As he turned the key, Flick outstretched her hand and gently touched his cheek. Their eyes met, a smile but no words as she walked away. Tubal closed the door behind him and turned on the TV as he undressed for bed.

It was the early hours of the morning. The national anthem had played out and there was zilch on the TV. As Tubal snuggled into bed, the evening recounted like a waking dream. Hunger or pheromone overdrive must have been playing tricks on him. Questions filled his head. Was he missing something with Felicity Francis? *Am I that bad at reading signs?* Tubal laid his head on the pillow and waited for sleep to consume him.

Tap, tap, tap. Tubal heard somebody at his door. He sat up startled. *It's too late, or too early, for maid service*, he thought. Perhaps it's another double-booked room. He slipped on his jeans and quietly called out, 'Yes? Who is it?'

'Mac, it's me. Open the door,' Flick whispered.

Tubal slid the door lock sideways and paused. Was this still a dream? Butterflies flitted within him as he pulled the door handle down. She was there, dressed as she had left him.

'I know it's late, but I know how much you need this.'

Tubal clasped his hands over his face and rubbed the corners of his eyes. Flick brought one hand from behind her back and pressed it towards him.

'Quick, take these.'

'What?'

'I've been down to the kitchen and grabbed some chicken legs out of the fridge. Throw the bones out the window to get rid of the evidence. Goodnight.'

And with that, she was off.

Chapter Fifteen

'Morning, Mac. How are you doing?'

Berwyn from Special Branch had rung early. Tubal had only managed a snatched two-hour sleep overnight. Paddy had them all out on one of his cases to find the address of a dealer up in Kilburn. Unluckily for the team, his man decided to trip the light fantastic at the Galtymore dance hall in Cricklewood until the early hours. Tubal would rather have been cocooned at home in bed than tailing a battered Mercedes at twenty miles per hour around Little Ireland's side streets. Thankfully, such events were rare and he felt glad that he'd sacrificed a late start as he would have missed Berwyn's call. There was something his new Welsh friend could tell him after all. Boteler Urban Regeneration Limited was a company registered in the UK, but the majority shareholder was a Cayman Island gatekeeper guarding a web of entities that might, he said, lead to the eventual owner. Tubal shouldn't hold his breath though. All Berwyn could tell him, he said, was that there were some indications that the owner was based in the Middle East. Somebody with power, influence and limitless supplies of money that choose to conceal their investment. If Berwyn did know who, then it was likely to be a State secret and he was not saying. Did Tubal feel the need to know? He thought not. If he couldn't legally pursue miscreants over the Irish Sea, the Arabian Desert was certainly a no-go area for him. It was beyond his pay grade anyway, so one for Allonby. Those within reach of Tubal in London are the ones that would have to explain their dealings with Sweeney and Martindale. And that day would be soon. Tubal's report had been okayed by George, who had allocated teams ready for what Tubal hoped would be his showstopper event or, if it went tits up, his swansong. Still, there were no thoughts of failure in Tubal's head. The whole office would be drafted in, but Group Five IOs would lead the charge at each location. Tubal would head up the raid on Sweeney; not that the photos snapped by Flick would help much. The night vision lens had, as she thought, sucked up the light, exposing a corpulent Space Invader glowing green as he sidled across the kitchen. Useless for an identity parade but uncannily managing to capture Sweeney's finer distinguishing points.

DI Henry Hammacott and his team at Wood Street Police Station had been lined up to provide the muscle on the big day. Ever since the 'Neville Brown' case, a continuing relationship had been maintained with the City of London Police. Earlier in the year, they had worked alongside Group Five after a consignment of high-value tax repayment cheques were purloined from the Royal Mail. These had been destined for large charities but, by the time the forgers had sucked up the payee details with mounting putty, the name 'Mr Phillips', or other such innocuous British-sounding monikers, replaced them. Each subsequently falsely addressed to one of a number of diverse council flats spread about London. For months these altered cheques turned up, each triggering a race against the clock to catch the villains collecting their stolen booty: IOs tipped off and ensconced behind bank counters in wait and Henry's lot blue lighting across London to collect the bodies. All based on the assertion that, as the money was drawn from the

Bank of England, the City of London Police had jurisdiction. A premise open to interpretation and manipulation, but it made life simple. Henry's Fraud Squad trusted that if BIO sought their help, there were enough grounds for a good collar. It was also better than cold-calling a local nick and elucidating the suspected offences to a puzzled detective with no idea who they were or what they wanted. No, not for them. Visits to Wood Street were met with mutual respect. No waiting at the front desk with lost Americans. The desk officer would buzz them through into the bowels of the building on sight, leaving the IOs to weave their own way to the Fraud Squad office. Case meetings were sealed with a few pints and a spot of lunch at The Globe on Moorgate before they literally set off on their merry way. Their drinking buddies were predominantly grafted from military stock, no-nonsense, old-style City coppers dwarfing Tubal's modest five-feet-eight-inch frame by at least six inches. All, that was, except Henry's diminutive sergeant DS Louden Stevens, a northern hobbit transferred in from Wigan. Standing bolt upright, he could nestle the tight curls of his permed and highlighted blond locks just below Tubal's chin if he came too close. Always smart in his grey, wide-lapelled, double-breasted suit and kipper tie, DS Stevens was normally puffing away like a modern Sherlock Holmes on his briar pipe, the terracotta-hued bowl topped with a shiny sterling silver band reflecting the ginger hairs of his moustache. Always one for lively banter, he was quite averse to the 'Northerner' tag, pointing out that Scotland was 'up North' and that was a one hundred-mile journey from Wigan. It would be DS Stevens that accompanied Tubal to arrest Sweeney.

The job was all set for the following Friday, the expected payday at the Pilgrims Pyramid site. Tubal's Operational Order detailed the logistics for the day and would be delivered in the Wood Street Police Station briefing room at midday on the

Thursday before. Each team would rendezvous near their target address at 4.30am ready for a 5am knock. If Sweeney started to move before then, his end of the operation would kick off early. Tubal, a small search team and the even smaller DS Stevens would stay over in Dunstable the night before, ready to serve Sweeney his morning porridge. At 9am, the site raid team would hit the Pilgrims Pyramid development to coincide with the execution of a search warrant at BUR's site and head offices. Team leaders had been agreed by George as follows:

Tubal McArthur: address of Joseph Patrick Sweeney, Barton-le-Clay

Felicity Francis: address of Tony Martindale, Stonepound Oldland

Padraig Smith: Pilgrims Pyramid site, Rotherhithe

Zahid Khan: Boteler Urban Regeneration Limited head office, Westminster

Stevie Nixon: Boteler Urban Regeneration Limited site office, Rotherhithe

George Craig: Control Room, Wood Street Police Station

The teams would consist of IOs from other groups backed up by at least one of DI Hammacott's men. All prisoners would be taken back to Wood Street for interview, where Paul Ramell and Terry Burton would assist Tubal and Flick respectively with Sweeney and Martindale. The search seizures, and Tubal *was* banking on locating Sweeney's stash of illicit documents, would be taken to Wood Street before being conveyed back to Hinchley Wood for sifting. The only omission to the plan was Grenville Allonby and his parting shot, 'I don't want you to approach the BUR directors without speaking to me first.'

George deliberately kept Allonby in the dark about the extent of the operation but felt obliged to inform him about the site raid at Pilgrims Pyramid. His logic being that the press might contact Somerset House for information. Technically, no directors of BUR were signposted for interview, let alone arrest, so the small matter of searching BUR's offices could be kept from Allonby's radar until, and if, he needed to know.

Tubal felt greatly relieved that the whole package had been coordinated together. The neural butterflies lay dormant within him, confident of success. On the Wednesday night they awoke, flittering around his stomach until Thursday midday. Then, as he walked onto the rostrum to give his briefing to the assembled officers, a calm descended upon him as he spoke. All nervousness subsided. He had reached the point of no return. Now was the time to relax, confident that no more could be done. Interview questions had been prepped, teams briefed and Tubal had a night away with some good mates. All he had to do beforehand was not drink too much and keep a clear head for Friday morning. And this time, there was a good reason to fill up on a hearty meal with their ale. Like spirits in the night, they'll slink away from the hotel into the dark way before breakfast was served. The morning driven by expectation that a '999 Special' breakfast had their name on it at Wood Street when they arrived back with one obese and disgruntled dealer and his stash.

Chapter Sixteen

The convoy left their muster point on the A6 and headed into the isolated cul-de-sac. Washing Meadow was bathed in a fine grey mist that danced around the street lamps' sodium-yellow glow. Three cars slowly moved into position, backed up by a van containing two uniformed officers sent up from the City of London early that morning. It was almost 5am, and there were no signs of life at number 10. The Landcruiser sat idle outside. Sweeney should be home; fingers crossed. As the vehicles parked up, Tubal spotted the twitch of a curtain from one of the neighbours before they skulked back into the shadows. Stealthily, Tubal and DS Stevens left their cars and glided towards Sweeney's front door. Another plain-clothes officer gingerly lifted the bolt back from the gate leading into Sweeney's back garden. Without instruction, he moved to cover the back exit. Tubal felt sure that Sweeney lacked both the speed and agility to escape. He kept the thought to himself as he could be wrong. A desperate man could find the inner strength to defy expectation. He imagined Sweeney crashing through the feather-edged fencing and escaping into the woods. They would soon find him, but the thought of transporting Sweeney back to London with his pyjamas caked in an entomological soup of putrefied badger and fox shit was not a pleasant one.

No, best to cover the back exit. DS Stevens signalled to the uniformed officers to stand by. One pulled a sledgehammer from under the van's passenger seat and moved towards the address. As DS Stevens and Tubal reached the front porch, the hammer-wielding officer held back to await a signal.

DS Louden Stevens stretched himself up to clasp a lion-head brass knocker. He banged it three times heavily against the black gloss painted surface of the hardwood door. The noise reverberated against the eerie silence. They waited for a response. Nothing stirred from within: everything stirred from without. Washing Meadow's inhabitants overtly peered out at the developing floor show. Lights flicked on and bodies appeared in shadow behind net-curtained glass. No need for furtiveness now.

'Mr Sweeney. It's the police. Please come to the front door,' DS Stevens bellowed through the letter box and into the dark.

Tubal moved along to a front window. Through a gap in the curtains, he spotted a shape moving around, making no effort to comply with DS Stevens' demand. Then the white phosphorous glow of a struck match head flashed momentarily. He saw a flame abruptly consume the aspen stick and then snuff out as it dropped to the floor.

'Somebody's trying to light a fire,' Tubal shouted.

DS Stevens stepped back as the sledgehammer swung and smashed against the door lock. Wood splinters flew back, but the door resisted until strikes two and three popped the hinges and the door submitted inwards. Strident footsteps echoed against the wood as the team traipsed into the building to search for the occupants. DS Stevens swiftly entered the dark front room as Tubal flicked a light switch. Before them lay a bulbous shape concealed by a duvet lying on a king-size mattress filling half the room. An empty bottle of Jameson's and discarded Guinness cans were strewn around in front of the flickering

TV. An ashtray overflowed with cigarette butts. On a small pine table rested a molten cheese-and-tomato-stained food plate, greasy pizza boxes and an open box of sleeping tablets. It must be the cleaner's month off. In one corner, amplified clicks and pops emanated from a discarded stylus, scratching round and round on a spent record on the stereo system. As they approached the shape, a call came that the rest of the house was clear. There were no other occupants.

'You can wake up now, Mr Sweeney.'

DS Stevens pulled back the duvet to find their man huddled in the foetal position, his head clasped between his hands. Sweeney's glasses perched precariously on his nose at an angle as he looked up to face his unwanted guests. Nestling between his thighs were the remnants of a burnt match resting on the scorched outer cover of a small pile of 715 voucher books.

'I've got to get to the toilet; I've a shocking hangover.'

Sweeney pushed himself up onto his knees and forced himself upright as the duvet fell to the floor. He swiftly grabbed a corner and pulled it towards him to cover his nakedness. DS Stevens extended a hand to steady Sweeney as he stumbled slightly towards the pint-sized detective.

'In a minute. Just listen to what I have to say.' DS Stevens stretched himself to his full height. 'Joseph Patrick Sweeney, I am arresting you on suspicion of conspiracy to defraud and handling stolen property.'

Sweeney was cautioned and informed of his rights. When asked if he understood, he managed to spit out the words, 'yes, sir', before lunging forward and vomiting in a bucket. As Tubal looked away, his eyes locked on to a group of cardboard boxes of differing size. He pulled back the lid of one to reveal a printer's note resting against a pile of newly produced Gilmore Angell Limited invoices. To the soundtrack of Sweeney retching, the search team moved in to record and bag up the evidence. From what Tubal had seen so far, things were definitely going to plan. The voucher books tucked up with Sweeney in the bed included those for Thomas Cole and Robbie Quinn. Six books were found altogether, with a couple of original 714 cards issued to names that Tubal did not recognise. Whatever their origin, they had no legal reason to be with Sweeney. They were seized for further investigation.

Sweeney raised himself back up, his face ashen with beads of sweat peppering the lines of his forehead. *Not much of an insomniac*, thought Tubal, *but excess booze and sleeping pills are a risky remedy for someone with Sweeney's lifestyle.*

'Can I get dressed, Mr Stevens, sir?' he asked. 'I overdid it a bit last night.'

'I really wish you would, Joseph, or is it Patrick?' Louden responded.

'My friends call me Patrick.'

'OK, Patrick, one of the officers will need to come with you.'

'No need, sir, I've all I need in here. I can't get up stairs, bad legs.'

As the duvet fell back to the floor, the naked Irishman prised open a battered cardboard box and pulled out a pack of new multicoloured Y-fronts. Selecting a fetching pale-blue pair, Sweeney ripped open the polythene wrapping and extracted his underpants. He placed his left, then right, foot into the openings and pulled them up towards his waist. They wouldn't budge past his thighs. Not to be defeated, he lifted a pair of scissors from the floor and cut through the waistband to give him the inches required to haul them over his valuables. The rest of his clothes were where he had left them. He dressed quickly, leaving a pair of white, urine-stained, waistband-slit pants on the living room floor. These he picked up and threw into the bucket holding his stomach contents.

'Get through a lot of pants, do you, Patrick?' Tubal felt obliged to ask.

'No, no, not many. It's just once I've worn them, they're not worth keeping.'

You could buy a bigger size and wash them occasionally, Tubal thought to himself. Once he was dressed, DS Stevens notified Sweeney that he was to be taken down to London by police van whilst a search of his premises and vehicle was concluded. He made no response to this and quietly exited with the uniformed officers after handing DS Stevens his keys; not that the front door had any useful purpose anymore.

The next few hours were spent methodically covering every inch of 10 Washing Meadow in the hope of finding financial information or any further tax exemption documentation. In a small cupboard, a grubby, oil-stained rucksack was found tucked away: empty except for a one-way open London Gatwick to Waterford airline ticket. The Landcruiser, loft, and even inside the pristine drum of the washing machine, were meticulously searched, but the original 714C certificate for Gilmore Angell Limited was nowhere to be found. It could be anywhere. A thin credit card-like piece of plastic could easily be secreted away in any available nook or cranny. Conversely, if something did lie hidden away, the first rule of concealment states that it should easily be accessible when needed. Having witnessed the ne'er-to-be-forgotten sight of Joseph Sweeney's undulating arse crack as he spewed his guts, Tubal knew it wasn't kept up there. Sometimes, though, you just have to stand still and scan the scene presented to you. Tubal's surveying experience taught him that houses on the inside shouldn't be significantly smaller than the outside. If they are, there could be a hidden room or void. No evidence of that here. They needed to think outside the box. Tubal walked around the house checking skirting boards, window ledges and wardrobe tops. He lifted carpet edges to look for loose floorboards. Nothing. Back in the kitchen, Tubal pulled out the detergent drawer from the washing machine. Clean. He opened the cooker door. Nothing but a pan filled with solidified fat. The only place left was the dustbin cupboard outside the front door. Tubal wondered if anybody had searched there at all. The question drew blank expressions and shoulder shrugs when mentioned. He moved outside, pulled the black plastic dustbin out onto the grass and lifted the lid. Only takeaway containers, drink cans and ripped underpants.

'Right, we're done here, Mac. The landlord's sending someone to fix the door, and the clock's ticking on Sweeney at the nick.'

Louden began loading the car with the evidence. The local police had sent a uniform over to secure the house, ready for when they returned back to the City. By now, Tubal reluctantly gave up on finding the 714C and headed back towards his car.

'You know what, Mac,' Fraser, one of the IOs partnering him on the search, lingered by the dustbin shed as he spoke, 'Sweeney can't ever do any cooking for himself.'

Tubal paused and swiftly moved himself back towards the house.

'Fraser, you're a genius.'

'Why, what did I say?'

'Think about it. Sweeney doesn't do any washing, so the washing machine is spotless. If he doesn't do any cooking, why is there a dirty roasting pan in the oven?'

Tubal beckoned Louden Stevens towards him and led him towards the kitchen. Opening the oven door, he pulled out the fat-filled pan before moving it over to the kitchen sink. Tubal turned the pan upside down, spilling the congealed mess out onto the draining board. Through the whiteness of the lard, a dark shape revealed itself. Using a spoon, Tubal dug down and extracted an object wrapped in silver foil. As he carefully peeled back the foil, the 714C certificate for Gilmore Angell Limited emerged. Bingo! After photographing and recording the find, they finally got on their way back to London for breakfast. Sweeney could sweat a bit longer, and he needed to sober up anyway. It would also give Tubal time to catch up on the rest of the operation with George. They followed DS Stevens at speed down the M1 and back through the arch into the Wood Street Police Station car park.

George was on the telephone as Tubal arrived in the Control Room, a grand name for an unused classroom allocated to BIO for the day. On a whiteboard propped up against the wall, Tubal noted that both Sweeney and Martindale were now in the cells.

'How's it going, Mac, still missing us?' It was Harry, the SIO from Group Two. 'I'm giving George a hand. It's going to get a bit manic once the site raid witness statements and BUR paperwork comes in.'

'That's great. Thanks, Harry. Do you know the latest?'

'Yeah, it seems like all hell broke loose at Martindale's. The whole family were screaming abuse, and Martindale and his missus were arrested. She's been taken to a local nick in Sussex for obstruction. The grandmother also got herself nicked but was de-arrested so she could take care of the kids.'

'Sounds like some party,' was all Tubal could think to say. 'Is Flick OK?'

'Of course she is; I'm unbreakable,' Flick muttered from behind him.

Tubal hadn't seen Flick arrive, but her presence pleased him. The two main players were in custody, and they could hold the keys to the BUR workforce set-up at Pilgrims Pyramid.

'Find much at Martindale's?' he asked.

'Very little: a few diaries, address books, bank statements.

It all needs going through. He says that he's just a bookkeeper with an office next to Boteler Urban Regeneration Limited in Rotherhithe. Doesn't know what this is all about.'

Tubal didn't think that Martindale would roll over and comply. Not with his track record. The interviews would be important, but experience told him that the case would rely heavily on the documentary and surveillance evidence to get it into court. Always work on the principle that your suspect was not going to talk. *Sweeney must be bang to rights though,* Tubal thought, *with the statements from the booksellers and the documents found in his possession.* He would work with Paul to have a crack at him later in the day, but first, Tubal's hunger pangs were crying out. Must have been late breakfast time.

Chapter Seventeen

Tubal finished his brunch, sighed and sank back into the chair, gastronomically fulfilled but growing increasingly weary. It had been a long day, and there was no end in sight. Paddy had arrived back from Rotherhithe and had perched himself opposite Tubal on the long trestle table. On his way in, he had popped into Control and given George details of the Pilgrims Pyramid site raid for the operational log. It was Tubal's turn now, and he jotted down a few notes ready for the Sweeney interview as Paddy updated him. Paddy reported that the Pilgrims Pyramid site agent fully cooperated and made no bones about calling the workers back into the canteen to speak to Paddy's team. Those that refused were identified and tracked down by the IOs. Inevitably, a few shy ones scarpered in the process. This was to be expected. Some people have their reasons for concealing their identity and not engaging with what they class as the establishment. They would also be unreliable witnesses and of little value to Tubal's case. Overall, thirty witness statements were taken, all telling a familiar tale. They were picked up from Cricklewood Broadway or made their own way to site early each morning before reporting to the offices. On a Friday, the foreman paid them cash in an envelope. Their name and the amount was scribbled on the outside but no tax deductions were shown. Each man testified that they did not know their boss's name but assumed they worked for the main contractor, BUR. The names Gilmore Angell Limited, Robbie Quinn and Thomas Cole meant nothing to them. All standard fare. That was, Paddy related, until two of the labourers decided to throw punches at each other for some unexplained reason. It was over in a thrice as two uniformed coppers restrained one of them, inadvertently giving the other open access to throw a right hook full in his face. Both were then carted off to cool down. Turned out that one of them was disrespectful to an old lady that had walked in front of his digger at the site entrance. Poetic justice. Now another story for the Tea Club and Tubal couldn't help spotting the glee on Paddy's face as he recounted the memory. The time had come to get down to the business at hand.

As Tubal joined George in Control, news was coming in from Stevie at BUR's Rotherhithe office. The contents of Martindale's office had been seized and included a cardboard box full of wage packets ready to go to site. All of these were as described by the men with no evidence of tax deductions. It would take a bit of time to sift through all of the records held, so Stevie would update them later in the day. The only news from BUR's head office in Westminster was that Sid had got into the building, but their office door was locked. He was waiting for someone to open up so that the search warrant could be executed.

Down in the cells, Sweeney waited to see the police surgeon to get his health checked before Tubal would have the chance to speak to him. The custody sergeant, a formidable Scot eking out his days before retiring back to the shores of Loch Fyne, was not happy with the pallor of Sweeney's skin and the radiating fetid smell and protestations about pains in his foot. After what he had drank the previous night, it was hardly surprising. *Probably gout*, Tubal reasoned to himself.

'I'm not going to mess about with him,' Tubal spoke quietly to Paul. 'I'll just run through what we found at his place and put all of the 715 vouchers that have been submitted from the stolen books to him.'

'Yeah, I'll keep his mother out of it. Don't want another wrestling match,' Paul joked.

'I think you're safe with this one. Sweeney probably sold his mother years ago,' Tubal fathomed.

Given the condition of Sweeney, in Tubal's estimation, if his mother was still alive, she'd likely give Methuselah a run for his money.

'I don't think that he's as old as you think,' Paul pre-empted. 'The custody log has him down as fifty-six. He's just, shall we say, well worn.'

'Or worn out, more likely.'

Just then, DS Louden Stevens stuck his head around the door.

'Police Surgeon wants Sweeney taken to hospital. He's got gangrene in one of his toes,' Louden updated Tubal. 'She's given him a shot of antibiotics, but it needs a proper assessment.'

Great, thought Tubal. What an anticlimax. He knew that nothing else could be done until Sweeney was deemed fit for interview. How long that would be rested in the hands of the doctors. All Tubal could do was wait back down in the canteen, top up his caffeine level and grab a couple of those pain aux raisins that had been eying him up.

Down in the cells, Flick and Terry were in full flight interviewing Martindale about his meetings with Sweeney and connection to BUR. Interviewing was perhaps a misnomer as he repeated the one monotone retort each time Flick spoke. Not to be outdone, she pushed onwards. Every so often,

Martindale fidgeted in his seat or stared randomly around the room, only pausing to stare contemptuously into Flick's eyes at every question.

'I've got some nice holiday snaps of Mr Sweeney in Southwark Park over a number of weeks, always on a Thursday.' Flick fished out a composite of random surveillance photographs from her briefcase. 'Tell me who the man in the black suit with the brown briefcase is.'

'No comment.'

'Looks like you to me.'

'No comment.'

'Is that you?'

'No comment.'

'What is Sweeney taking out of his rucksack and passing to you?'

'No comment.'

Flick placed three close-up photographs of Sweeney passing bundles of cash to Martindale onto the table between them.

'Each week, Pat Sweeney withdraws over £37,000 in cash from the Midland Bank in Harlesden and hands it over to you. Tell me about that.'

'No comment.'

'Is that what happens, Tony?'

'No comment.'

'Officers went to your office in Rotherhithe this morning and seized wage packets for the Pilgrims Pyramid site ready to be paid out. What is the origin of that money?'

'No comment.'

'Who makes up the wage packets?'

Martindale stayed silent.

'They were in your locked office.'

'No comment.'

'Why are no tax deductions shown?'

'No comment.'

'Tell me about the 714C company, Gilmore Angell Limited.'

'No comment.'

'Financial records from that company show that Boteler Urban Regeneration Limited, or BUR, pay a cheque to Gilmore Angell Limited each week for between £40,000 and £41,000. What is BUR paying for?'

'No comment.'

'And every week Pat Sweeney collects £37,500 in cash and hands it over to you. Is that fair to say?'

'No comment.'

'That is the amount paid by BUR to Gilmore Angell less 10%. Tell me how this money laundering scheme works.'

'No comment.'

'Are you laundering money to cover a cash-in-hand workforce on behalf of BUR?'

'No comment.'

'Tell me about payments made by BUR under cover of the exemption documents of Robert Quinn and Thomas Cole.'

'No comment.'

'Come on, Tony, you know the score. You wouldn't be sitting here if we hadn't done our homework. Man with your form must have an opinion on this.' Flick used her finest vicarious tone with just a little smile.

'No comment.'

It hadn't worked, but hey, a man like Martindale might only turn when jammed in a tight corner to save himself. To keep the pressure up, Flick laboriously presented each of the Gilmore Angell Limited invoices to him, each viewing resulting in either silence or the comment 'no comment'. Time to wind things up for now, she decided.

'You told us back at the house that you were just a

bookkeeper and didn't know what this was all about. Yet, my colleagues found the wage packets in your office and no evidence of any tax deductions. What's the truth, Tony?' Terry added his rather late contribution to the proceedings.

'No comment.'

There was no point carrying on. Terry could go back in his box. Flick had put all the questions she wanted for now. Martindale was handed back to the custody sergeant and ensconced back in his bijou yet secure accommodation. Flick would have another crack at him if further evidence was turned up by the IOs still out on the job.

Whilst Martindale wasted his chance to come clean, an ambulance had pulled up to take Pat Sweeney to hospital. Tubal joined them in the custody suite as DS Stevens tasked an officer to watch over Sweeney whilst the medics assessed him over at St Bartholomew's. As soon as they had left, Tubal climbed the stairs back to the Control Room. There he faced a sombre-faced George pacing the floor like a zoochotic wolf.

'I don't fucking believe this, Mac.'

'What's up, boss?'

'I'll tell you what's up. Sid rang from the Westminster head office. They've had to bust the lock to get in.' George tossed his spent cigarette in the bin and grabbed another from behind his ear. 'Place was deserted, safe left open and papers scattered all over the floor. Security said that the managers came in overnight and left with dustbin bags of stuff.'

'What stuff?'

'How the fuck would I know? All I do know is that the directors are nowhere to be found. Total shitstorm.'

Tubal held his tongue. As far as he was concerned, a major dealer had been taken out and stolen documents were now back in the Revenue's possession. Surely all was not lost at BUR. If Tubal could prove that the illicit 715 vouchers and the 714C certificate of Gilmore Angell Limited had covered the wages of BUR's cash-in-hand labour force, the company could still be held liable for the Exchequer's six-figure tax loss. Tubal was well aware that finding culpable evidence against individual company directors was rare. That could be the problem. George had stuck his neck out to get search warrants for the BUR premises despite the warnings of political sensitivity from Allonby. As for the directors, Marty's searches at Companies House had given him only 'care of' addresses for an office used by BUR's accountant, one of the major players with offshoots throughout the globe. Nat was already making his way over to the accountants with Debbie. Tubal expected that the balloon would go up with Allonby before the end of the day. Hopefully Nat would behave himself. George was already having kittens without an early fireworks night.

'We'll head over to the Registry at the London office to see what more we can find out from Companies House.' Tubal beckoned to Paul to grab their coats.

'Good idea, but stay the fuck away from Somerset House and Allonby,' George spat.

'You don't need to tell me that, George. Give us a call if they bring Sweeney back,' Tubal shouted as they headed out towards the exit.

Chapter Eighteen

The information available about BUR was much as indicated by Berwyn at Special Branch. A detailed search through the Companies House records had identified the beneficial owner and majority shareholder as another company registered in the Cayman Islands. Tubal had no authority to dig deeper, and he already knew that this was a fruitless exercise. Nat had been given the run-around at the accountants and they divulged nothing of relevance, spouting client confidentially. They would not discuss anything without a court order; little chance of Allonby agreeing to that in the circumstances. Anyway, the chances were that the directors have been spirited away, likely stooges brought on board with no definable profile or history in the UK. That's what everything indicated to Tubal at that moment. He had the uncomfortable feeling that his failure to fully research the absent directors earlier had let himself and the team down. Everything had been focused on Sweeney and Martindale, leaving those pulling the strings at BUR ensconced outside of the jurisdiction and protected from BIO's reach. BUR had vanished, and Tubal had no doubt that over the following few days, a phoenix company would rise from the ashes to complete the Pilgrims Pyramid development. Life would continue unabated for the controlling money men.

This time, though, they would have to play by the rules or learn to cover their misdemeanours more covertly. What Tubal couldn't fathom was how BUR had got wind of his operation. He knew that he had not inadvertently leaked information and couldn't believe that it was one of his Group Five colleagues. What would he or any of the BIO colleagues gain from this? Nothing, was the simple answer. It must just have been a coincidence. Perhaps BUR were in financial trouble. Perhaps the plan all along was to liquidate BUR without surrendering to the UK tax burden, then resurrect a new company with a clean slate. But that made no sense at all. There would be no need to use the documents and laundering operation Sweeney supplied. Tubal then remembered what Abbie Scott had said at the Dunstable letting agent: 'There's only a few weeks left to run as the tenant is moving abroad.' That must be it. The strategy all along must have been to bring the company and Sweeney's involvement to an end after a period. This still made no sense to him, but Tubal began to feel heartened that he had brought Sweeney down before he had flown off to County Waterford.

'I've just taken a call from George Craig at Wood Street.' Paul broke Tubal's ruminations. 'Sweeney's having his toe amputated. There'll be no interview today, but Solicitors Office has agreed to charge him with Conspiracy to Defraud and Cheating the Public Revenue amongst other things.'

'Conspiracy? Who with?' Tubal enquired.

'Tony Martindale and/or persons unknown. George wants us back over at Wood Street.'

Tubal thanked Maggie, the London office Registry clerk, and they both headed back to the car inconspicuously tucked away in a side street off the Strand. George decreed that they stay away from Somerset House, so job done; his budget will just have to suffer the parking costs. As Paul pushed out into the London traffic to crawl the two or so miles back to Wood Street, Tubal reflected further on the day.

'You know, we've probably done Sweeney a favour,' he randomly piped up, breaking the silence between them.

'What do you mean, mate?'

'Well, he's lost a toe, but without today's soirée, the gangrene might have cost him his leg, or even his life.'

'You reckon?'

'Yeah, I think it's very public-spirited of us to arrest him *and* save his life. All part of the service.'

'Fuck off, Mac. I'm not so sure that Sweeney sees it like that.'

'Well, he should.'

The Portland stone facade of Wood Street Police Station eventually stretched out before them; a neoclassical idiom belying its 'swinging sixties' origin. Paul wound his window down and buzzed the intercom, prompting the languid car park shutters to judder skywards. As Paul eased into a spare parking bay, Tubal collected the discarded food wrappers and drink cartons that had punctuated the day. Eat when you can was a philosophy he had learnt to abide by, married to his other edict of never wasting the opportunity to piss when on active operations.

'Right then, matey, let's go and see George.' Paul lit his umpteenth cigarette and led Tubal towards the steps up to their base for the day.

As they entered the room, George ambled towards them accompanied by a slim, blonde woman, running pale, willowy fingers through her frowzy hair as she approached. Before George could speak, a hand shot out and grabbed Tubal's wrist.

'Hi there, I'm Rebecca Franks from Solicitors Office. I must tell you, I've been run ragged today.' There was urgency in her voice, but the reason remained concealed within her.

'Yes, Rebecca has kindly travelled over here from Somerset

House to assess what we have,' George cut in. 'She has drafted charges on Joseph Patrick Sweeney, and the plan is that he is brought from hospital, charged and bail refused with an appearance at City of London Magistrates tomorrow morning.'

'What about his toe?' Tubal asked.

'Doctors have agreed to sort it out in the next few days,' George replied. 'Rebecca will oppose bail at court, and we'll be looking at a remand before trial. His medical issues can be dealt with then.'

'Well, he can't run away yet, but there is mention of a plan for him to go back to Southern Ireland soon, and we found an open ticket to Waterford.'

'Rebecca's aware of that, Tubal. At court, the magistrates will be told that he is a flight risk and of the potential multimillion tax loss resulting from his actions.'

'Well, let's hope that they listen. What about Martindale?'

'I'd like you and Felicity to have another go at him,' George directed. 'Let him know he's also facing a conspiracy charge and needs to start talking as this time he could be banged up well into his old age.'

'I hope I didn't hear any threats or inducements being planned, gentlemen,' Rebecca interrupted.

'Strictly by the book, of course.' Flick had snuck in behind Tubal, catching the tail end of the conversation to put in her two pennyworth.

'Ah, a kindred spirit. I'm Rebecca, the solicitor sorting this out.'

The two women locked eyes and loosely shook hands. Rebecca held Flick's gaze a little too long for Tubal's liking.

'Let's get him up from the cells then, Mac, then you and I can have another crack.' Flick turned away from Rebecca, ushering Tubal back towards the door. 'You can take the lead and see if he'll cough now that he's had time to reflect.'

Tubal's earlier negative thoughts abated as adrenaline coursed back into him. Perhaps he had a chance to recoup some ground, he concluded, particularly if Martindale felt inclined to grass up the architects behind the fraud operation. Despite his self-perceived failings, Tubal still believed that he had reached the zenith of his short career to date. It also felt good to be ending the day back in Flick's company.

'You coming then, or what?' Flick jolted Tubal's thoughts.

'Yes, ma'am, on me way.'

'Cheeky bugger, let's just get on with it.'

By the time they had reached the interview room, Martindale was sat waiting for them and sharing a joke with the custody officer. As they entered the room, he stood up and nodded in Flick's direction.

'Thank you, Officer, we'll take things from here. Please, Mr Martindale.' Tubal waved an arm, inviting Martindale to sit back down. 'I am Tubal McArthur, the officer in charge of this investigation. Miss Francis is already known to you.'

Tony Martindale sat, placed his hands on the table and, eyes down, studied the remnants of his chewed fingernails.

Tubal continued. 'I understand that you have waived your right to a solicitor. I must remind you that you are still under caution, but we need to clear up what's been going on. Do you understand, Tony?'

Martindale looked up at Tubal and spoke quietly. 'Yes, I do.'

'Miss Francis has detailed the evidence against you. You know that Pat Sweeney was also arrested this morning, and we have recovered items that incriminate you.' Tubal spoke measured and firmly. 'We are not going to put anything else to you now, Tony, as shortly you'll be charged with Conspiracy to Defraud with Sweeney and others.'

'What others?'

'Does it matter? Thing is, the BUR directors have scarpered and left you hanging out to dry. The buck now stops with you. Is there anything else that you wish to say?'

Martindale dropped his eyes to the floor and ran his hands over his face. Tubal stayed silent, giving time for the reality of the situation to sink in.

'You bastards nicked my good lady wife and her mother this morning. Angels both. Obviously, they got a bit upset when you lot traipsed into the house in the early hours, but they've got fuck all to do with this.' Martindale sat bolt upright, paused momentarily and continued. 'Here is my statement, but I will say no more after that without some assurances from you. It is true that BUR engaged me to facilitate a way of keeping labour costs down and I used Pat Sweeney's services. In the early days, he provided 715 vouchers to cover BUR's own men. I made up the wage packets and told BUR head office the name on the tickets being supplied by Sweeney. As the Pilgrims Pyramid site developed, they needed greater amounts of cash and, if you like, I helped launder the payments using the 714C certificate of Gilmore Angell Limited. The company name didn't matter, just as long as there was a vehicle to cover the men's cash-in-hand wages. Sweeney provided invoices totalling the weekly wage bill, plus a cut for both of us. He skimmed 10% off the top, and I took whatever I felt I deserved from the men's pay packets. Nothing much but something to supplement what BUR paid for my indulgence in their scheme.'

'So how did BUR know how much to make the weekly pay cheque out for?' Tubal interrupted.

'I would ring the Westminster office with the details, and they couriered the cheque over.'

'Who signed the cheque?'

'One of the directors. I could never read the signature, so don't ask me for a name. Sweeney, or a runner, provided invoices and collected the cheque from my office early in the week. Sweeney personally paid back 90% of the cheque value in cash to me at Southwark Park each Thursday.'

'But you must have discussed the arrangement with the directors.'

'I've already said too much but might remember more if you help me out a bit.'

'A deal you mean. Can't make deals with you, Tony, you know that. It's getting late and I think that we are finished here.'

Tubal conferred with Flick to make sure that they had enough to keep Rebecca happy and brought the interview to a conclusion. Flick switched the recording machine off.

'I'll take you back to the custody sergeant,' Tubal informed Martindale.

'If you must, but I think that you will want to hear the ace I have up my sleeve.' Martindale moved away from the doorway and back into the corner of the room. 'I'm not just a crooked bastard, you know. To some, I'm more like a keeper of secrets, shall we say.'

'Too late to put it on record though, Tony. What are you getting at anyway?'

'Well, let's just say that one of your number is quite happy feathering their own nest.'

'And how do you know that? You'll have to be more explicit if you want to get our attention.'

'I'm tired now. You see what you can do for me first.'

And with that, he walked out the room and surrendered back to the custody desk. Next time Martindale saw Tubal was thirty minutes later when Rebecca's charges against him were read out. It would be a night in the cells before he faced the magistrates' court next morning.

'What do you think he meant, Flick?' Tubal whispered as they climbed the stairs back up to the Control Room.

'I don't know. Look, keep this between us for now while I have a think,' she replied cautiously. 'What are you doing over the weekend?'

'Nothing much. Washing my hair and sleeping probably.'

'OK, meet me at The Old Ferryman at one o'clock tomorrow.'

Chapter Nineteen

Tubal and the team didn't arrive back at Hinchley Wood until gone midnight. He slept well overnight until breakfast pangs beckoned, and his head again filled with speculation about Martindale's disclosure. It might just be grandstanding on Martindale's part, but Flick felt sufficiently concerned to warrant interrupting her Saturday schedule to discuss it with him. This was a first; despite the familiarity at work and the geographic proximity of their homes, contact at the weekend with anybody from the office was normally off limits. Martindale had suggested that somebody was on the take. The two of them had to decide who, if anybody, could be trusted within BIO. The reputation of the perceived noncorruptible might be tarnished by the actions of a colleague. It was unthinkable. Tubal had seen the effect on workplaces where a corrupt colleague was suspected. Everybody was treated with suspicion. Rumour-mongers thrived on misinformation and conjecture until the perpetrator was exposed. The culprit's trusted workmates became victims of a deception they had unwittingly endured in the believed safe environment of their daily life. A deception that might tear at their soul and faith in common man. And now the finger of suspicion pointed at those Tubal had adopted as his alternative family: those who had moulded his imperfections and laid a path to follow.

As he walked down to The Old Ferryman, the rain buffeted against the hood of Tubal's parka. He kept his head down, walking briskly, his thoughts unconsciously marrying the patter of rain to the beat of random rock anthems floating out from his memory: a gambit of the earworms driving him forwards. He was early as the oak door of the pub swung inwards, but there she was, already secreted in a nook, wiping a moustache of Guinness froth from atop her bare lips. Tubal silently studied Flick momentarily until she realised that her 1pm date was at the bar.

'Am I late or were you early?' Tubal called across to her.

'Early bird and all that. Get yourself a drink so we can talk before the place fills up,' she called back. 'And a packet of salt and vinegar crisps wouldn't go amiss.'

Flick hadn't asked for a drink, but he bought her one anyway. Tubal clasped two crisp packets between his teeth and tentatively walked towards her to avoid spilling their pints. Once sitting, an uncharacteristic silence prevailed, as if each didn't know how to kick off the conversation. Finally, Tubal broke the impasse.

'Well, what are we doing here?'

'What do you mean? You heard Martindale as much as I did. Some things just haven't been adding up lately, but I didn't think that it would come to this.'

'Do you believe him?'

'It's too risky not to.'

'So, who do you think it is?' Tubal had no suspicions of his own, but Flick might be more astute as the longer-serving IO.

'I dunno. But while we are both here, I need to ring Rebecca to see what happened at court this morning.'

'You have her number?'

'No, I'm telepathic.' At that, Flick wandered over to the

payphone and, hooking a business card from her purse, began dialling.

Tubal finished his drink and moved over to the bar to replenish their empty glasses. By the time Flick had replaced the receiver, he was sat back down and waiting expectantly.

'Yet another drink I've bought. I'm not made of money, you know,' he teased.

'Oh, come on, you love it.' Flick winked as a Guinness froth-framed smile cracked across her face. 'Do you want to hear what Rebecca said or not?'

'Of course. Good news, I hope.'

'Well, sort of. Sweeney has been remanded in custody, but Martindale is out on bail. Duty solicitor managed to convince the magistrate that he does have an angel at home after all, plus three oversized cherubs to nurture.'

'I just wish that we had more time with him yesterday. Custody clock was ticking down, and I didn't even ask him if he was involved in BUR's liquidation.'

'To be honest, Mac, I don't think that he had a hand in that. A company like that is way out of his league, and Martindale is not one for mixing with the big accountancy boys.'

'So, what's the plan?'

The pub had started to get busy now and deliberations ceased as they surveyed the sights and sounds around them, each pondering what the other was thinking. Finally, Flick broke in, her voice lowered to not much more than a whisper.

'We've got to tell George.'

'I don't know, what if it's him,' Tubal replied.

'I can't believe it's George; I've known him long enough and he's as straight as a sea turtle's erection.'

'A what? Oh, never mind,' Tubal conceded, never one to challenge Flick's occasionally abstract metaphors. 'Perhaps Martindale being released on bail could work in our favour.'

'In what way?'

'What about if, before we speak to George, we make contact with Martindale off the record.'

'George would blow a gasket if he found out.'

'Yeah, but what have we got to lose? Currently, all we have is a cryptic remark from an untrustworthy source. He could just be playing us. If he is, then all the upset and suspicion it will cause is not worth it.'

Flick cradled her drink against her breast and fidgeted back into her seat. Tubal waited to hear her thoughts.

'OK, here's what we'll do,' she said, pausing for a swig of her drink. 'On Monday afternoon, you will telephone Martindale at home and tell him we have some of his property to return.'

'What property?'

'That's what we'll be doing during the morning, going through the search seizures from his home. We'll try to find something that we don't need and give it back to him.'

'What if we need it all?'

'No matter, we just want to draw him out so that we can meet somewhere neutral.'

Tubal felt happy with that and had no qualms about deceiving Martindale if he had to. Now he had the rest of the weekend to enjoy before Monday and the need for another pint.

'Your round I think.' Tubal lifted his glass and moved it towards Flick.

'I'll get you a drink, but I've got to get back. Ross is coming round to see me.'

'Thought you were on a break.'

Flick walked off to the bar without answering. Tubal leant across to an adjacent table and grabbed a recently discarded newspaper. By the time he'd found the TV page, Flick had returned holding a perpetually effervescent Stella Artois, inviting, chilled, resplendent within its glass chalice. The 'wife beater' lager bemoaned by the gutter press, but to Tubal an elixir driving the rest of the day.

'Don't forget to eat.' Flick gently placed her hand on Tubal's shoulder. 'I'll see you Monday.'

Tubal watched Flick saunter towards the pub door and smiled as she paused, turned and waved to him before exiting. He settled back and people-watched during the fifteen-minute lifespan of his pint; a slow death by Tubal's standards. It was time, he decided, to catch the bus down to Chessington and have a drink with his grandad at The Harrow. If he was lucky, his nan might be cooking one of her famed rabbit stews with dumplings to finish the day off. Tubal knew he was always welcome, and The Harrow fascinated him. Bob, the ex-Flying Squad landlord, courted a smorgasbord of characters from all levels of the criminal fraternity. Last time Tubal was there, one of the Great Train Robbers, over from Spain, popped in. People in The Harrow just knew Tubal as 'the grandson' and his job never came up. He was happy to keep it that way – far less embarrassing for all concerned. So that was decided, Saturday with his nan and grandad and a day's rest on Sunday. Monday could be forgotten for now.

Chapter Twenty

Having spent most of Sunday in bed, Tubal was up and into work extra early on Monday morning. The evidence seized on Friday had been brought down from Wood Street nick and was now sitting in the storeroom behind the Registry. It was of no use yet to Tubal as Marty needed to surface with the key so that he could book Martindale's property out. As he sipped his morning coffee, Tubal hoped that Flick was right about George. It would be far easier pursuing the allegation, if that is what it was, with the boss on board giving strategic direction and batting it up to board level. Tubal was conscious that Flick wanted to tell George, yet she had bowed to his persuasion and held back. He hoped that she hadn't developed second thoughts since Saturday.

'Morning, Mac, good weekend?' George's unmistakeable voice resonated as he briskly passed by the door to the Group Five office.

'Oh, morning, George. Fine thanks,' Tubal called out, hoping that George was too occupied to chat further.

Tubal's plan was to keep away from George as much as he could. Once Flick arrived in, the two of them could ensconce themselves away out of his gaze in one of the interview rooms. That way they could avoid the awkwardness of the situation and, if George was clean, their later approach to him could firstly be on the basis that they had to check their facts and, secondly, that everyone was so busy that they hadn't yet had a chance to speak to him. He would still blow up, but Tubal felt prepared to take the risk.

'You making the drinks then? You obviously couldn't sleep after a weekend of debauchery.' She was in.

'Morning, Flick,' Tubal responded boldly, then lowered his voice down to almost a whisper. 'Well, you kicked it off. I would have been quite happy going to my Saturday morning knitting class.'

'Nice, you could have knitted me a boob tube for work.'

Tubal decided not to linger on the image his puerile imagination had thrust upon him.

'I couldn't afford the amount of wool needed. And where would I get enough poles for the support scaffolding?'

'Ooh, you're getting brave, young man.' Flick frowned, feigning displeasure before a smile cracked across her face. 'Are you saying my tits are too big?'

'As if I would be so rude.' Tubal felt the tinge of warm blood flushing his cheeks and felt he should change tack. 'Come on, let's grab our drinks and get this done.'

The pair snuck down the corridor, passing George's open door. Thankfully, he had his back to them. As they entered the Registry, Marty was in; hungover but functioning as he always does. It didn't take long to get the storeroom key from him before booking out Martindale's seized items from his home address.

'There's not much here, is there?' Tubal handed the bag of documents to Flick.

'I told you, mostly diaries and so on. I'd have put his missus in a bag, but the cops wouldn't let me,' Flick replied. 'They've probably released her by now unless she kicked off at the nick.'

As they scoured through the paperwork, little of value was found. Any names, phone numbers or potentially useful calculations were extracted, copied and recorded, leaving a pile of tat ripe for an urgent return to its owner. Tubal left it until they returned from a light lunch at the Orleans before finding an empty office and making his call to Martindale. Surprisingly, Tony answered the telephone and was uncharacteristically responsive to a meet the next day on neutral ground, The Hole in the Wall, a pub secreted into the Waterloo Station arches within a tulip's bloom of the infamous Buster Edwards flower stall. Well, Tony Martindale might deduce that it's neutral ground. Tubal knew it as another BIO haunt. Well, it was once, until a Channel 4 documentary paraded a source claiming that an IO had attempted to buy unauthorised electronic scanning devices from them in there. Total bollocks, Tubal knew that, but enough for Allonby to invite a batch of journalists down to Hinchley Wood to observe the surveillance equipment. The five senior investigating officers had flown into a collective frenzy of incredulity. Allonby, true to form, remained rectitude in declaring that the Department must be seen to be beyond reproach.

'You might as well have stamped fucking "Inland Revenue Property" on everything, including the IOs,' George was heard to bellow through his office wall in a customary fit of pique.

This blip soon passed, and even if Joe Public were in any way interested in spurious surveillance techniques, that curiosity soon waned. No, it had to be The Hole in the Wall, quick route from the office into London and fast train back to Surbiton. George could blink and miss them. If he did ask, Tubal and Flick agreed to say that they were going into London to follow a lead on BUR. That should suffice, although both believed that keeping out of George's way would be the most prudent option. Fortuitously, the plan worked, and as soon as

George left for his liquid lunch, Tubal and Flick headed up the back path to Hinchley Wood Station and caught the train into Waterloo. Martindale was due to meet them at 2pm, so they had time to get into the pub and secure a cosy corner. By then, the office drinkers should be back in work, leaving the diehard drinkers cradling the bar and out of earshot.

Tubal loved the buzz of Waterloo Station, spitting distance to his birthplace and cocooned by streets that bled his ancestry. Railway stations and airports, places where you could watch and not be noticed, fascinated him. To Tubal, unsuspecting players about their daily routine invited an anodyne voyeurism in him to consume time. There was no room for a brief encounter under the station clock though. Flick was briskly walking ahead; she had already exited out of the station through Victory Arch under Britannia's torch of liberty and was bouncing down the stone steps into York Road. Tubal finally caught up with her outside.

'You in a hurry or something,' he gasped.

'Time waits for no woman as they might say; I need to grab a quick pork pie before Martindale gets here. Anyway, why are you puffing? Started smoking or something?'

'I don't need to smoke when the air is thick with nicotine every way I turn.'

'You and me both, Mac. We breathe in more smoke than an asthmatic dragon in a caravan.'

Tubal shook his head but couldn't think of an appropriate riposte.

As they entered the pub, the distinctive smell of stale beer and yet more cigarettes filled the air, trapped within the grubby arched ceiling. Little had changed here over the years, ripe for the weary commuter, lonely local or blagger planning the next job. A drinker's pub with no thrills. Decor appearing as though it hadn't been touched in years, remaining faithful to its late-1940s origins. Tubal took the lead now and secured a table and chair set in the sparsely inhabited back bar whilst Flick serviced her pork pie craving. Two o'clock was fast approaching but there was still time for a pre-meeting drink to sooth any trepidations around what Martindale might divulge. That's if he turned up and, if he does, still has the temerity to repeat his intimation about one of their own outside the confines of police custody.

The answer came soon enough as Martindale swung open the door into the bar and furtively looked around. Flick raised an arm to invite him over. This must be the casual Martindale, faded, fur-trimmed denim jacket, black, open-necked shirt, jeans and leather cowboy boots stained with patches of God knows what and run down at the heels. He walked to the bar and bought himself a pint before moseying towards them, his heavy steps echoing on the wooden floor.

'You've got something for me then,' Martindale spoke abruptly as he stood in front of the table.

'Sit down, Tony, all in good time.' Flick gestured towards him. 'Enjoy your drink; there's plenty of time.'

'Wasn't aware it was a social visit,' he replied curtly.

Where'd you park your horse? Tubal thought to himself before adding, 'I'm glad you've been able to meet with us today; magistrate must have been looking on you kindly.'

'What do you mean? I've got a good solicitor.'

'Think about it, Tony, man with your record on a conspiracy charge. Do you think that your solicitor is a miracle worker?'

'Or might it be that a good word was put in for you on the basis that you have information that might be of use to us,' Flick added, fuelling an illusion that they had anything whatsoever to do with his current freedom.

Martindale sat down and took a mouthful of his pint as if to buy added thinking time.

'I don't follow you,' he finally spoke. 'Where's my stuff?'

'All in good time; I'll have to write out a receipt but, in the meantime, would you care to elaborate on what you told us at the police station?' Tubal answered.

'My solicitor says that you can't ask me any more questions now I've been charged.'

'That's true in relation to the conspiracy, but that's not what we're talking about, is it, Tony?' Tubal added. 'You made a reference to one of our colleagues being on the take, "feathering their nest" I think were your words. That's right, isn't it, Miss Francis?'

'Indeed, Mr McArthur.'

'Ah, it was just bluster. I meant nothing by it,' Martindale replied.

'Well, that's a pity, Tony, we've got to go back to the magistrate now and say that you are not cooperating after all. They won't like that.' Tubal compounded their deception.

'Might add a few years once the case gets to Crown Court, do you think, Mr McArthur?'

'I do, Miss Francis. Let's hand back Tony's diaries and not waste any more time.' Tubal slowly and methodically wrote out a receipt to give Martindale some thinking time.

'Look, wait a minute, Mr McArthur. How do I know I can trust you?'

'You don't, but we're the best chance you've got,' Tubal lied.

'Alright, give me a minute.' Martindale downed the rest of his drink and gestured for another from the barman.

'Well in that case, I'll get us all a drink.' Flick collected the glasses as she rose from the table. 'You've more chance of getting pregnant than getting table service in here. Tony.'

An uneasy smile cracked across Martindale's face. revealing nicotine-stained, uneven teeth peppered with food debris. Tubal handed over the returning documents in exchange for his scribbled signature.

'Right then, Tony, let's just relax a bit and see what you want to tell us,' Flick said as she placed the drinks on the table. 'Where would you like to begin?'

Martindale began his tale with the claim that he had been contacted on behalf of the money men behind the Pilgrims Pyramid development via an intermediary: a man he named as Clive Lamptey, an English businessman based on an island in the Bermudian cays. Martindale said that he had only ever spoken to Lamptey on the telephone and his knowledge of him was gleaned from the directors at BUR. They held Lamptey in some esteem and had alleged to Martindale that he had made his money as a 'fixer' for the powerful, whether they be princes, billionaires or both. Martindale said that he had no doubt about this as others had confirmed it.

'There was talk that Lamptey built his reputation brokering deals with the oil producers in the Middle East. People who were nomadic, feudal tribes in the 1940s and '50s before oil created untold riches. I heard that Lamptey was well placed, through family military connections, to tap into their new-found wealth and help them create a platform on the world stage. Oil led to the need for weapons; both led to power; and Lamptey creamed his substantial commission off the top,' Martindale explained.

'OK, so how is this of any relevance to us?' Tubal enquired.

'One of Lamptey's strengths is his ability to make sure that his clients get what they want. One thing they don't want is to squander their wealth paying taxes to countries they have little respect for. That includes this country.'

'Well, you've orchestrated your fair share of tax evasion over the years, Tony,' Flick butted in.

'Yeah, but nothing on his scale. All I've got is a poky little house I rent in Sussex. He's got an island.'

'You should up your commission rate, mate, might get

you a caravan plot on the Isle of Wight.' Tubal added his two pennyworth.

'So, Tony, how does this Clive Lamptey fit into our investigation?' Flick asked.

'Listen, I only have a nickname. Lamptey asked me to provide some girls that could travel to France at short notice to sweeten the "Revenue Man".'

'When you say girls, you mean toms, prostitutes,' Tubal interrupted.

'Indeed, I have a few girls on my books in Brighton that work independently and were more than happy for a trip abroad,' Martindale replied. 'I brought two of them up to London and they were collected by a chauffeur-driven Bentley outside Charing Cross Station. Lamptey told me that they would be very well looked after if they kept the Revenue Man sweet during a business trip to Paris.'

'Whose business?' Flick asked.

'Lamptey's client's business,' Martindale replied. 'In return for the incentives on offer, the Revenue Man would be coerced to drop any tax investigation.'

'When you say "coerced", the term blackmail comes to mind,' Flick countered.

'Well, that depends on how complicit you believe this man is. Lamptey told me that he had someone on the inside of the Inland Revenue, a highflyer who is known for recovering millions of pounds back to the Exchequer. A man who hounds rich, fiscally non-compliant people and recovers megabucks in tax from them. This reputation, and the free hand afforded, has corrupted his loyalty. Blackmail is when you've literally been caught with your trousers down. No, this is payment for services rendered, not the girls' services but Revenue Man's.'

'So, the girls are the payment, the bribes if you will?' Tubal asked.

'Not just the girls but the whole package. All-expenses-paid trip to Paris, overnight stays, the whole caboodle,' Martindale replied. 'The girls were in their element, the Bentley collected Revenue Man from a side street near Admiralty Arch and they drove down to Lydd Airport before taking a private jet to Paris. Over in France, they stayed in an upmarket hotel and were taken to the Crazy Horse nightclub in the Latin quarter. Revenue Man paid for nothing, and the girls could order as much champagne they liked. You know, the kosher stuff at £60 per bottle.'

Sounds like my sort of weekend, Tubal thought before enquiring further. 'So, you've had dealings with the likes of me and Miss Francis over the years, Tony, with BIO, and you know what we do. When you said that one of us was feathering our nest, are you now saying that it wasn't one of us at all?'

'No not one of your lot, way out of your league.'

'Thanks for that,' Flick mumbled. 'So how would we contact this Clive Lamptey?'

Martindale gulped at his drink and shook his head.

'You wouldn't. He operates in a very clandestine world.'

The answer was not unexpected, but Tubal and Flick at least felt some relief that they could now consult with George Craig. What they had to fathom now was how to identify this 'Revenue Man'.

'So, are you being straight with us, Tony?' Tubal asked. 'Do you know the identity of Revenue Man?'

'That's a "yes" and "no" to both questions.'

'How about your girls? They must have called him something,' Flick asked. 'Can we speak to them?'

'You'll be lucky,' Martindale responded. 'Look, I've got to go. Thanks for the drink and all that, but I'm done.'

Tony Martindale rose from his chair and swiftly moved to the exit. Tubal caught him as the door swung inwards.

Grabbing him by the wrist, Tubal leant towards Martindale and warned him, 'We've not finished with you yet. We'll be in touch soon,' before releasing his grip.

Martindale rubbed his sleeve, turned frontwards and propelled himself speedily back into the anonymity of Waterloo Station.

Chapter Twenty-One

'So, what do you think about Martindale's story?' Tubal murmured as he supped the final lager dregs from his glass.

'Well, I think that the BUR directors are not as blind as we thought they were to what has been going on,' Flick replied. 'Following a premeditated plan all along I reckon.'

'You're probably right. So, what are we going to do about this bent bastard, Revenue Man?'

'Well, Mac, we find out who he is and bring him down,' Flick replied. 'That's if we can corroborate what Martindale has said.'

Tubal felt distain and excitement in equal measure at the thought of identifying and bringing down a corrupt higher-ranking officer. He thought back to Eric's training school lectures and recounted that an investigation such as this was the principal reason BIO was created. All IOs knew that cases of dishonest tax inspectors helping themselves to feed debt, addiction or pure greed would cross their desk every now and then. A smattering of disillusioned souls gratifying their own financial affliction without considering the ruin awaiting them once detected. Each only concerned with satisfying their own perceived need to steal from the State. Taking what they think is theirs. *This 'Revenue Man'*, Tubal thought, *plays in a different league*: blatant venality at the Department's higher echelons and stratosphere length from the low-hanging fruit of subbies selling a few tickets. Tubal felt vindicated over the BUR situation. Unknown forces had been at play, and he knew now that they'd been tipped off.

The journey home to Surbiton found Tubal and Flick locked in reflective silence; a mean feat for them, given a train journey of nearly twenty minutes. Occasionally, each caught the other's glance; a smile exchanged without words. Both knew that the only conversation worthy of discussion was the knowledge they shared, and that was not for public discussion. In fact, not for discussion at all until they saw George in the office the following morning. This suited Tubal. The previous few days had been hectic and, after saying his goodbyes, he headed off home from the station for a microwave meal in front of the TV and an early night.

Tubal slept well overnight, waking on cue at 6am with a muzzy head followed by the spontaneous release of a deep sigh as the magnitude of the day ahead hit him. Martindale's allegation played over and over as Tubal showered, dressed, shovelled his porridge down and travelled into the office. Silently, he planned and rehearsed how he would broach the subject with George. For the first time in months, nerves were getting the better of him and Tubal felt random twinges as his intestines gurgled and squirmed inside of him. But Tubal had travelled a long road since his seventeen-year-old persona sat before the man with the pyramidal moustache. Now he revelled in knocking on strangers' doors chasing down and locking up the bad guys: His confidence shielded by the perceived protection his position in law enforcement afforded him. But this was George, his boss, a man who, although he didn't yet know it, would certainly take umbrage once informed of Tubal and Flick's deception or, as they saw it, omission, albeit for the right reason.

Tubal arrived at Hinchley Wood at 8am sharp, followed

minutes later by Flick. The rest of the team trickled in over the next forty-five minutes, but there was no sign of George until just after 9.30am. What's more, he was singing to himself.

'Morning, boss, you're sounding chipper this morning,' Terry jumped in as George made for the kettle.

'Chipper indeed, old bean.' George batted back Terry's retrogressive vocabulary. 'I had a bit of a win on the gee-gees yesterday.'

George loved his horse racing, not quite as much as Heart of Midlothian Football Club but almost on a par. Tubal and Flick momentarily locked eyes, both instinctively deciding that this was the time to strike.

'When you've got your coffee, George, could we have a word in private?' Tubal waved a finger in Flick's direction to show which 'we' he meant.

'Of course you can, but I can't marry the pair of you. You must be confusing me with a ship's captain.'

'No, it's alright, boss, you're safe for a few years yet,' Flick reassured him. 'We'll give you time to master a pedalo on the Thames.'

George turned his back and gestured for them to follow him back to his office. As they entered, Flick shut the door behind them.

'It must be serious,' George said. 'What have you been up to now, Mac?'

Tubal only felt slightly peeved at the assumption that he had done something. True, he got away with the unauthorised search of Pat Sweeney's Landcruiser, but at least this time there was bilateral responsibility. Flick answered first, seizing the mantle as the more experienced officer.

'Yesterday afternoon we met Tony Martindale up at Waterloo. He somehow believes that we had some input into his making bail on Saturday.'

'Which of course you didn't,' George interrupted. 'Go on.'

'His assumption might have followed on from his interview at Wood Street on Friday,' Flick continued. 'Something he said after the tape recorder was switched off and our response to him. He basically implied that there is a corrupt officer amongst us.'

'And what did you say to him?'

'Well, I told him that he would have to be more explicit if he wanted our attention,' Tubal interjected. 'Martindale said that it depended on what we could do for him.'

'A deal?'

'Yes, but we told him that we couldn't offer him a deal,' Flick replied. 'Then he was charged and unexpectedly made bail at City Magistrates on Saturday.'

'So, you met him yesterday.' George now had more of a familiar scowl returning to his face. 'And the reason was?'

'On the pretext that we had some property to return but ostensibly to find out more about the alleged bent officer,' Tubal said.

'So let me get this right. On Friday you received information that there might be a corrupt officer at BIO.' George was slow and measured in his words. 'It is Wednesday, five days later, and you now bring this to my attention.'

'Yes.'

'And why would Martindale tell you anything more if no deal was struck?'

'Because of the intimation that we might actually have had a hand in his getting bail,' Tubal replied.

'OK, I'll let that one slip.' George paused to compose himself. 'Why the fuck was this not reported to me at Wood Street on Friday?'

'To be fair to Mac, boss, it was a joint decision, and we agreed that we couldn't tell anybody until we had more concrete information,' Flick answered.

'Not even me?'

'I'm sorry but not even you, whom I trust implicitly,' she continued.

'And what do you know now?'

'It's not one of us,' Tubal said. 'We know that now, but until yesterday, we had no idea who we could trust with the information.'

George rose from his chair and walked over to the window. He stared at the hailstones drumming furiously against the glass and paint-chipped metal frame. Without turning, he lit a cigarette, inhaled and blew smoke upwards into the yellowing ceiling tiles.

'Glad to hear it, the bit about it not being someone at BIO, I mean. How could either of you ever believe it was?'

'That's not fair, George. We were in a really compromised position,' Flick countered.

'So, do you now know who it is?'

'No, just that they are one of the higher up tax inspectors dealing with the corporates and millionaires. Someone who has a no-questions-asked, free reign to travel, chasing down the big money,' Tubal replied.

'Well, there's too many of those for my liking, the old boys club no doubt, probably Tories. Still, way above our pay grades. Can you find out who?'

'We'd have to put more pressure on Martindale. Currently, all he is saying is that he knows this person as "Revenue Man". Not very original but that's it,' Flick said. 'So far, we know he's been to Paris all expenses paid and is being supplied prostitutes. The only "in" we might have comes through some of the women Martindale has procured to soften up our man. Part payment on account, if you like.'

'More like harden up,' Tubal quipped.

'I'm currently experiencing a sense of humour bypass, so

'I'll ignore that, Mac,' George grumbled as he returned to his desk. 'Right, I want you both to work covertly on this and find out as much as you can. For now, we'll keep this in-house, and you only report to me, understand?'

Both nodded their heads in agreement.

'And the other thing is, we'll have to find some other appellation than the "Revenue Man",' George continued. 'Sounds a bit too close to home for my liking.'

George reached inside his desk and pulled out a ring binder where he kept an alphabetical list of operation names ready for allocation. At that time he was using an A to Z of baby names.

'Right, here we are, it's not the next name on the list; Operation "Innocent" won't quite cut the mustard. So, we will call him "Irandi".'

'What about the rest of the team?' Tubal enquired. 'Won't they think something's strange if Flick and I are pulled off other jobs to work on this?'

'Don't worry about them; I'll sort it on a need-to-know basis. Once we have a name, I'll need to contact the DCI of B1 Squad SO6 at Scotland Yard.'

'That's the Public Sector Corruption Unit at the Met Fraud Squad,' Flick enlightened Tubal.

'There is another aspect but, from what Martindale says, I assume it will be off-limits to us,' Tubal added. 'A man called Clive Lamptey, acting for Middle Eastern businessmen, is bribing "Irandi" to stop any investigations into untaxed money and assets they hold in the UK.'

'Off-limits how?' George asked. 'I rather think that's for me to judge.'

'Well, Lamptey lives in Bermuda,' Tubal replied.

'Right, OK, that's probably another one for SO6 if the evidence holds up. For now, I'll set you both up in a spare office over at Spur B. As far as Group Five and the other teams are concerned, you are working on a project for Solicitors Office. You still have the Sweeney and Martindale papers to get ready for trial, so nobody should question it.'

'So how should we proceed with Tony Martindale?' Flick enquired.

'You can tell him that if he cooperates and his allegation is substantiated, your SIO will submit a letter to the judge outlining that his information has facilitated the exposure of corruption at a senior level. It's now up to you two to find the evidence.'

George dismissed the pair with an order to return to the group office and stay clear of the BUR investigation and Martindale's case until the Spur B office was set up. Not, Tubal concluded, too difficult to manage, as the Orleans, wholly neglected over the last week, enticed them like a siren to a horny mariner. There was just the small matter of the lunch break still being another hour away; tea and biscuits had to suffice until then.

'So, George has got his sense of humour back then,' Tubal said as Flick chucked a custard cream over to him.

'How's that?'

'Irandi, could be an acronym; Inland Revenue and I, or I Randy, which seems appropriate in the circumstances.'

'Mac, your mind amazes me sometimes. Come on, let's sneak away from here to avoid the others for now.'

Chapter Twenty-Two

It was no surprise to Tubal that the decor in Spur B looked just as archaic as the BIO offices. George had appropriated a redundant office by the fire escape of the 'Post War Credits' section. Tubal had no idea what they did there. Some process linked with World War Two, they said. Tubal could have guessed this by the musty bouquet skulking the passageways and small group of extra-matured civil servants ensconced in a time warp. Each poring over crumbling files to mollify an antediluvian fiscal commitment until retirement or death released them. But this was of no concern to Tubal. The adjacent fire escape would provide a handy egress to the car park without the need for small talk or unwelcome curiosity from their temporary hosts. To further keep them away from prying eyes, Flick and Tubal shifted a bank of dusty grey metal filing cabinets into an 'L' shape at right angles with their doorway. This gave enough cover to set up an operations centre where they could work without being overlooked. It was clear that nobody had used the room for a while. The desks belonged to a different age, sturdy, crafted wood affairs with a leather infill for fixing sheets of blotting paper with a patina of tarnished lacquer; not like the grey, metal-framed chipboard and veneer furniture installed elsewhere as 'modern' sometime in the 1960s. Flick soon got to work on the accumulated grime with a tin of Pledge and a faded yellow duster she found in the office cleaners' cupboard. From then on, this room was out of bounds to all but a select group of two.

'Well, Mac, this is cosy,' Flick said. 'Our own little fiefdom.'

'You're right, we could get a few crates of beer in and set up a bar in the corner. No one would be any the wiser,' Tubal jested, but the idea held a certain attraction.

'Yeah, I could come to work in my pyjamas if I can't be arsed to get dressed.'

'Well, that wouldn't work for me.'

'Why not?'

'I don't wear pyjamas. I'd scare the life out of some of the biddies amongst this lot.'

'Oh, I don't know, there's probably some right ravers under those pearls and twinsets.'

'Well, Miss Francis, I'll just stick to my jeans or a dark-blue, thin pinstripe number for now, height of sartorial elegance I reckon.'

'Yeah, you reckon, more like an extra from *The Long Good Friday*, methinks.'

Tubal had managed to keep his weight at a manageable level in recent months. He was determined to look good in the clothes he already had without splitting his trousers. Granted, this had only happened once when climbing into a pool car, but walking like a penguin with dysentery into a meeting to curtail a flash of vivid red man briefs had left an indelible imprint. No, he decided that his body must fit the clothes in his wardrobe, even if it meant sacrificing the occasional naan bread.

'You sure? I seem to remember you wearing jeans when I got you out of bed up in Dunstable,' Flick reminded him.

'Well, I'm too modest to answer the door naked. I had no idea who had come calling, let alone the Robina Hood of chicken leg rustlers.'

'Would it have made a difference?'

Tubal felt unable to answer. He could only reflect on his perplexity at that time and how fate had conspired to draw them closer together. So close, that Tubal knew he must suppress the increasing urge to cross the line from work colleague to potential lover, even if such a dalliance turned out to be unrequited. In truth, Tubal couldn't separate Flick's natural charm, coquettish banter and cheeky quips towards him from the way she might respond to any of their other teammates. He could hardly ask around or conduct a straw poll. No, he just had to bat her banter off with an appropriate retort. If she was at all interested in him romantically, Tubal resolved, she would have to be more explicit in her intentions. Undoubtably, he knew he would succumb, but for now, they had a case to solve.

'We need to find a way to draw out Irandi, and Martindale's our only hope.' Tubal changed the subject. 'Let's see if we can draw out a bit more from him on the girls involved.'

Flick twiddled with her pen, tapped it against the desk and picked up the handset of the ivory Bakelite telephone before tossing it in Tubal's direction. This landed short of its target before slinking back slightly as the curled connecting cord recoiled towards Flick. Tubal reached across to retrieve it as Flick spun the dial to connect with Tony Martindale.

'No time like the present. I'm dialling the number; you talk,' she said.

Tubal clutched the phone to his ear and waited for the *bur bur* tone to click in. As it did, he hoped that Martindale would answer rather than a member of his abrasive pseudo family. He got his wish as a rasping male voice spoke.

'Yeah.' A man of few words.

'Tony, it's Tubal McArthur from the Revenue.'

'What do you want?'

'Well, you know what I want, access to the girls that looked after our corrupt officer.'

'What, you feel horny or want some of the same?'

'Don't mess with us, Tony, it's in your own interest.' Tubal dropped George Craig's words on him. 'Help us, and at your trial, we'll pass a letter in your favour to the judge.'

'Oh yeah, so you say. Why should I trust you?'

'Listen, if you can prove what you told us, you will be exposing a bent officer at the highest level. Not being funny, but wouldn't it be sweet revenge against the taxman, present company excepted of course.'

'Can you get down to Brighton?'

'I can get to Timbuktu if you come up trumps.' Tubal had no desire to go to wherever Timbuktu was, but Brighton was within budget. 'Brighton will do for now. When?'

'Give me your number and I'll call you back.'

Tubal gazed at the telephone's centre dial and relayed the number printed there back to Martindale before writing it down in his notebook. It always took him months to remember telephone numbers and this one had just been thrust upon him. Martindale read the number back and was gone, no goodbyes, kiss my arse or pleasantries. The actions of a man reluctantly accommodating those he loathed most. Tubal couldn't care less. It was a means to an end.

It didn't take long for the phone to ring. Well, just long enough for Flick to beat Tubal at rummy three times but, who's counting? Martindale had set up a meeting at the Derby Arms in Brighton. When he came off the phone, Tubal let Flick know that he knew it well; a 1920s-built Kemptown Brewery inn crowning the path into Brighton's sprawling cemetery. Before she became too unimpressed, he followed up with the revelation that, when he was a child, one of his uncles was the landlord there. Tubal fondly remembered the cinema opposite where he first saw Judy Garland on the big screen in *The Wizard of Oz* with his older cousin Marlene. Oh! And, not so fondly, being trapped in an upstairs room of the pub with a psychopathic German shepherd while downstairs the adults drank the place dry. All that later came to an end after a mystery fire. The dog met a sticky end and Tubal's uncle moved to pastures new at Her Majesty's pleasure. So, the Derby Arms it was, 6pm that night. Just time for a quick pint and a sandwich before hotfooting it down to the South Coast.

'You been overdosing on Paco Rabanne?' Flick said.

'What do you mean? I always wear aftershave,' Tubal replied.

'There's wearing it and drowning in it; I'll need to throw you a rubber ring at this rate. I can't concentrate on the road.'

'Just been freshening up, that's all.'

'Amazing what meeting a few toms does to you,' Flick countered. 'I'll sit downwind of you. Bit of luck there'll be a downpour to wash it off.'

'I don't know who or what we are meeting yet. Could be a trap.'

'Well, they'll need to be wearing hazmat suits then.' Flick floored the accelerator as they hit the M23.

Brighton soon found them and the fight for a parking space near the pub was won when Flick disgorged a Morris Minor-driving clergyman who stalled when distracted by two nubile, bare-legged, ripe-breasted teenagers bending down to pick up bags from the pavement.

Wait until they get a whiff of my aftershave, Tubal thought but didn't say.

Parked up and facing eternal damnation, the pair headed towards the door to the Derby Arms lounge bar. Two Neanderthal cave dwellers lurked by the door, each innately grinning and nudging the other as Flick led the way. Tubal drew alongside her, all puffed up, metaphorically staking his claim. The gargoyles lifted their pints and washed the drool that leaked from the corners of their mouths.

'Nice scent, love,' one was heard to say as Tubal pushed open the door.

Flick turned towards Tubal and winked, as only she, in Tubal's mind, can.

'Looks like you've pulled,' she muttered before heading for the bar.

Tubal had already spied Tony Martindale sitting alone in a corner of the room. He knew he'd been clocked as their eyes momentarily locked. Clearly, Tony had no desire to advertise their brittle, somewhat artificial, relationship. But this was of no concern to Tubal. He was here to find answers and marched straight over, followed by Flick with their drinks.

'All alone, Tony? Thought you were bringing some friends,' Tubal asked.

'All in good time. They are, after all, working girls, so this is going to cost me,' Martindale countered.

'What, no mates rates?' Flick added. 'You understand that our expenses won't be able to cover it.'

More's the pity, Tubal thought but dared not repeat. How much easier his love life would be if temporary solace could be hired at the firm's expense. Still, at least the £10 meal allowance satisfied one of his needs.

Tony Martindale stood up and beckoned to the barman who, on cue, walked to the door of an anteroom located at the end of the bar and tapped twice. As the door swung open, Martindale signalled to Tubal and Flick to follow him through the doorway into a small corridor that led to a private lounge. Once inside, a table set out with a tray each of neatly quartered sandwiches and savoury titbits took centre stage. Martindale picked up an egg mayonnaise on white bread sandwich and posted it through his wonky molars before inviting his guests to join in.

'I could only get one of the girls to speak to you and she wants a favour in return,' Martindale spluttered through mashed egg. 'She has a little immigration problem. She also has a contact number for your man.'

'Not sure that our influence extends to illegal immigrants, but I'll see what we can do.' Tubal knew that this was beyond his authority, but the risk of losing this contact overweighed all else.

'She's not illegal, just overstayed her visa,' Martindale replied. 'And talking of which, may I introduce you to Kat.'

In the doorway stood a woman, probably late twenties, a cliché in bright-red lipstick and black patent knee-high boots over faded denim jeans. Pretty, in pink cashmere V-neck sweater with a cleavage of pale breasts peppered with delicate freckles that snaked up to a face as sweet as honey. All crowned by a mop of blonde hair, curls spawning from a pink woollen beret tilted jauntily over her left eyebrow. Her large, deep blue eyes stared directly at Tubal, who noticed a raised scar like a red liquorice shoelace extending below her hairline. She smiled and held out a hand as if Tubal was expected to kiss it.

'Hello, my name is Aikaterini Vlachos, but you can call me Kat,' the woman spoke with a faint foreign accent.

'That's not a British name,' Flick said. 'Where are you from?'

'I was born in Limenaria on the Greek island of Thasos. My name means "pure" but I'm sure my family back home will have other descriptions for me now. I came to England to teach little children.' Kat spoke directly to Tubal, holding his gaze. 'Are you wearing perfume?'

'Yes.' Tubal nodded.

'It's nice,' said Kat, pouting and pausing for Tubal to respond if he wished. He didn't. She continued. 'Tony here is my friend. That's correct, isn't it, darling?'

Martindale nodded agreement. Flick couldn't imagine Martindale having such an exotic acquaintance but thought he had obviously worked his magic in the bookkeeping department. And that's not a euphemism.

'So, Kat, I believe you can help Tony and us with information about a client, the man you know as "Revenue Man",' Tubal asked.

'No. No. I call him Teddy, my little bear.'

'Is that his real name, Edward or Ted or whatever?'

'I don't know what his real name is; I just do what he wants, and the nice people treat me well.'

'Pay you for lying on your back you mean,' Flick said.

'Oh, I'm much more adventurous than that. You obviously don't approve, darling?' Kat answered. 'I'm sorry about that, but you don't know me.'

'That's true, but I don't wish to.'

Tubal couldn't pinpoint why Kat appeared to have hit a raw nerve with Flick. She seemed pleasant enough, and Flick hadn't expressed any views on the work choice, if that's what it was, of the women Martindale helped. Yet something was pricking Flick's conscience. Perhaps she thought Kat was distracting him and he'd end up crowing like a rooster in a hen house: putty in her £10-a-handjob grip. Maybe it was more personal than that, or Flick's hormones were playing up. Staying focused was the best strategy.

'Kat, we're here to do a job,' Tubal said. 'We need you to help us and you will also be helping Tony,' Flick continued. 'How can we identify this Teddy of yours?'

'He gave me his telephone number,' she replied. 'In Paris, he said that he would like to see me again back in London. I told him that this would not be possible. I told him that I am reserved for certain corporate clients. He was sad.'

'Do you still have the telephone number?'

'I do,' Kat said. 'But not here. Tony said that I should keep it for, how do you say it, insurance. That's it, insurance for the future.'

'OK, we need you to call him and say that you would like to meet with him after all,' Tubal forced the issue further. 'You will also give us the telephone number.'

'And you will help sort out my visa, yes?'

'No promises, but we'll see what we can do,' Flick said. 'But please, don't be under any illusion. If you do not cooperate, you'll be on the first plane back to Greece and the judge will lock up and throw away the key for your friend Tony.'

'So dramatic.' Kat grinned. 'But I get the point. I tickle your back, you tickle mine.'

'Something like that.'

'Scratch,' Tubal said. 'Scratch my back.'

'So, when will you make the call?' Flick said.

'I'll sort something out with Kat, and we'll get back to you within the next few days,' Martindale interrupted.

'OK, we want the meet to be somewhere in public, say a restaurant, as we need to identify this man. What arrangements you come to afterwards is up to you,' Tubal said. 'Do you understand?'

'Of course. A girl must make a living, my love,' Kat replied.

'And, Tony, something else is bugging me,' Tubal said. 'If Lamptey tipped off BUR, why didn't they let you know?'

'Oh, why didn't I think of that?' Martindale mocked. 'I am expendable, shit on their handmade shoes. Do you honestly think that I'm helping you because of your meaningless incentives? I know what's in store for me this time.'

And with that, the meeting was over. All made their way

out of the Derby Arms and blended back into the cosmopolitan Brighton air.

Tubal and Flick barely spoke on the return journey, each mentally churning through their personal inquest of what had been discussed. Could Tony Martindale and Aikaterini Vlachos be trusted? Would the telephone number lead to anything? They could only hope that the number rang at a Revenue office. On the other hand, if Martindale passed the telephone number on to him, Tubal could run a reverse number check through the Registry. That might take a week or so, losing valuable time, but it might be the only viable option. All they could do in the meantime was wait.

Chapter Twenty-Three

As the door swung open, Tubal saw the blink blink of the answerphone pulsing red. They had pulled the blinds down the previous night to stop curious eyes, so the room was unnervingly dark. As Tubal felt for the light switch over the top of the filing cabinets, he knew that the flashing beacon could only mean one thing; Martindale had been in touch. It must be him as nobody other than George had the number, and he wasn't likely to call, given that debriefings were now face to face, closeted within their domain. It had been ten days since they'd been in Brighton. Tubal had rung Martindale during that time, but there was no answer. He pushed the 'answer' button on the machine and waited as a familiar drawl rang out.

'It's Tony. Kat left a couple of messages on the man's number, but he hasn't returned the call. Don't want to push the issue, might look suspicious. His number is 071 438 7607. I'll be in contact if I hear any more.'

Tubal quickly scribbled a file note and pushed 'save' on the answerphone in case Martindale's message had any future evidential value. Not the answer he wanted, but at least he had something to play with. Tubal carefully wrote out a request for the Registry to conduct a reverse telephone check on the number to locate the address it was registered to. Once completed, he tossed the request into his 'out' tray, knowing that nobody would be calling to collect it. No post clerk had visited this room in decades. This end of the corridor was designated as 'off-limits' to the general staff, and although it might arouse general curiosity, few would encroach BIO territory. So, the telephone request would have to wait until Tubal or Flick ventured back over to their home spur. That way, any awkward questions were avoided, particularly if Tubal asked George to hand over the request to the Registry. Marty would never challenge George. It'd be akin to Vlad the Impaler's stake sharpener challenging his workload: there'd be no point, and the outcome would be messy.

'Morning, Mac, been here all night?' She was in. 'I've got some news.'

'So have I: Martindale has left us a message with a telephone number,' Tubal replied. 'What news?'

'No, it will keep for later. Tell me what he said.'

Tubal played the answerphone message back to Flick. She unearthed a sparkly pink hairbrush from her handbag and dragged it through her honey-blonde locks. Tubal watched as she pulled the loose hair from the brush and held it up to the light before tossing it into the wastepaper basket.

'Get dressed in a hurry this morning, did you?' Tubal asked.

Flick threw him a smile and winked. 'We'll get the number checked out.'

'Already in hand. It's in the tray, I've just got to take it over to George.'

'No time like the present then. Quicker we get the ball rolling, the quicker we can get down to business.'

They locked the office and retreated over to the BIO spur. The Group Five room was empty. *Must all be out on a job*, Tubal thought. George was in his office, humming a tune to himself in the misguided belief that he was alone.

'I'll name that tune in one,' Flick called out.

George grabbed for his pen as the two pushed his door open and entered the room.

'I just said that I'll name that tune in one,' Flick repeated.

'What you on about, girl?' George said.

'You know, Lionel Blair, the game show *Name That Tune*, used to be on the tele.'

'I don't have time for the television, hen. Now what have you come to tell me?'

Tubal ran through Martindale's answerphone message and pushed the reverse telephone number request across George's desk.

'And you want me to sign this?' George scanned the paper and passed it back over to Tubal. 'I'm not going to. This is too sensitive, and if it comes back as an internal number, alarm bells could be triggered.'

'What should I do then, boss?' Tubal questioned.

'Put it through your Special Branch contact on a need-to-know basis. They'll just think that you're following up on BUR and Sweeney.' George stood and walked towards his office door. 'Chances are you'll get the details back today if you catch them before lunchtime.'

Tubal and Flick took their cue and headed back to Spur B to call Berwyn. Luckily, he was in the office and promised to call back pronto with the result. As is the wont in these cases, Berwyn traded a favour in return, tracking down a work address for an individual on Special Branch's radar. An easy trade-off, especially since all IOs now had covert computer access to the national tax database. All dealt with at the tap of a keyboard. Favour for a favour, plus a promise to meet up for a few pints soon.

Within the hour, Berwyn had called back. The number checked out to a telephone forwarding service at a business centre right by South Lambeth Estate off Dorset Road, Kennington. Tubal noted the address, but he knew the area well. In days of old, before he was born, his grandad ran a second-hand car lot on Dorset Road. Tubal still had a blank 'Dorset Autos' invoice he had found when he was a kid. At the time, he'd scribbled down the details of an old MGA Roadster his grandad bought at auction to sell. In those days, during enforced respite from home, he tagged along to car auctions with his grandad and uncle. He must have imagined himself the fancy spiv, Tubal McArthur selling *his* MGA on to a grateful punter. Tubal knew it all looked very childish now, but he didn't have the heart to dispose of his crumpled memory. In an eleven-year-old's scrappy blue Biro writing, 'MGA Bought as Seen £50', as if such a bargain could be found.

'Put your face on, Felicity Francis, we're going out.' Tubal tossed his note of the address across the desk.

'What you see is what you get, cheeky bastard.' Flick grabbed the car keys and they both headed out. 'Natural beauty this.'

It didn't take them long to get up to Kennington. The address, the grandly named 'Dorset Business Centre', was found to be a run-down corner shop long since redundant. A metal bank of letter boxes, each secured by their own keylock, stacked up against the shop's grimy facade. Tubal pushed open the front door and into an open-plan room fitted out with a counter that ran all the way round, leaving a space for the doorway and a void in the middle for customers, of which none were obvious. Behind the counter sat two women, each knitting an unidentifiable garment and chatting to each other in a language unknown to Tubal; well, it wasn't French, the only language offered to him at school. On the wall behind the counter stood five telephones, each in their own booth with an answerphone. For each booth, a dog-eared record book hung from a cord screwed into the masonry.

'Can I help you, sir?' A voice heard from the direction of the shop door.

Tubal looked behind him to find a paunchy, brown-skinned man blocking his exit. Sweat marks stained the armpits of a grimy nylon shirt, open to his chest and sprouting dark hair where the material parted. He looked Middle Eastern but sounded like a native 'sarf' Londoner.

'Alright, mate, I'm trying to speak to someone on one of your numbers.' Tubal dispensed with any introductions and pulled a scrap of paper from his back pocket. 'The number is 071 438 7607. Is that one of yours?'

'Our client list is confidential. What makes you think that it belongs to someone here?' the man asked.

'Well, Miss Smith here and I are enquiry agents acting for solicitors trying to locate living members, and potential beneficiaries, of a deceased relative's trust fund. That's right, isn't it, Miss Smith?'

'Indeed, Mr Jones, and as you can appreciate, our sources are also confidential but, let's say, we have reason to believe that the person using your facilities is happy to keep themselves out of sight of the authorities.'

'Well, I run a legitimate business here.'

'Exactly, of course. Could be a finder's fee.' Tubal improvised.

'There *could* be a finder's fee, Mr Jones,' Flick concurred.

The man beckoned one of the knitters over and murmured an unintelligible instruction in somebody's mother tongue. She lifted one of the ledgers and stretched its restraining cable to reach the desk. On the front cover the number '7607' had been written in red marker pen.

'I have got to move my car; it's on double yellows and I

sense that the local parking Hitler is on the prowl.' The man turned tail out of the door and the knitters resumed their natter.

Tubal flicked through the pages in the hope of identifying the subscriber. Kat Vlachos's message and telephone number sat as the latest entry. Other entries listed numbers and first names but no clue to how the messages were forwarded. All of this meant nothing to Tubal. All he could do was copy as much as he could into his notebook.

'What's that stapled to the rear cover?' Flick turned the book over and pointed at a slip of pink paper noted with a two-digit number.

'Twenty-seven, what do you think that is then?' Tubal said.

'I dunno, give me a minute.' Flick left the shop and walked round to the metal postboxes.

Tubal looked towards the two ladies, hoping for guidance, but none came. He skimmed through the empty pages of the ledgers, hoping to find anything that might help.

'That's it, dead letter box.' Flick beckoned to Tubal to join her outside. 'Look, box number twenty-seven.'

'What do you mean?'

'I mean that messages are left via the telephone and notes of the call are placed into the dead letter box to be picked up by the intended recipient,' Flick explained. 'Key holders have access to those boxes twenty-four hours a day. They never need to come into the shop and collect messages.'

'Great, so we put the box under constant surveillance and see who turns up,' said Tubal. 'Only problem with that is that only you, me and George know what we're looking at. And I can't see George giving up his forty winks.'

'No need if we find out who pays for the box and telephone service.'

Just then the man from the shop emerged from a pale-blue Volvo estate that had pulled up outside.

'I hope you found what you were looking for, my friends,' he said as he passed them.

'Not quite,' said Tubal. 'I was just wondering who you invoice for the telephone and postbox service?'

'Ah, you have worked it out. On that 7607 number we don't forward the messages by phone. The client likes to remain discreet. It suits him to collect messages and post from the box.'

'Well, I can't take the credit. Not much gets past Miss Smith, a right Miss Marple.'

'Only fifty years younger and prettier, I think,' said the man.

'Well, gentlemen, it takes a woman's eye. So, if you could give Mr Jones the details, we'll be on our way.'

'I've already been more than generous.' The man paused, looked momentarily at the floor and lowered his voice. 'You mentioned a finder's fee.'

'That's right,' said Tubal. 'For successfully locating the person conducting his affairs through 071 438 7607.'

'Come over to my car; I might be able to assist if we can keep this amongst ourselves.'

The man leant through the open passenger window and pulled a leather-bound ledger from the glove compartment. Flicking through the pages, he stopped midway to run his finger down the entries.

'There,' he said. 'Six-month rental of telephone service and postbox facility. Company called Nevaeh Scent WLL, pay by bank transfer.'

'Who do you deal with there?' Flick asked.

'I don't deal with anybody, all done over the phone,' said the man. 'The box key was posted off to a PO box. If they're paying, it's of no concern to me; that's the nature of these things, miss. So, what about this finder's fee?'

'Well, we haven't found anybody yet, have we,' Tubal

answered. 'We'll pass on the information to our client, and if it checks out, someone will be in touch.'

'But you don't have my details.'

'Don't worry about that; we know where you are,' Tubal said as they made a quick exit towards their car.

The man briefly started to follow them but stopped as they put into practice their well-rehearsed synchronised getaway technique. They left him on the pavement gesticulating his dissatisfaction as he moved back to the shop entrance.

'What do you make of that, Mac?' Flick said.

'I can't see that we're any further forward other than knowing about yet another company. All part of Clive Lamptey's smokescreen, I suppose, and protecting his clients.'

'We could put a remote camera somewhere to watch the boxes, but you'd never pick out who was going to which one. It would be a nightmare.'

Tubal knew that Flick was right. Plus, how would Irandi know there was a message for him in the box? There had to be a missing link, unless the level of corruption was greater than they had anticipated. What if Irandi expected to see messages on a regular basis and visited weekly, or even daily? That would indicate that his corruption went deeper than scuttling the BUR investigation. Lamptey would have deep claws in him, and that was a serious risk to the Department.

Back at the office, Tubal tossed his notebook down on the desk and put the kettle on. As he sat back down, he spied George walking along the path from the other spur. He guessed that George had seen them drive back in and wanted a debrief. Flick opened the back door to let him in.

'The prodigals return… what have you got to tell me then?' George loomed at the foot of Tubal's desk.

'Well, we turned the number round to a dead-letter business in Kennington that fields the telephone calls,' Tubal started. 'All we've got is another company name that pays the bill, Nevaeh Scent WLL.'

'WLL, that's a Bahraini company, With Limited Liability.'

'How do you know that, guv'nor?' Tubal piped up.

'Goes back a long way to my Customs days,' George said. 'Difficult to find out who's behind them. If you've got the right amount of funds, the WLL can be wholly owned by foreign investors. Chances are that the shareholders are other offshore companies in yet another jurisdiction.'

'So, I won't be packing the sun cream and budgie smugglers then,' Tubal replied.

'That's right, Mac, you'll have to make do with galoshes and a wet arse in London.'

'Bit harsh, she's not that bad.'

'I am here you know,' Flick chipped in. 'Thing is, George, to find out who's collecting the phone messages, we'll need a covert device on or inside the dead letter box.'

'This is not *Space: 1999*, you know, those fuckers at Channel 4 would definitely be onto us if I could access such a thing,' George replied.

'Well, just a thought,' Flick said. 'I thought that Stevie might be able to tap up his old colleagues.'

Just then, Tubal's phone rang. The room went silent as he picked up the receiver and pushed the loudspeaker button.

'Yes.'

'It's Tony Martindale. Lamptey's been in touch. He wants me to bring Kat up to London for an overnighter on Friday evening to meet up with your man.'

'Where's the meet?'

'Jack's Bar, Jermyn Street, Piccadilly at six o'clock.'

The line went dead.

'Looks like we're on after all,' said Flick.

Chapter Twenty-Four

Friday came soon enough. Tubal put on his best suit, silk tie and jewellery and drifted into the office just before 10am. *This was going to be a long day,* he decided, *so no point rushing breakfast and catching the early cattle train to work.* As he creaked open the back door at Spur B, Flick's presence wafted to him. He snared the tang of Opium at the back of his throat. He loved that smell. It clung to everything that was her.

'Morning, Mac. Ready for our date night?'

Gone were the jeans and the baggy top, back to the red lips and backcombed curls. This was Felicity Francis all dolled up. All dolled up for a night up the Dilly. If only Tubal had the courage to say that to her, such was the connotation, even in jest. Particularly, given the company they would be keeping with Martindale and Kat, his *belle-de-nuit.* But there she was, pink minidress, pink opaque tights, a cropped black leather jacket and pink kitten-heeled sandals. Barbie On Her Majesty's Service.

'Yes, Miss Francis, I am, and I must say you scrub up well.'

'Well, thank you kindly, sir.'

George was soon round to their room with the obligatory Operational Order detailing the mission ahead. The three of them would tackle this together. Flick and Tubal inside Jack's

Bar and George parked in a side street, radio linked to Tubal's covert communications set. It was George who held the ace card in identifying Irandi. He attended the management briefings in Somerset House so should know this man. As soon as Tubal signalled that the meet was on, George would discretely head into the bar and observe from a distance. As a plan it was basic, but this was no ordinary case. They had no way of knowing who would turn up or even if this was some fool's errand orchestrated by Tony Martindale. Normally, Group Five would act as a team to cover public transport as well as vehicle movements. Not tonight. George still deemed this too sensitive. And it wasn't just about surveillance. The request for Martindale to bring Kat meant that Irandi might not be going home that night. No, this assignment had one aim: finding out who Revenue Man was. Mission accomplished and then the real work would start: investigating the extent of his corruption.

After their briefing, George returned to his office with an instruction that he would meet them by the rear entrance of Fortnum and Mason at 5pm. Before then, he said that they should get themselves up to Waterloo and fit in a meal before the evening's work. Tubal needed no prompting for this and slipped behind the filing cabinets to take off his shirt. *Might as well get prepared now*, he thought to himself. After de-robing, he slipped a thin white linen holster over his head and ran the securing straps around his body before fixing Velcro tabs tightly against the chest plate. He placed a fully charged battery to the base of his radio handset and clicked the two together. This he slipped into a cloth sheath beneath his left armpit, the rubberised antenna snuggling against the apex of his shoulder. A thin wire ran down his arm. Tubal secured this beneath his watch strap, leaving the bulbous tip of the transmit button dangling under his wrist. When the time came, this will be eased down into the palm of his hand. A diminutive flesh-coloured earpiece decked with a tiny volume control switch was tucked into Tubal's breast pocket, snug within its muslin carry-bag. He carefully replaced his shirt, smoothed himself down to hide any revealing lumps and put his suit jacket on. By the time he had come out from his makeshift dressing room, Flick was standing there, waiting. She now clasped a pink clutch bag to her side. Tubal pulled a bottle of Paco Rabanne from his drawer, poured the liquid into his palm, rubbed his hands together and massaged the scent into his jawline. That's it, they were ready to rock and roll.

As the afternoon was reasonably pleasant, they chose to walk along the South Bank after leaving Waterloo Station and crossed over the Thames towards Embankment Tube Station before emerging up on The Strand. Just off Trafalgar Square, they entered The Chandos in St Martin's Lane for lunch. This wasn't Tubal's choice. As a lager man, he found real ale pubs a bit challenging as the choices felt alien to him. No good for a Stella Artois man. But the surroundings were agreeable, and the food filled a hole. Both were limited in their conversation as everything was focused on the anticipated scenario in Jack's Bar. The time for banter and ribbing will come later, as the adrenaline was kickstarted. Before then, each inwardly ran through a series of events and consequences so that they were best prepared for what may lie ahead.

Leaving The Chandos, Flick hailed a cab to take them to Piccadilly. They got out short of Jermyn Street so that they could survey the area and familiarise themselves with landmarks that might be relevant. The Ritz and The Cavendish, both within striking distance. Other quaint establishments are noted, but they imagine that Lamptey's clients patronise the time-honoured residences of the privileged. Much more clout to influence a corrupt taxman and hold his compromised balls to ransom.

As they walked towards the rear entrance of Fortnum and Mason, they spotted George parked in a loading bay within sight of Jack's Bar. They both climbed into the rear of the car. It was just after 5pm. George informed them that he had spoken to SO6 at Scotland Yard and would brief the DCI if a positive ID was made. First of all, they needed to check radio communications before going in. Tubal undid the middle two buttons of his shirt and slid a hand in to turn his radio on. He took the earpiece from his pocket and flicked the switch to 'on' with one of the only unchewed nails left on his fingers. This he popped into his left ear canal. Leaving the car, he walked towards Jack's Bar and stood outside as if waiting for a date.

'Mac to Boss, are you receiving me?'

'Loud and clear,' George replied.

'Are you looking for business, love?' a third voice says.

Tubal is joined by a much older woman, literally tarted up and smelling of cheap perfume and fags.

'No, I'm fine thank you,' replied Tubal, shocked into politeness.

'Please yourself.' She spurted away.

'Who's your girlfriend?' Flick appeared beside him.

'Just shows I still have it,' Tubal replied.

'Yeah, darling,' was all Flick could say.

As she spoke, George drove past them to find a more discrete place to park up. Flick loosely pulled at Tubal's jacket sleeve before cautiously leading him into Jack's Bar. Inside, the bar opened up into a spacious meeting place built over two levels. All white leather seating and cosy enclaves lit by multicoloured camed glass Tiffany lamps. Behind the bar stood a slim, balding man in a crisp white shirt, blue waistcoat and black bow tie, his face lined with experience of life and listening to the lives of the inebriated. They moved to the bar, and each climbed onto the inviting bar stools, all polished chrome and sumptuous seated. Ideal for the discerning customers on their nightly trawl of the bars.

'Hello, sir, madam. I am Charles. What can I get you?'

'Hello, Charles, what do you recommend?' Flick replied.

'Speciality of the house is my own special cocktail, the Charlie Alexander.'

'We'll have two of those then, Charles,' Tubal said without having any clue what he would be drinking.

Charles placed two coupe glasses on the bar and set about pouring the ingredients into a stainless-steel cocktail shaker. Tubal noticed gin being poured, but his attention was primarily focused on the clientele for any sign of Tony Martindale. He was not there. There were still some minutes to go before 6pm.

'Sir, if you would like to find a comfortable seat, I'll send Jasmine over with your drinks.'

'Thank you, Charles, we'll be up on the balcony,' said Flick.

They climbed up a spiral staircase leading to a mezzanine lounge area and took a table with a clear view of the entrance.

'I'm not that keen on gin to be honest,' Tubal shared. 'Plus, it's going to cost a small mortgage if we're here too long.'

'Sip your drink slowly and look like you're enjoying it,' Flick said. 'Just think of England.'

As they sunk into the upholstery, a waitress arrived with their cocktails on a silver tray and placed them on the table before them. She slipped the bill to Tubal as he pulled some notes and change from his pocket, counted out the exact amount and handed it over. There was an uncomfortable pause as Jasmine hovered for her tip. Disappointingly for her, Tubal's inbred Scottish frugality and shock at the cocktail price had kicked in. She left unrewarded yet retaining the fixed smile mandated by the management.

'You meany,' Flick commented.

'Yeah well, we can't claim this on expenses, and I'm not drinking Coke all night.'

Down below, the entrance door swung open, and Tony Martindale entered, followed by Kat. Both dressed soberly in black suits. Tubal deduced that Martindale must have visited Moss Bros since the days of following him through Southwark Park. He appeared remarkably well turned out for a man of his pedigree. Definitely there to impress somebody. Kat's suit didn't quite compare with Martindale's as it shimmered with sequins and was tailored to expose her inviting attributes. A large silver cross hung around her neck like a defrocked nun. The pair eased themselves over to the bar as the two IOs watched discretely from above, their position such that they could observe without being seen.

It was 6.10pm. The pair were still alone, sat at the bar but not talking. Tubal picked up his drink, took a small sip and grimaced his distaste. From underneath their balcony, a figure appeared, shook hands with Martindale and embraced Kat before planting a kiss upon her cheek. Tubal shifted round to get a closer look. He could see it was a man, but the face was obscured by the upturned collar of a beige trench coat and the brow of a brown trilby hat. As Tubal watched, Martindale rose from his stool, touched Kat gently on the shoulder, made his way towards the front door and exited.

'Do you think that this is Irandi?' Flick asked.

'I dunno, could be him or it could be the fixer,' Tubal replied. 'I won't contact George yet until we know what's going on.'

The man stood up, removed his hat and coat without turning round and placed them on the floor in front of the bar. As he sat back down, Kat billed and cooed around him, her movements tactile and attentive. Charles placed an iced bucket of champagne and two glasses before them, then proceeded to fill each glass.

'I'm going down to have a closer look,' Flick said.

As she stood up, Jasmine the waitress came over.

'Please, madam, can I get you anything else?'

'No, I'm just visiting the ladies' powder room,' she replied before adding, 'Isn't it lovely, those two down in the bar with the champagne, proper lovebirds.'

'Oh yes, not seen them before, but it must be a special occasion. Charles said that a friend is picking up their bill at the end of the evening so to give them anything they want.'

'Oh, how nice, I might go down and congratulate them,' Flick said. 'My bloke here is a bit of a miser.'

Jasmine winked knowingly at Flick, cast a glance at Tubal and hurried over to a group of men gesticulating at her.

Flick made her way down the stairs and walked over to the bar. It was quite crowded by then and she stared straight ahead at her refection in the mirrored wall behind the optics. After a few moments, she turned her head in the direction of Kat. At catching sight of the man's face, she quickly turned away and slowly made her way back to Tubal. Before she reached the top of the stairs, she waved at Tubal, as if beckoning him to come to her. He didn't move. Flick continued towards him, bent down to his ear and whispered something. Tubal stood up, grabbed a handful of peanuts from a dish on the table and walked away, leaving the remnants of his Charlie Alexander. Both exited Jack's Bar separately, with Tubal radioing George to pick them up on the street corner.

The pair moved quickly to the rendezvous point. Flick climbed into the front of the car and Tubal slipped in the back behind her.

'Well,' said George, 'what's going on?'

Flick composed herself, turned slightly to face George and spoke. 'It's Allonby.'

'What's Allonby?' George said.

'Grenville Allonby, he's Irandi, he's the Revenue Man.'

Chapter Twenty-Five

Things were starting to make sense. Allonby's corruption explained why he had taken such an interest in Boteler Urban Regeneration Limited. BIO had stamped upon his domain. He couldn't be seen to influence their subcontractor misuse work but equally he couldn't let them aggravate his illicit relationship by badgering the company directors. That's why the company pulled the plug on the day of the raid. On the journey back to base, the three of them dissected all of their recent dealings with Allonby. George reminded Tubal and Flick of the surveillance job Allonby had tasked Group Five to do in Hampstead. The one they had to abort when their radio signals were jammed. With hindsight, could this have been Allonby? Putting pressure on a prospective target for his greed. Letting them know that he was watching. Letting them know that he knew that they and their wealth were here in the UK and not the Middle East. Now, Tubal thought back to the surveillance on Joseph Patrick Sweeney at the Midland Bank, Harlesden. Who was it that tipped off the Flying Squad to say that the bank was going to be robbed that day? Perhaps, Tubal surmised, Allonby thought that BIO would arrest Sweeney at the bank when they caught him carrying the cash being laundered for BUR. That would have greatly affected his candour in protecting the owners of the Pilgrims Pyramid development. But would he really have risked the police shooting a BIO officer at the bank? The possibility caused each one of them concern. All they could do was report their findings to the relevant authority. George ordered Flick and Tubal to stay away from the office on Monday. He would go directly to the Board and report Allonby to the Public Sector Corruption Unit at Scotland Yard. A briefing for Group Five would be held on Tuesday at 10am sharp. Tubal and Flick should attend then.

As they drove towards Surbiton, Friday evening was coming to an end. The night sky was clear, and London's smog gave way to the infinity of the stars. Just time, Tubal decided, for one more drink before last orders. Tubal asked George to drop him on the riverbank by The Old Ferryman. Flick said that she would walk home from there but, true to form, she fancied a nightcap once they had wished George a good weekend. The two felt quite drained as the magnitude of their discovery hit home. They sidled into the pub, and for the first time that day, Tubal enjoyed a lager of his choice.

'You know,' Flick said, 'we all know that he's a smarmy bastard and takes liberties with the typing pool girls, but who'd have thought he was also a corrupt bastard.'

'I know. I remember that smirk on his face. "I really don't think that BUR would be involved in anything criminal, do you?" he said to me. Bent bastard.'

'You know, we make a great team, you and I,' Flick said.

'We do, but it will be back to the old routine next week.'

Tubal lifted his glass and pushed it in Flick's direction.

'Cheers, Felicity Francis, and thank you.'

'What for?'

'Making me the IO I am today.'

'Well, I can't take all of the credit,' Flick said. 'I think there's a bit of a rogue hidden under that sensitive facade.'

Oh, if only you knew, Tubal thought to himself. 'Do you think so?'

'Don't get too big-headed, tiger.'

Tubal felt happy inside with her little idioms for him and always enjoyed their time alone. But the pub was closing and it was time to go home. As they walked back to the Thames path, the night air took on a chill and Tubal spontaneously shivered.

'You need a good woman to cuddle up to, keeps the chills off,' Flick said.

Tubal smiled but didn't reply. It might be too much if Flick was offering. As they parted, Tubal called after her. 'You never told me your news the other day.'

Flick turned and walked back towards him.

'Oh, Ross has asked me to marry him.'

With that, she resumed her journey home.

Epilogue

The police investigation into Allonby was protracted and complex. Such was his reputation, colleagues working in Allonby's office were happy to misdirect the direction of play. All of his cases had to be re-examined for evidence of corruption. It became clear that those actors protecting him had also benefited from the spoils. The whole department came under scrutiny and the policy of allowing Allonby and his team to travel unchallenged around the world at public expense fuelled great media interest. But essentially, the buck stopped with him. It was Allonby who accepted the services of prostitutes. It was Allonby who accepted luxury holidays for himself and family in the USA and Caribbean. It was he who received envelopes of cash, hospitality at £120-a-head Michelin-star restaurants and designer suits. Tubal felt a great sense of pride as Allonby was sent to prison for eight years.

As for Martindale, he turned Queen's evidence against his 'Revenue Man' and Kat's 'Teddy'. And just as Tubal promised, the judge looked favourably upon his cooperation to the extent that his guilty plea to the conspiracy charge only cost him a more-than-generous eighteen months in chokey.

Aikaterini Vlachos, 'Kat', had her visa renewed. As a key witness against Allonby, the Government expressed their gratitude without any intervention from the Revenue. This was fortuitous as neither Tubal nor BIO had any means of influencing the Home Office. She was now back teaching 'little children'.

The tax exemption documents recovered from Sweeney produced enough cases to keep Group Five going for the best part of a year. Each subcontractor was visited as a potential culprit. Most were victims of a system that allowed organised crime to flourish, 'low-hanging fruit' ripe for picking and propping up departmental prosecution figures. Without the likes of Sweeney, temptation to illegally sell their documents would not present itself. In recognition of this, Sweeney was sent down for five years' incarceration at public expense. Well, 99.9% of him was. His gangrenous toe escaped to the St Bartholomew's Hospital incinerator. Sweeney no longer needs to make self-tailoring adjustments to his underpants.

Tubal McArthur was promoted and was still learning his craft. Felicity Francis has not announced if the proposal from Ross was accepted. Tubal works on the premise that one day she will.

Thanks to Allonby, the Department's investigative arms endured a reorganisation. The technically adept were later conjoined with the wily street hawks of BIO. Tubal's skills were proving invaluable. He had come a long way. Is he an enigma? That's for others to judge. Introversion still caged him in the outside world, but as an IO, he was on a ride. A switchback ride in a clandestine world of catching criminals, disrupting racketeering and enjoying the esprit de corps of playing fast and loose with a skilled and highly effective group of misfits in dirty, dangerous places. Is his imagination still running away with him? Not one iota; everything was real.

Sté McCoinnich was born and raised in South London. He has over thirty years' experience as a criminal investigator for Government departments and the NHS. *Revenue Man* is his first novel. Sté lives in East Sussex with his wife, Sue, and two demanding Border Collies.